MEMORIES OF MY GHOST BROTHER

MEMORIES OF MY GHOST BROTHER

Heinz Insu Fenkl

A DUTTON BOOK

DUTTON
Published by the Penguin Group
Penguin Books USA Inc., 375 Hudson Street, New York, New York 10014, U.S.A.
Penguin Books Ltd, 27 Wrights Lane, London W8 5TZ, England
Penguin Books Australia Ltd, Ringwood, Victoria, Australia
Penguin Books Canada Ltd, 10 Alcorn Avenue, Toronto, Ontario, Canada M4V 3B2
Penguin Books (N.Z.) Ltd, 182–190 Wairau Road, Auckland 10, New Zealand

Penguin Books Ltd, Registered Offices:
Harmondsworth, Middlesex, England

First published by Dutton, an imprint of Dutton Signet,
a division of Penguin Books USA Inc.
Distributed in Canada by McClelland & Stewart Inc.

First Printing, November, 1996
10 9 8 7 6 5 4 3 2 1

Parts of *Memories of My Ghost Brother* have previously appeared, in various forms, in the following publications:
"The Mosquito" in *Vassar Review* (1981)
"In the House of the Japanese Colonel" excerpts in *Bridge: An Asian American Perspective* (1983)
"Dead in August" in *One Meadway* (1992)
"In the House of the Japanese Colonel" in *Writing Away Here: A Korean/American Anthology* (1994)
"Image from a Stolen Camera" in *Asian Quilt* (1995)

 REGISTERED TRADEMARK—MARCA REGISTRADA

Library of Congress Cataloging-in-Publication Data
Fenkl, Heinz Insu
    Memories of my ghost brother / Heinz Insu Fenkl.
      p. cm.
    ISBN 0-525-94175-4 (acid-free paper)
    I. Title.
    PS3556.E4778M46   1996
    813'.54—dc20   96-24865
                               CIP

Printed in the United States of America
Set in Palatino
Designed by Leonard Telesca

PUBLISHER'S NOTE
This is a work of fiction. Names, characters, places, and incidents either are the products of the author's imagination or are used fictitiously.

For Anne

明月

1

Moon

In the House
of the
Japanese Colonel

月

Outside, in the moonlit courtyard, the snow is falling again, bluish white and heavy as flakes of coarse sea salt. Slowly and silently, it covers the red clay storage jars, the water basin left out, the tops of the slender cherry branches. No wind. No sound. This is the third month of winter in the lunar Year of the Pig. My mother lies unconscious in the warm side of the room, dreaming of springtime in the old city of Seoul. She is walking along a palace wall, on an avenue white with fallen cherry petals. She breathes the springtime fragrance and sings a country song until, turning the corner, she is silenced by the magnificence of the palace gate; and there, hearing a strange noise, she stands quietly to listen. A giant serpent, thick as a pine tree, dangles its head from atop the palace gate and whispers to her in human speech, "I have something to tell you." The serpent is so long its glistening body encircles the entire palace grounds; its tail dangles just opposite its head. "Come here, I have something to tell you," it says. "I have something very important to tell you." My mother takes a cautious step forward. But before the serpent can speak again, she returns to consciousness and, enduring the last contractions of her day-long labor, she gives birth to me.

✧

The last snows of winter still lay in gray patches along the path that wound from the train station up the hill into Samnung. There was a house where the nameplate had fallen, leaving a rectangle of bright wall, there a gate with red peppers dangling on straw rope to show a son had been born, and over there, along a stretch of urine-stained wall, fliers carelessly posted, half torn, advertised the movies of last autumn. At the very top of the hill a strangely clean wall began, detached from the other walls that all ran together. It followed the gentle slope of the hill down toward the stone embankment that kept the road from crumbling into the paddies; and here, where the other houses ended, the wall turned sharply left and became the great gate of the Japanese Colonel's house.

We had arrived. While my uncle, Hyongbu, rang the bell and waited for the door to open, I looked out over the embankment. The rice paddies below had just thawed, and the dikes had turned dark and muddy under the tread of many feet. Thin strands of smoke rose high over the thatched roofs of the mud-brick shacks. Near the embankment, an old man in white stood in his yard, breathing steam, looking up at the pale hills with their tufts of scrubby trees receding, like a chain of grave mounds, into the distance.

This was more beautiful than the lower neighborhoods near the American Army post. The first hills stood so close I could make out single pine trees and even the narrow trails. I breathed the cold air and began to count the trees, chanting made-up syllables when I passed the numbers I knew.

"Let's go in," said Hyongbu. "We're the last ones here."

I stooped in after my uncle through the small door in the gate. And for the first time, I saw the beautiful house of the Japanese Colonel.

Before we moved in, we had heard rumors about why the rent was so low. Everyone said the house had been built during the Japanese Occupation by a Colonel who tortured and murdered tens of thousands of Koreans for his amusement. He would gloat in his rock garden, pretending to meditate, and then he would have some tea before seeing to the next victim. When World War II began, Emperor Hirohito rewarded the Colonel's loyalty by sending him first to Burma, then to defend Iwo Jima against the Americans. But he lost the island to the U.S. Marines and committed *seppuku* in his bunker on Mt. Suribachi.

Mr. Hwang, the new owner, knew all the stories because he was the nephew of the wealthy merchant who had bought the house cheap by agreeing to spread the Japanese Colonel's ashes in the rock garden. The merchant uprooted the old Japanese-tainted trees and planted a new orchard, spreading the Colonel's ashes as fertilizer. He also hired a *mudang* to perform a day-long exorcism of the ghosts of the Japanese and their victims. During the Korean War, the merchant ran away to Taegu, then farther south to Pusan where, by some unlucky turn of fortune, he was mistaken for a Chinese spy and shot by a GI. The house had, by then, become a haven for refugees of the war. Many died there from disease and starvation.

Mr. Hwang had inherited the house after the war. He renovated it, adding a shed and another room. But because he was a Christian he refused to have a traditional *mudang* exorcise the war ghosts. There were so many stories and rumors about the house that no one who believed in the old superstitions would rent it. Mr. Hwang assured us that the Japanese Colonel had been a rather quiet and philosophical man who practiced Zen meditation in his garden and had never murdered anyone. Mr. Hwang was on good terms with a Catholic priest of the Maryknoll Mission, and if there ever was a problem with ghosts, he said, he would arrange for a Western-style exorcism.

At first, my mother had decided not to take the house, but we had little money back then; because the price was so low, she said yes and rented three rooms. My mother's older sister, Emo, would live in one room with her husband Hyongbu and their two children, Yongsu and Haesuni; one room was for Gannan, a niece from the country; and one was for us. The owner's family lived in another room, and in the last room lived a couple who had moved back to Korea from Nagasaki with their crippled son whose name was Chonghi.

What had been the rock garden during the Japanese Annexation was now overgrown with pine, maple, chestnut, and ginkgo. In the back of the house by the shed stood a wonderful white Russian birch, and beneath it lay a terraced vegetable garden which Emo soon cultivated each day. The walls around the house, rebuilt to a height of three meters, were newly studded with shards of colored glass to keep thieves out.

During the day, the house was quiet and parklike. I spent the warming afternoons exploring the hiding places, climbing the trees, leaping among the small boulders in the garden. But at night the trees lashed in the wind and the house became a frightening place, and I would forget about the town beyond the walls. With the sinister shadows under the trees and the reflections from the pale boulders, the grounds of the house seemed a wilderness where tigers and evil ghosts might appear at any moment. I seldom went outside at night. From behind the barred windows, I would look out into the trees, thinking myself into a folktale or a goblin story, shivering each time I saw something move. Stormy nights were especially frightening, because then, through the sound of the wind and the spattering rain, I often heard whispers which I knew were the lamentations of the refugees who had died during the war. Sometimes when I looked toward the boulders, I would see the ghost of the Japanese Colonel standing quietly under the trees, gazing at me with his sad and lonely eyes. I told Emo about the ghosts, and she stopped going out to open the gate by herself at night.

On warm mornings, a mist would rise from the old rock garden. Before the sun climbed high enough to make the day clear, I would glimpse the mist spirits dancing between the beams of light that shone like revelations through the gaps in the tree branches. One evening, in the rust-colored light just before dark, I stood outside the front door of the house and listened while the owner told me that the sky was endless. I stared up through the branches of my favorite ginkgo tree at the stars, trying to imagine a darkness that went on forever and forever.

Winter ended and the spring passed quickly. One morning, when the spring rains had become the torrents of the monsoon, I found a sick magpie under the largest chestnut tree. I went out into the rain and brought it inside. I tried to feed it, but it wouldn't eat. When it was dry I took it to the owner's room and asked how to make it well again.

"It didn't like the bread," I said. "Owner *ajoshi*, when will it fly and sing again?"

Mr. Hwang touched the magpie tenderly. He stroked it and lifted its wings, and then he looked at me, the way the ghost of the Japanese Colonel looked. "Keep it warm and dry," he told me. "And we'll pray and hope that God up in the sky will bless it."

"What about the Swallow King up in the sky? Will he bless the bird, too?"

"The Swallow King isn't real. All prayers go to God. Shall I teach you one?"

I shook my head and took the magpie back to our part of the house. I made it a small perch and placed different sorts of food in front of it, but the bird still would not eat anything. In the evening when my mother returned, she said to put the bird on the window ledge so it could look outside. I moved the perch and even opened the window the tiniest bit to let in the fresh smell of dirt and rain. The magpie sat very patiently as if it were waiting for something. It would turn its head from side to side, but never moved from its place.

That night, I dreamt of a wide, still river with banks of white pebbles, and a face that looked like my own looking up at me through the clear, rippling water, and when I woke the next morning, the magpie was dead. I trembled when I touched it. I thought I might wake it from sleep, but it was too cold to be sleeping—and strange, as if it weren't the same bird I had seen sitting so quietly on the perch at night. I wrapped it in a handkerchief and placed it in the curve between two broken rooftiles. I buried it under the chestnut tree where I had found it, and I whispered a prayer to the Swallow King to take the magpie's spirit to a good place. I even tried to cry, but I could not. Perhaps I had begun to understand at that moment, as I crouched in the rain and heard the whispering ghosts, that the magpie's death would go on and on forever like the endless sky.

✧

Each day during the monsoon, I went out and stood by the magpie's grave. Emo saw me one morning and gave me an umbrella so I wouldn't get too wet. "It's not good to stand so long in the rain like that," she said, "even if your bird is dead. Go and sit in the warm side of the room." She frowned and hurried back inside, drenched with rain.

When I came in, Emo dried my hair with a small towel and gave me a bowl of hot water to warm me. I held the bowl under my chin as I drank, feeling the steam on my face. "Emo," I said, "when will the rain not come anymore?"

"Next month," she said. "Then you can stay outside all day if you want."

I took off my white rubber shoes and stepped up onto the wooden *maru* floor. Emo wiped my feet. "Now go into the room," she told me. I went and lay on the hot *ondol* floor where the heat rose up into my body, making my head heavy on the cushion I used as a pillow. I started to sing a bird song that Gannan had taught me.

> Magpie, magpie, your new year
> Was on yesterday.
> Our, our, new year's day
> Has arrived today.

I sang the song again and again until my eyes closed and my mouth hung open in sleep. I awoke quietly when I heard Gannan's door sliding shut. She usually brought me Fig Newtons when she came back from the club in ASCOM, the American Army post. I left our room and thumped across the *maru* to her door and stood there for a moment. A little noise, like the snuffling of a small animal, came out of her room. I slid the door open and poked my head inside. "*Nuna*, why are you crying?"

"It's nothing," she said.

"Did somebody hit you?"

"No. It's nothing." She sniffled, and now her shoulders heaved up and down as she put her hands over her face.

"If somebody hit you, then I'll beat that bastard up!" I stepped inside.

Gannan tried to smile, but only her cheeks twitched.

"It's . . . nothing," she said again. I wanted her to stop crying. Her tears made something crackle and sag inside my chest. I didn't know what to do.

"*Nuna*, is it because of your yellow-haired boyfriend? Did he say he didn't want to marry you?"

Gannan gave me a hopeless look and then she hugged me and cried into my belly while I stood helplessly, watching her shoulders heave. "*Nuna*," I said, patting her dark hair, "let's sing a song. If you sing a song, it makes you happy." The corners of my mouth turned downward each time Gannan sobbed, but I did not want to cry with her. I started singing the song about the wild rabbit going home.

> *San-tokki-tokki-ya*
> Where are you going to?
> Hopping, hopping, leaping so,
> Where are you going to?

It was much easier after the first verse. I sang it again, loudly, and I heard Gannan's breaking voice join in.

> Over the hills, the hills,
> All by my self, my self,
> Hopping, hopping, leaping so. . . .

And when we had sung the song three times, Gannan wasn't crying anymore. My heart felt lighter. Even if the yellow-haired GI didn't marry her, I knew she would get married soon because she was beautiful and her face was like the moon.

When I came back to her room later that afternoon, she was rubbing Vaseline on her face. "Is your face burned?" I asked.

"You stupid, I'm just taking my makeup off." She put the Vaseline jar on top of her note pad.

"Did you bring me some Fig Newtons even though you were sad?"

Gannan smiled quietly and pointed toward her handbag. I found the cookies next to a white envelope in her bag and I sat in the corner to eat them, crunching the tiny seeds between my teeth.

"Go play in your room," said Gannan. "I want to be alone for a while."

"What are you writing?"

"A letter."

"Is it for me?"

"Yes, it's for *you*. Now go to your room if you want to read it later."

"*Too* loud!" I said, covering my ears. I went back to our room to play with the hook-nosed puppets my grand-mother had sent from the German country.

My mother came home after the rest of us had eaten din-ner. She ate alone from the table Emo brought for her. I sat at her side, taking pieces of *kimchi*, spinach, and chewy bellflower root to eat with the spoonfuls of rice she offered me.

"Did you win, Mahmi?"

"No. No jackpot today. Maybe I'll take you next time for luck. Didn't you eat enough?"

"*Ungh*, but I'm hungry again."

"I told you to eat more," said Emo. She sat and smoked a cigarette, looking worried. Or maybe she was just think-ing about something. The mole over her right eye made her seem always thoughtful. "Go and see Gannan before you sleep," she said to my mother. "Something must have happened today, again."

"When did she come in?"

"After I came in with the umbrella," I said. "She was crying hard and I—"

My mother gave Emo a tired look. I looked down for a moment at the floor, remembering how Gannan had cried.

"Maybe she should be sent back home," said Emo, watching the dark, wet window glass behind the magpie perch. I could see our reflections and the bright electric bulb that hung in the middle of the room. It seemed that we were all sitting out in the rain. My mother's reflection turned toward me, and I could see the night through the blacks of her eyes.

"It's no good being a *yang saekshi*," said Emo. "It's not as if those GIs will buy her a homestead. If she'd stayed in the country with Country Sister. . . ."

"There's nothing we can do now," said Mahmi.

"Mahmi," I said, "what's a *yang saekshi*?"

"You don't have to know. That's adult business. Go play in the other room with Yongsu and Haesuni."

"I want to stay here."

The windowpane rattled in a gust of wind. Trees hissed outside. I could hear the refugee ghosts wailing because they had lost their homes in the war. Then, through the streaks of rain on the window, beyond our reflections, I saw the ghost of the Japanese Colonel watching us with his sad eyes. Why was he always so sad, I wondered. Was it because his ashes had been scattered under the tree roots and he had no way of getting them back? Or was he just lonely? Did he miss the house and want to come back and live here? Now the wailing of the refugee ghosts quieted as it always did when the Japanese Colonel appeared. I could hear rain dripping from the trees, and the faint sound of someone shouting far away. The Japanese Colonel nodded good-bye, then walked toward the garden and was gone.

". . . I even collected the money for her at first when she couldn't speak English," Mahmi was saying. "I can't do more than that."

"If you hadn't introduced her. . . ." Emo picked a lump of spilt rice off the floor and stuck it to the rim of the table. Mahmi put her chopsticks down. I took one and tapped on the table next to the rice until she said to stop.

Emo took the Salems out of her vest pocket. "One for me, too," said Mahmi.

While they smoked, I remembered proudly that I had

been there in the NCO Club when my mother had first introduced Gannan to the yellow-haired GI. He was stand-ing in the lobby under the painting of the coiled dragons, shaking his leg the way my father did when he was im-patient. Gannan looked shyly at his shiny black shoes while he looked down at the top of her head. "Hello," said Mahmi, "this is my young daughter of sister. Her name Gannan." "Hi there, baby-san," said the yellow-haired GI. "*Olgul chom ollyo pwa,*" Mahmi said in Korean to Gannan. "Lift your face and look at him. He's a decent man, con-sidering he is an American soldier." Gannan lifted her head, and with a half bow, said, "I am happy to meet you." He smiled. "Hey, you talk American good-good," he said. "This kid yours, baby-san?" "*My* son," said Mahmi. The yellow-haired GI gave me some money before he went to the bar with Gannan. Mahmi played slot ma-chines, so I bought a Coke and ran outside to wait. Later the yellow-haired GI came to our house and spent the night in Gannan's room. I saw him the next morning while he was still in bed without a shirt on. He had curly yellow hairs all over his chest just like a monkey, and he smelled even more like an animal than my father did. I jumped on the bed while Gannan made him breakfast in the kitchen. "Hey, baby-san," he said, "let's play a little game. I throw these and we'll see how fast you can pick 'em up, okay?" I nodded eagerly as he picked up a pack of cards and tossed them across the room. I leapt out of the bed and gathered them by the handful, working frantically, scoot-ing this way and that way on the floor, sticking my arm under the cabinet where some had slid. When I breath-lessly brought all of the cards back, the yellow-haired GI was sitting dressed on the edge of the rumpled bed, put-ting his black socks on. "Now *you* do," I said, holding the cards out. He smiled. I smiled too, and hurled the cards as hard as I could, scattering them across the entire room. But the yellow-haired GI just sat and laughed, especially when Gannan came in with the table and yelled at me for making the mess. He didn't pick up a single card. He laughed harder and harder until my face turned red and I hated him.

". . . before the war we lived well there," said Emo. "If there were only as many plots of rice as there used to be, she could stay in the country."

Mahmi nodded and exhaled through her nose. The smoke came out in two plumes that mingled into one cloud before it faded. Suddenly, Mahmi looked up at Emo. "What's that noise?"

"What noise?" said Emo.

The rain seemed to get louder and louder as I listened for the noise. In a moment, we could hear it. Hyongbu was outside, singing "The Man in the Yellow Shirt."

Emo sighed and arranged the table to take back out to the kitchen. "He's come over the wall again," she said. "Sometime he's going to fall and hurt himself."

"*Yobo*, open the door!" cried Hyongbu. "I've returned!" He banged against the doorframe. "Look here, I'm getting wet in this TYPHOON out here! I said OPEN THE DOOR!"

"I'll clear the table," said Mahmi.

Emo went out to open the door. "Where have you been all this while?"

"Shut your mouth," Hyongbu slurred. "Don't meddle in my business."

I listened to the rattle, the loud argument, and the thumping as Hyongbu staggered to his room. In a while I heard muffled noises, then the soft crying of Yongsu and Haesuni.

My mother cleared the table and put out the bed mats. The soft weeping of the rain, drowning out the noises from Hyongbu's room, lulled us to sleep. I dreamt that I saw Hyongbu standing in the rain, chanting,

> I am wearing a yellow shirt.
> I am wearing a yellow pants.
> I am wearing a yellow hair.
> I am wearing a yellow heart.

He was naked except for his underpants, the way he was when he washed outside, and he danced in the traditional Korean way, waving his arms and taking little steps. The chant wasn't at all like "The Man in the Yellow Shirt." It meant Hyongbu's heart was strong and he would live for a very long time. But when I looked again, I saw that his hair was black, not yellow. His pants were white, not yellow. When I said, "Hyongbu, where are your yellow things?" he answered, "*Shhhhh . . .*" and pointed up to the sky as if someone were listening.

> Black, white, blue, red, yellow,
> You, too, come and dance with me.

chanted Hyongbu. "And be quiet. *Shhhhh . . .*" *Shhhh* was the peeing noise.

When I awoke in the midst of a comfortable warmth, I found the bed mat soaked. I tried to stay asleep until it was dry, and I was ashamed when Mahmi made me get up and help her put the mat out in the kitchen near the big stove. Haesuni and Yongsu laughed at me on their way to school.

"You drew a good map," said Haesuni. "Look, it looks like Australia."

"No," said Yongsu, rubbing his eyes. "It's Greenland. Insu-ya, are you going out to borrow some salt today?"

"No!" I cried. "I'm not going!" I already knew the trick of sending bed-wetters out to the neighbors for "lots of salt." They would get beaten for peeing, and when they came back home they would get beaten for not bringing salt. As Haesuni and Yongsu went out with the plastic and bamboo umbrella, I noticed their fresh bruises in the outside light. I looked up at Mahmi.

"It's because he gets drunk," said Mahmi. She went in to put on her makeup. While I sat watching the bed mat dry, Emo came into the kitchen with another mat that had an even bigger map on it. I heard Mahmi laughing.

"Who peed?" I said, pointing at the stain.

"*You* peed. You couldn't just piss on *your* mat, you had to come and wet *ours*, too."

"I *didn't* do it!"

The day's rain hadn't yet begun. I went outside to look at the magpie's grave where the night's rain dripped slowly, in large drops, making a fresh patting sound against the earth. I wondered how many drops were in the sky waiting to fall, and why it always had to be cloudy and dim during the monsoon. Why couldn't the rain drop from a bright and sunny sky? I would ask the owner. If the sky was endless then how far did the raindrops have to fall? I crouched under the chestnut tree and checked around the roots to make sure the magpie's grave was safe. I had put another roof tile over the grave to keep it dry because I knew that although they liked to splash in the summer, the birds didn't like to get too wet. "Magpie, Magpie," I sang.

"Insu-ya!"

I turned around.

"Magpie's or ours—New Year won't come for a long time," said Hyongbu through the window bars. "Come inside and eat. Then I'll tell you a story."

"I'll come in after I pee," I said.

Hyongbu laughed loudly. "All that and you have some left? Hurry and pee before the rain comes. There was a fool once who started to piss just when the rain started. He thought the rain sound was the sound of his pissing and he stayed there all afternoon and evening holding his pepper until the rain stopped. 'Must have drunk quite a lot,' he said when he finally pulled up his pants."

"What a stupid. Is it true, Hyongbu?"

"Of course it's true. The fool was a country relative of mine."

I looked up at the sky, then peed hurriedly and went back into the house. Hyongbu chuckled from the window. After breakfast, he led me down the hall to his room. "Gannan's been doing bad things again," he said. "Hasn't caught a husband yet. You and I are going to talk like men while your Mahmi and Emo scold her."

"Gannan will marry a *good* man," I said.

"She should just marry one of those Black bastards who're glad to get anything with skin whiter than theirs."

"Why? Why do they want people with whiter color skin?"

Hyongbu sat cross-legged on the floor and lit a Salem he had stolen from my mother. Between puffs, he scratched his blue-black hair. "Later, when you grow up, *you* tell me, *ungh*? You can stick it in some white women, yellow women, and black women. You tell me which ones you like best, all right? And with those American women, remember they have lots of different hair colors." He made a ring with his thumb and forefinger, then stuck the cigarette through it. "You stick it right in, just like this."

"Stick what in?"

Hyongbu laughed, exhaling a huge cloud of smoke. "I'll tell you in a few years when you're old enough to know."

"Why can't you tell now? I can do that, too." I imitated him, using my finger instead of a cigarette. "Look here— stick it in, just like *this*."

"You learn fast," said Hyongbu, "but now I'll tell you a story. You want to hear a story?"

"Yes," I said.

"Then get me one of your mother's American cigarettes and a cup of coffee."

I went back to our room, where Mahmi, Emo, and Gannan were talking in quiet voices. They had all been crying about something. "Mahmi," I said, "Hyongbu wants some cigarettes and coffee."

She pointed to the Salems which lay under a handkerchief smudged with makeup. "I'll talk to someone I know at the 121st Army Hospital," she said to Gannan. "Maybe he can do it."

"I'm afraid," said Gannan. She looked toward me and began to cry again. I heard a sound like the tinkling of tiny bells. Emo was stirring the Maxwell House coffee with a tiny sugar spoon.

"Here," said Emo. "Take this coffee and go to Hyongbu. And not so many cigarettes."

I put back two of the five I had taken from the pack and, carefully lifting the coffee on its saucer, I went out the door. Emo closed it behind me. I felt like sitting down and crying, but even with the heavy sadness in my stomach, I managed to take the coffee to Hyongbu without spilling a drop.

"Hyongbu, Gannan is sick," I said. "Mahmi said something about the 121 Hospital."

"That's right. She's sick all right. She's been careless and now she's got something growing in her belly. I suppose they want to take it out." He smiled as he tucked the three Salems into his own cigarette pack.

She must have swallowed too many seeds, I thought. "Hyongbu, what if she eats the terrible medicine and throws up? Will that get it out?"

"It's too far down inside. Now let's see about the coffee, *ungh*?" He took a small sip and said, "Ah, it's good. Shall I tell a story?"

"No." After hearing about Gannan, I was in no mood for a story.

Soon, Mahmi and Gannan left for ASCOM. Emo cleaned up the breakfast tables out in the kitchen and Hyongbu got dressed to go out. Since the rain had not started and the day looked clear, I asked Emo if I could go outside to play.

"Go ahead, go out and play," she said, sniffing as she washed the rice for dinner. "Don't go too far."

I watched her for a while from behind the kitchen door. Every few moments, she would stop her work and look far away beyond the walls of the kitchen. Her puffy eyes would brim with tears, her breasts would heave; and then, squeezing her eyes so the tears beaded out of the corners, she would go back to her work, saying to herself in a mourning voice, "*Aigo, uri Gannan-ah, aigo uri Gannan-ah. . . .*"

Emo's sadness made my heart feel heavy. I promised to myself that when I grew up and became a dark-haired GI, I would make lots of money and buy everyone everything they wanted so they would be happy always. We would have servants so Emo wouldn't have to work in the kitchen; Mahmi could stop going to the PX to buy things for other people; Hyongbu would have his American cigarettes and whiskey. And my father, by then, would surely be a great general with white hair and a beard instead of only his short yellow hair. He would tell me wise things and we would kill many enemies together. Since they said I was growing each day, all I had to do was eat plenty of food and wait patiently until I was big enough. Then they would give me a green uniform and a cap—I would be a GI. I could go to America to see the many, many PX's, NCO Clubs, and all the tall people in green with their sharp, pulled-out noses.

But I had forgotten Gannan. No—I had saved her for last because she was special and deserved the most special things like the filmy American dresses with the colors I couldn't name, the fancy shoes with heels as thin as bird legs, and the most fashionable handbags, the kind that glittered like fish scales when the light shone just so. Gannan had worked hard in the rice paddies and now she worked hard here in Pupyong, waiting outside the ASCOM gate each day until a GI took her through, getting searched each evening on the way out unless her special MP friend was working.

I wandered aimlessly around the house for a while, thinking about this and that, sometimes trying to remember a word or a sound with the insides of my ears, sometimes seeing memories in the darkness behind my eyes. Today I even tried to find pictures or words for the feelings beneath my heart, but it was too hard to do. Those feelings had no words or pictures for them, only darkness and a noise like the sound of rain. I went down to the rice paddies beyond the thatched houses and watched the farmers repairing their paddy dikes.

✦

"**G**annan came! Gannan came! Hurry! Everyone come out!"

I ran out of the room, nearly crashing through the door. Gannan had arrived with a bag full of wonderful things: bananas, oranges, apples, rice cakes—even two bottles of Johnnie Walker Red. While Yongsu and I were pushing and pulling at each other to get to the fruit first, Haesuni quietly took the best ones.

"Where did you get all this?" asked Mahmi. "It's from the Army post, isn't it?"

Gannan nodded. I couldn't hear what she said, but Mahmi smiled and took one of the rice cakes.

Soon Emo, Hyongbu, and Mr. Hwang's family came out to share the things. Hyongbu and Mr. Hwang drank together and talked more and more loudly while Emo and Mahmi helped Gannan peel the apples and oranges. Everyone was very happy because something good must have happened for Gannan to bring home such expensive presents, but Gannan never told us what it was. She just said it was nothing, even when Emo asked if the yellow-haired GI had changed his mind and promised to marry her.

Gannan looked at each of us and gave us each a piece

of fruit she had peeled and cut, but she didn't eat any
herself. "Here, Insu-ya, eat this." She gave me a crescent
piece of white apple, and I just held it dumbly in my hand
until she said again, "Eat it."

I ate it, and a piece of orange. Gannan took some fruit
and rice cakes out to the room where the family from Nagasaki lived. Emo followed her, and after a few moments
the two of them returned with Chonghi's father.

"Chonghi's father! Come in!" called Hyongbu. "Drink
a bit with us. It's precious stuff!"

"Have you all been well?" asked Chonghi's father, half
bowing.

Mr. Hwang gave him a glass of whiskey even before he
had taken his shoes off. Chonghi's father sat with them,
and they began to sing loudly about the rainy park of
Chang Ch'un Tang. To help them, I cracked the chopsticks
against the table and joined in the *jjajajang-ch'ang* parts. It
was just like a party.

Soon Chonghi and his mother came and joined us on
the *maru* under the glare of the fluorescent light. While the
older people drank and sang around the table, Yongsu and
I had fun throwing pieces of fruit at Chonghi and watching
him try to clasp it between his hands. Chonghi had been
born with no bones in his right hand. He had no knuckles
or even creases on his palms, just a rubbery hand that
looked like a half-inflated hospital glove, so we called him
"Rubberhand." When he ran or got excited, he would flap
the hand like a flipper and laugh wildly. Now he clasped
an orange so tightly that his rubber hand bent and the fruit
fell on the *maru* with a thump.

"*Ya*, Rubberhand, watch this!" Yongsu flapped both
of his hands until Chonghi imitated him. We all laughed
together when the boneless hand started to slap against
Chonghi's arm.

Now all the adults, even Gannan, had joined in song.
Haesuni fed slices of apple to Mr. Hwang's little boy, who
had just grown his first teeth. The fluorescent light began
to swing back and forth on the chain as a cool wind blew

in from the garden. The fruit smelled even more sweet and delicious; the sound of the song grew hushed just as rain began crackling in the trees.

Suddenly, Chonghi's mother started singing alone in a raspy voice that came from the *han* deep in her heart. As she sang, tears rolled down her face and her voice cracked, but she kept singing until the song was done. All the women cried, especially Gannan. The men looked down at the wooden *maru* floor, hiding the wetness in their eyes as the rain and the trees sighed outside. Everyone sat quietly while the crying stopped, and then they all told Chonghi's mother what a wonderful singer she was.

"*Nuna*," I said to Gannan. "Will you read me the letter you wrote me now?"

Gannan's face had swollen from the crying. She rubbed her eyes once more. "You don't have to hear the letter now, Insu-ya. I'll tell you a big secret, instead, *ungh*?"

"All right," I said, "but only if it's better than the letter."

"It's much better. And more important."

"What is it?"

Gannan bit her lip for a moment. I thought she would cry again, but she said in a very calm voice, "When you're grown up, you must have compassion. Good things and bad things will happen, but you must remember this always, *ungh*? You must have *injong*."

I frowned. I would much rather have heard the letter she had written to me, but now there was this big secret. "What does that talk, *injong*, mean?"

"It means you have to be a kind person and think of others. Will you remember that word *injong*? It means compassion."

"*Ungh*."

"You won't forget?"

I nodded. The word for compassion was easy enough. I mumbled it a few times to myself: "*Injong, injong, injong*." Maybe the yellow-haired GI had suddenly gotten some of this *injong* and agreed to marry Gannan after all. I hoped it wasn't true because I hated him—I didn't want him to be a good person. But what else could it be? Where could Gannan get all the money to buy the expensive things for the party?

"You really won't forget, Insu-ya?"

"I won't forget!" I said loudly. "Will you read me the letter now?"

"You'll have plenty of time to read the letter some other time." Gannan turned away from me. Her skin looked very white under the fluorescent light. Her arms and shoulders, even her fingers, glowed the way things glow under the big moon. I could tell she had been to the bathhouse that day.

I was annoyed. If Gannan wouldn't read the letter to me, I would learn how to read it by myself. I went to our room and found one of Haesuni's old reading books and opened it to the beginning. I already knew the stories in it. I had memorized every word, and all I had to do was to remember what mark went with which word. Then I would look at the marks on Gannan's letter and know what it said. But the noise from the *maru* bothered me and all the marks in the book looked the same. Many of them seemed to be the same mark put sideways or upside down. If the number seven mark made a sound like *ka* as Haesuni had explained, then how could you make that sound upside down? I turned the book this way and that way, and finally put it back.

I went out to the *maru* where they were singing and dancing. Mahmi told me to put out a bed mat and sleep with Chonghi. His parents would take him home later. Yongsu and Haesuni had already gone to bed and Mr. Hwang's son slept soundly in his mother's lap. Chonghi helped me get the blankets out of the cabinet and lay them out on the floor. We lay down, curled against each other under the bright, dangling bulb; and listening to the singing, the rain, and the rustling trees, we fell asleep.

Sometime late in the night, I awoke with a start in the

dark and silent room. The rain had stopped. Rubberhand had gone, and in his place Mahmi lay at my side. She had turned her head the other way. I couldn't hear her breathing. It was too quiet, and I was afraid. I lay still, afraid even to close my eyes, hoping that Mahmi would turn in her sleep or a tree would move or the wind would blow to make the silence go away. For the longest time, the silence drew on and on; but then, just as I prepared to cry out for Mahmi, the moon came out and its light streamed in through the wet windowpane. I heard a gentle creaking sound, and in the moonlight, I saw Gannan, dressed in white, waving to me from under the branches of the chestnut tree. I smiled and fell, unafraid, into a deep sleep.

Shortly after dawn, Emo's loud wailing woke everyone but Gannan.

✧

I did not cry once before or during Gannan's funeral, and I was not afraid, either, when I saw her body tightly bound in the burial cloths. All the relatives had come up from the country, making our house a busy and noisy place. I spent my time running from room to room watching the preparations and listening to the new voices keening and chattering. Everyone from the country had the country smell and their odor, with the fragrance of *hyang*—the funeral incense—mingled with the smoke of Korean and American cigarettes, the sulfurous stink of struck matches, and the intoxicating fumes of spilt lighter fluid. From the kitchen came the steam of cooking rice, the sharp deliciousness of *kimchi*, and the subtle aroma of roots and grasses. I went outside to breathe fresh air until my nostrils and head cleared so that I could go in to smell all the strange smells once again.

On the morning after the funeral, my mother's eldest brother, Big Uncle, who had had much experience with ghosts and evil demons, sawed down the thick branch from which Gannan had hanged herself. He split the wood into small pieces and arranged them into a rectangular pile. Here were placed all of Gannan's clothes and personal possessions. Gannan's mother, Country Aunt, wept as she brought the things out of Gannan's room; and she laid them in the pile gently, as if they were Gannan's body. Before Big Uncle poured kerosene over the pile, Country Aunt held one of Gannan's blouses against her cheek and looked up into the sky.

Mahmi, Emo, and all the other women stood on one side while the men stood on the other. When Country Aunt finally put the blouse down, Big Uncle nodded to Hyongbu, who struck a match and tossed it into the kerosene-soaked pyre. The flames began almost invisibly with a tiny wooshing sound. It was quiet at first, but in a matter of moments the fire began to roar, and though there had been no wind, the flames began to blow in every direction.

Big Uncle chanted something in a soft and powerful voice. Country Aunt keened loudly, almost singing a t'ar-yong. Hyongbu lit American cigarettes and passed them out among the men, who smoked them thoughtfully in silence.

The green chestnut wood sizzled and crackled now. I watched Gannan's clothes turn black and crumble into ash. Her high-heeled shoes burned with a smelly black smoke; her thin nylon things puffed and shriveled into tiny puddles that looked like melted sugar. As the heat beat against my face, I suddenly remembered she had told me something very important. It was a word I was supposed to remember—a very easy one—that meant to be a good person, and yet, even though I knew how easy it was, I could not remember it no matter how hard I tried. I scratched my head, closed my eyes, and began reciting, one by one, every word I knew, beginning with "fire," which I felt against my face. "Fire hot wood smoke wind mountain tree bird fly cloud rain cry water river ocean. . . ." The fire crackled and I went on and on until I forgot the words I had already listed. I had begun to repeat myself. I knew now that I could name easily only the words that had pictures or funny sounds. When I needed a word that was just an empty spot in my mind, I hesitated and was filled instead by a memory of something I did not want. Soon, I felt as if I were spinning in the dark the way I did when I was sick with fever. I saw picture after picture of Gannan, and now when I remembered she was dead forever and forever just like the magpie, I began to sniff and sob. I tried not to cry, but a moan came out through my throat, growing louder and louder until someone heard and said, "Insu-ya, don't cry. Don't cry, don't cry. Gannan has gone to the Heavenly Kingdom."

When the fire had died down and all the relatives had gone in to eat before their trip back to the country, Big Uncle gathered some ash from the fire and rubbed it into the stump of the chestnut tree branch. He and I were the only ones left outside.

"Big Uncle," I said. "Will Gannan be a ghost and come back?"

Big Uncle cleared his throat and looked up at the chestnut tree, mumbling something to himself. "Let's you and I pray she doesn't come back," he said at last. "She's left this unhappy life behind. Why would she want to come back?" He said these last words quietly.

Mahmi had told me that when he was younger, Big Uncle had been bewitched by a ghost while he was walking home at night. Something had struck him in the back of the head, and he had run as fast as he could down the narrow mountain trail. But the ghost had caught him and tied him up to a tree trunk until morning. When he woke up he found that he had been tied up by nothing but some strands of long grass. Since then, Big Uncle had learned all about ghosts, and now he often helped in exorcisms.

"Big Uncle, do you think Gannan's spirit is unhappy?"

Big Uncle made a sort of humming noise. He looked down at me with his tired eyes and shook his gray head.

"Don't worry and go have fun, *ungh*? It's too early for you to be worrying about things like that." He led me to the place that was once the rock garden, and while I watched, he whittled me a guardian post out of a piece of fallen branch. "Whenever you're afraid of a ghost, you take this and stick it where the ghost will see it, *ungh*? Then everything will be fine."

I took the fresh, white guardian post and touched its frightening face. "It's a scary one," I said.

Big Uncle smiled, showing his stained teeth. "It's the *Ch'onha Taejang'gun*—the Great General of all that is under heaven. Now let's go in and eat."

I paused for a moment and stuck the guardian post into the soft earth at the foot of the chestnut tree where it belonged. I knew already that Gannan would never come back as a bad ghost, but if this was such a sad world like Big Uncle said, I thought it would be better if she didn't come back at all.

Big Uncle and all the other relatives except Country Aunt left early the next morning after staying up all night. When they were all gone, the house seemed too quiet. The sadness that they had kept out with all their voices came into the house and filled it completely full. Now, even when Hyongbu talked with his deep, loud voice, it sounded as if he were far away. The sad silence was so heavy that any noise, even the sound of a sliding door or the buzz of a fly, made me feel better. I spent the next days outside, taking food down to the old farmer's pig and playing with Rubberhand when his mother let him out.

But any time when I wasn't doing something, my thoughts would return to Gannan, and I would feel a great emptiness. I would cry, but the crying did not help, and after a time I would sit and stare dumbly up at the green hills. Now that Gannan was gone, Haesuni and Yongsu fought more and more. Hyongbu drank more often, and Mahmi and Emo had less to talk and be hopeful about. There was no one, now, to bring me Fig Newtons, or play

American games with me, or tell me stories about all the strange things the GIs did.

All that remained in Gannan's room now that everything had been burned and buried were a white folding screen, a white-clothed table, a black-banded portrait, and an incense urn with several sticks of *hyang* beside it. A few days after the funeral, I opened the door a crack and carefully peeked inside. I could feel the heavy silence and emptiness leaking out into the rest of the house, flowing gently over my bare feet. This silence and emptiness was warm, and it made the large room very bright. The light that shone in through the rice paper panels rippled each time the wind blew outside, shifting the shadows of the tree branches. I could still smell the thick odor of the funeral incense that had soaked into the room.

As I stood there with the door slightly open, I began to remember things about the room: where the yellow-haired GI had tossed the cards; where Gannan had sat, wiping the makeup from her face; where we had kneeled to throw dice against the wall to play the GI Number Seven game. In that corner near the window, Gannan had set up a stage for a puppet show which we performed with the ugly German puppets; there, in the other corner, she had sat while making things disappear by magic. I slowly closed the door and went back to the other room where it was cooler and less silent. I took a nap full of the tiredness I had gathered in the past days.

More days passed, and I grew used to the quiet of Gannan's absence, but for a while I still listened for the sound of her voice in the late evening, and when I woke in the middle of the night I would imagine I heard her moan or giggle from her room the way she had when her boyfriends visited.

✧

One morning when I had returned from feeding the pig and was sitting in front of the gate, a shadow fell over me.

I looked up into the shy, smiling face of the yellow-haired GI.

"Boy-san, your mama-san home?" he asked in pidgin, nodding toward the house.

I shook my head.

"When she be back? You know?"

I shook my head again, more slowly. I felt as if I should be doing something—crying, shouting, or beating him— but I felt too hopeless even to move.

"Boy-san, you *aroh* GI talk?" he asked anxiously.

This time I nodded yes.

The yellow-haired GI smiled briefly, then squatted down to make his face level with mine. "Me and my buddies—you *aroh* 'buddies'? *Ch'ingu*—you know that, right? *Friends*. Me and my GI friends *so so* sad Gannan dead. We likee her number one. She number one friend." He paused a moment to look through the gate into the house. "We *so so* sad." He pretended to wipe tears from his eyes. "We want to help out Gannan's mama-san, understand? We got all this money for her." Now he unbuttoned the shirt pocket of his uniform and pulled out a thick stack of colorful MPC bills. "You make sure you give this to *mama-san*, understand? This *t'aksan* money. You go give it to mama-san and say Gannan's GI friends brought it, okay?"

"Okay." I took the money he gave me in both hands, wishing that what I held were his entrails and that he would die in the most terrible way.

"Now you run inside and give that to Gannan's mama-san. This is for you." He pulled a pack of Juicy Fruit gum from his pocket and put it into mine.

I put all the money on my belly and folded my shirt up over it. "You wait," I said.

"Huh?"

"I got for you somesing."

"What?"

"*You* wait here." I ran as quickly as I could through the

gate and to the place where Big Uncle had buried the remains of the fire. I dug with a stick until I saw ashes, then
I poked around until I found some tiny scraps of burnt
cloth. I took these back to the yellow-haired GI and placed
all of them in his hand except one, which I saved.

"What's this?" he asked.

"Gannan dress," I said. "When Gannan die, we burn."

The yellow-haired GI frowned, then suddenly lurched
back and slapped the burnt cloth scraps from his palm.
"What the fuck!" he shouted. His fear made me very
happy.

"Not *Gannan*," I explained. "Just Gannan *dress*." When
the yellow-haired GI turned to go, I quickly put the last
scrap of cloth into his back pocket.

"What do you want now?"

I hoped he hadn't noticed. "You got gum, Hello?" I
said.

"I already gave you some, you little motherfucker. Now
you just get your ass in the house and take that money to
mama-san, hear?"

"Okay, Hello. I got gum. Okay."

"Better be fuckin' okay. Now get your ass in the house!"
He pointed to where I should go, as if I were a dog. I
hoped Gannan's ghost would come and punish him now
that she knew where he was. When she wore that dress in
the Heavenly Kingdom, she would see that part of it was
missing because it hadn't all burned in the fire. She would
have to come back and get the missing part. Then she
would surely punish the yellow-haired GI.

"*Hwuking* okay!" I shouted, stepping through the gate
as Emo came out of the garden to look. "So long, Hello, I
give *okay* money mama-san."

"I'll be seeing you, boy-san."

As he left, I made an evil gesture at his back.

Emo took the money, and that evening she and Mahmi
had a big argument, but they decided to keep the money
and give it to Country Aunt because she had no money at
home. Now that Gannan was dead, things would be much

harder in the country. Country Aunt worried that they might have to sell the mountain where the ancestors were buried. Emo and Mahmi said they would do anything to keep the gravesites. Mahmi would sell more on the black market and Emo would do sewing at home. To my father, they would say nothing.

2

Water

Blood and the River

The house grew even thicker with silence. I imagined at times that I waded through it, as if it were an invisible fluid that swirled between the rooms over the wooden maru *floor. I began to dream that I was looking down into a beautiful, clear river at faces that looked up at me from under the water. I knew these faces—Gannan, Haesuni, Emo, Mahmi—and sometimes the face would be my own reflection, sometimes a subtle distortion that I took to be myself but knew, in my heart, was really an older stranger. I would know that stranger soon.*

When my father learned of Gannan's death he responded with his own silence because it was far too late to do anything. Hyongbu became more moody, drunk, and violent for reasons I would never fully know. My mother and Emo did not talk as frequently because my mother would stay out late into the night and return only to sleep.

I do not really remember what happened in that world of silence. The images I recall must have been from my dreams. A ghost in white with long, black hair and an ethereally beautiful face would often come to me in the garden at night and smile at me with a sorrowful expression. She spoke only when it rained, and then her voice was always lost amidst the noise of the raindrops. Sometimes she appeared with the ghost of the Japanese Colonel, but they could not see each other because they belonged to different tragedies.

✧

I remember the river, the upper Han flowing beneath the green hills across from Big Uncle's village. It was late summer, after the monsoons, and the exposed riverbed stretched out into a vast field of pebbles—pure white like hens' eggs, speckled like robins' eggs—surprisingly beautiful and clean. The palest and lightest stones left a chalk-like dust on my palms and the largest were so heavy against my five-year-old strength that I thought they must be held to the earth by roots. I remember the riverbed as if I had been there a hundred years ago when the flat-bottomed boats still wound their way down the current on their way to Seoul, when short-statured men in white, their skin burnt dark by the sun, portaged their goods from boat to boat as they ran aground in the shallows.

That summer, the year after Gannan's death, I had sat naked through the hot afternoons in the water of the giant aluminum basin at home, never imagining that water could be so wonderful, so cool, so clear as the river. Big Uncle had come down from the country one evening with the news that it was time to move Gannan's grave nearer to the ancestors, and since my father was north of Camp Casey, near the DMZ for field exercises, my mother and I had joined the rest of the family for the visit to Sambongni, the home of the old Lee clan.

Now I played along the riverbank, stumbling barefoot over the smooth stones as Hyongbu squatted on the grass smoking a Salem he had borrowed from my mother. Between puffs, he scratched his glossy black hair and hummed to himself.

"Hyongbu, why scratch your head like that?"

He looked at me and smiled. "Insu-ya, you may think these lice are all I've brought back with me from the deep country. Ha! I've seen some things, too, and I have a story just for you. Want to hear?"

"*Ungh.*"

"Good. Of course you want to hear." His voice changed tone and cadence. He began to rock slowly back and forth, scratching his head with the same hand that held his precious cigarette.

"Hmmm. . . . So I'm on my way to the burial. A dozen mountains away from Sambongni, you see, so there is much walking. I walk faster than anyone else, so I'm alone at least three *li* in front of all the others.

"I see this chasm where the trail ends, and across it— over there—I can see what is left of a rope bridge. On this side there is nothing." He nodded. "Ah, now that the bridge has fallen, it will be all right if I don't go to the burial. I never wanted to move her grave anyway."

"Hyongbu, why did they move Gannan's grave?" My mother had tried to explain it to me earlier, but I could not understand why they would bury her near Pupyong only to move her again, far away.

"It was an auspicious time," said Hyongbu. "The fortune-tellers and the geomancers all said it was a good thing to do."

"But why?"

"It has to do with luck," he said. "I don't believe it myself, but you wouldn't want unhappy ghosts to ruin the family, would you?"

"No," I said.

"So let me finish my story, *ungh*? I looked over the chasm, scratching my head just like this. I had already caught lice from the night before, sleeping with those country people around. I tried to see if there was another trail at all, but I couldn't find one over the chasm. I thought maybe I would have to leap across and fix the bridge so that the others could cross. It was only twenty meters across—I can leap that easily.

"Suddenly, I felt something watching me." He squinted, then pushed his face forward at me and snapped his neck violently around to look behind him. I jumped.

Hyongbu chuckled. "I have very sharp senses, Insu-ya. I looked, and over behind a huge boulder—a thousand times bigger than the ones out here—I saw the huge, yellow, glowing eyes of a goblin.

"Ahhh . . . ," he said, making his eyes large and round. "Tiger eyes are hungry—the eyes of cats—but goblin eyes are very round and they blink very, very slowly."

I moved away as he made his eyes even larger and imitated a goblin looking for a victim.

"Now goblins are a little bit slow. They get stupid because they only eat up stupid people like that relative of mine—the one who pissed in the rain. Anyone who knows a little can get away from them.

" '*Ya!* Goblin!' I shouted. 'What do you think you're doing, *ungh*? Hiding behind a rock like that? Are you trying to scare me? Get up! Show yourself!' So this goblin, blinking his huge stupid eyes, started to get up. And up. And up. I thought he was flying into the air at first, but he was still connected to his long legs. He was taller than most of the trees on the mountain! Never, while I have been alive, have I seen a goblin that tall!" Hyongbu took one last drag of the Salem and mashed it out on a rock. "So this goblin is getting taller and taller blinking those huge, stupid, yellow eyes. And I was getting scared. Even your Hyongbu gets scared sometimes. For a moment I thought of leaping across the chasm, but I know that this goblin could *skip* across. I had a better idea.

" 'You stupid goblin, why are you here?' I said. 'You're much too tall for all these trees and rocks. You had to lie down on your stomach just to hide behind that boulder. Isn't that so? What will you do when tigers and foxes and people walk all over you while you're down like that, *ungh*? You stupid.'

"Of course this goblin was too stupid to answer me. He was having a hard time trying to think about my words. He just blinked and let his jaw hang open. His teeth were huge and monstrous. 'Look here, you stupid goblin,' I said to him. 'If you help me, I'll tell you where to go so you won't have to think about what I'm trying to tell you. You're too rock-headed to figure out these things for yourself. You must have eaten lots of village idiots to be this stupid. Maybe your brain got stretched, *ungh*? So will you help me?' The goblin nodded. What else could he do? He was dealing with your Hyongbu.

"So I told this goblin that what I needed was a bridge to get across the chasm. I told him to put down his club, which had an enormous spike in it, and stand at the edge of the chasm. I made him raise his arms to see if he would be twenty meters tall. Of course, he was. 'Now don't be afraid. You won't miss or let go. You may be stupid, but you're strong.' "

"Hyongbu, so what did you do? When did you kill it?"

"Shut up, brat. I'll tell you."

"You tied up his hands and beat him with his club?"

"A good idea, but wrong. Listen." He scratched his head some more. "So I *pushed* him and he toppled down down down—but just when you thought he was going to fall all the way into the chasm—he grabbed the other side with his horrible hands. Ha!

"So now I had a bridge. I walked back and forth over the goblin to make sure it was sturdy. I told him not to move or make any noise and made sure his backside was up so he wouldn't think to eat up the people who were going to walk on him.

"Now the others caught up to me. 'Ah,' they said. 'You walked so fast and now you're either tired or you have blisters.' So I said to them, 'You'd like that, wouldn't you, but I was just waiting because you're all so slow. In fact, I'm going to wait just a while longer after you leave. Then I'll follow along behind so you don't get lost.' Of course they thought I was bragging and all walked across the goblin bridge. And they didn't even know it was a goblin! Those stupids.

"Now when they were all gone, I went across myself and then helped the goblin up. He was very heavy, but you know how strong your Hyongbu is. Even if I don't eat so much meat like you Yankees, I'm stronger. Why, I was the village wrestling champion when I was young. I even won a cow.

"And now I told the goblin to go down south to where the Buddhist monasteries are and the trees go up into heaven. I told him to be kind and not to eat any monks, only nasty little brats who go outside late at night. The goblin wanted to thank me. He made scary noises and blinked his big eyes even more. '*Ya*, goblin. If you want to thank me, you can fix this bridge here for the villagers. There's plenty of wood all over the mountains.' So the goblin helped me fix the bridge, and now that village has the best bridge in the whole province.

"So I showed the goblin how to get to the south country, and he leaped into the sky and disappeared. He was a good goblin, *ungh*?"

"*Ungh*," I said. But now I thought of the goblin story again and had a question. "You didn't hit the goblin even *once*, Hyongbu?"

"Well . . . ," he said. "I did hit it once, but I wasn't going to tell you about it."

"Why not? Is it secret like when you hit Yongsu and Haesuni when you're drunk?"

"*Ya*, be careful what you say."

I looked down at my feet.

"I hit him with my knee," said Hyongbu. "But goblin skin is prickly and sharp just like that glass along our wall. I cut myself on that goblin's skin, and he didn't even know I'd hit him." He rolled up one leg of his trousers and showed me a fresh cut. "See. Don't ever hit a goblin without looking first. It's best to hit them in the face or poke their eyes out."

"Does it hurt?"

"This is nothing. I've been shot by guns."

"Bang!" I shouted. "When I'm a GI I'll have a machine gun and I'll shoot lots of bad guys with it."

"And you'll buy me lots and lots of cigarettes and Johnnie Walker, right?"

"Right. Black Label."

"And do you know what you say to GIs you don't like? You don't like that yellow-haired bastard who used to nail Gannan, do you?"

"No," I said. "I'll hit him with my fist."

"It's better to kick him right in the pepper," said Hyongbu. "And this is what you say." He curled his index finger and his third finger so his long middle finger stuck out. "You do this and you shove it at them like *this* and you say, 'Hwuk you, muddahwukka!' "

He helped me curl my fingers like his, and we practiced together, shouting, "Hwuk you, muddahwukka! Hwuk you, muddahwukka!" until I knew it by heart.

"If they don't listen to that, then you grab one side of your ass and you say, 'Eat my *shet*, muddahwukka!' Understand?" He showed me how to grab one buttock and make the gestures. "Next time your Mahmi takes you to ASCOM, try it a few times."

"All right," I said. I practiced several more times just for fun while Hyongbu laughed and occasionally corrected me before walking back to the village.

In a while, Yongsu and Haesuni joined me to show me the schools of minnow darting through the magically transparent water. I noticed how my legs seemed larger and bent at a funny angle in the water but became normal again when I lifted them out.

We waded and splashed. Yongsu skipped stones and Haesuni turned wet cartwheels in the shallows, but I was too clumsy to do either. I simply sat down in the cold water until I grew numb, then crawled out and lay on the warm stones to feel the strange sensation of my limbs coming back to life. This was the only game I could think of. I tried to describe it to my cousins, but they urged me to put on my clothes and come play with them instead.

✧

Late in the afternoon, Hyongbu came back from the village singing a song. He walked the way I had on the pebbles, stumbling and staggering every few steps, and when he came near, I could smell the pungent *soju* on his breath.

"Boat ride!" he said. "Boat ride! Let's ride a boat and *go* to the other side!"

Yongsu squinted and grinned, but Haesuni seemed worried. I put on my clothes and shouted, "Boat ride!"

"Good!" said Hyongbu. "Come here. I'll take you kids for a ride on the *boat*." Hyongbu led us upstream to where a weathered flat-bottom boat lay grounded on the pebbles. With our meager help, he pushed it into the water, slipping several times in the process.

He lifted us all inside and pushed the boat until we were clear of the shallows. When the water reached his knees, he jumped aboard, jolting us out of our seats and into the bottom of the boat.

"There," he said. "If you like, I'll row all the way to Inchon."

I looked over the side into the clear water. The pebbles on the river bottom shimmered with the light that shone through the ripples on the surface. The boat's shadow glided along the pebbles as the gentle current moved us toward the middle of the river.

"Father, take us to the other side," said Yongsu. "Big Uncle said that's where he saw tigers when he was little."

Hyongbu growled like a tiger and snapped at us. "Then let's go see the tiger!" he said. "Are any of you scared?"

My breast swelled with joy. To see a tiger! To be asked if I was scared and yet still remain brave! I splashed at the water, inhaled its pure smell and shouted, *"Yaa!"*

Haesuni looked toward the riverbank, then at me. "The water's getting deep," she said to Hyongbu. "Go back, *appa*. What if we fall out?"

"Then we'll swim like *fish*!" declared Hyongbu.

I stopped my shouting and looked carefully down into the water. The boat's shadow was a bit larger, but the bottom seemed just as near as before. When I stretched my arm down, the pebbles looked just out of reach. "Look," I said. "It's not deep."

Haesuni calmed, but still looked nervously at the riverbank, where, in the distance, the village seemed slowly to move away from us. Now Hyongbu began to row with one oar while Yongsu and I tried to manage the other one. At first we could only make it jerk and flap like a broken wooden wing, but soon we made it dip properly into the water. The boat spun in slow circles.

Hyongbu sang:

> Go to the mountains.
> Go to the ocean.
> When the rain's pouring,
> Go to the homestead.
> *Jjang jjang, wajang ch'ang!*
> If there's no rooftop,
> Let us get wet then.
> *Jjang jjang, wajang ch'ang!*
> If the hills crumble,
> Let's eat up the mud!

"Jjang jjang, wajang ch'ang!" I sang with Yongsu as we rowed. The oars creaked and lapped at the water.

"Appa!" Haesuni suddenly shouted. "Let's go back! I can't see the village!"

"*Ungh?*" said Hyongbu. "If you don't want to ride, *get off!*"

Haesuni was silent for a moment. She stared down into the water and looked sullen. When Yongsu and I stopped rowing, she grasped the side of the boat, turned, and climbed out feet first. She stretched her legs, trying to find the bottom, and for a moment it looked like she had managed to stand, but then the boat moved, sucking her legs underneath. Haesuni screamed and clutched frantically, her fingernails digging into the soft wood. Her wide eyes glinted in the sun. I could imagine them open, just like that, as she lost her grip and fell backward into the water so clear she would sink to the bottom without even seeming to recede. I could see Big Uncle pulling her out of the water with her long black hair plastered over her pale flesh.

"Hyongbu!" I shouted when Haesuni screamed again.

"Shut up!" said Hyongbu. Yongsu and I tried to pull Haesuni back up, but Hyongbu swatted at us. "You just hang on like that till we get back," he said. "If you two help her, I'll throw you *all* in! And if you cry, I'll just go farther into the river!" He grabbed both the oars now, and singing the song again, he rowed back upstream. All I could see now was the terror on Haesuni's face: her wide eyes, her lips pulled taut and quivering as she hung, grim and silent as a ghost, onto the boat.

"Hyongbu!" I called. "Hurry! Hurry!"

He rowed at the same pace, looking left and then right. The foliage along the far bank seemed not to move at all. I wondered if Hyongbu was just pretending to row.

Yongsu dipped his hands in the water and started splashing to make the boat go faster. He looked anxiously at me until I helped, too.

Haesuni continued to hang there, propped by her armpits, quivering and clenching her teeth. After a few moments she made a strange groaning noise through her nose. Again, I tried to help her, but Hyongbu gave me an angry look and I cowered.

"*Appa!*" said Yongsu. "Hurry!"

"All right, I'll hurry," said Hyongbu. He rowed a few quick strokes and then, with an expert flick of the oars, splashed water all over us. "*Hurry! Hurry!*" he shouted. When he saw us he laughed loudly. "Shall I hurry again?"

Even under the hot sun the water he had splashed on us seemed especially cold. Yongsu and I shivered and huddled together in the back of the boat. While Hyongbu went back to his leisurely rowing, I hid behind Yongsu's back and held on to Haesuni's cold hands as she grew weak and began to lose her grip.

Somehow, after the longest time, we finally reached the riverbank, and Haesuni walked unsteadily away with us to Big Uncle's house. We said nothing about what had just happened, but as we walked, something flashed between us, as if we had all realized, at the same instant, that we had seen Haesuni's spirit on the verge of leaving her body.

Hyongbu stayed behind to bathe in the river. He fell asleep and had to be carried back to the village before nightfall.

✧

The room was empty when I awoke in the darkness of late evening. Everyone—even Haesuni and Yongsu—had gone out somewhere, and the only one left behind was Hyongbu, sitting on the *maru* floor just outside the room, quietly puffing on a cigarette. All around him the walls were flecked dark with mosquitoes he had smashed. The large red splotches were ones that had bitten him.

"Come here," said Hyongbu. When I remained inside the sliding doors of the room, he said more loudly, "Come here!" and slapped the *maru* in front of him. I slowly walked over, looking down at my feet.

"What's the matter, *ungh*? Still sullen over the boat ride?"

"No," I mumbled.

"Afraid I was going to let Suni drown? *Ungh?*"

I was afraid to say yes, but I nodded slowly, not daring to look up. "I was scared," I said finally.

"I would never do that to you or my son, Insu-ya. Never. But she's just a girl. A woman. A woman can ruin an entire bloodline. A woman can suck you dry of your strength. And she's going to grow up into a bitch, just like the rest of them. She's already got that devious fox look in her eye." He blew smoke for a moment and lit another cigarette from the stub in his mouth. "Bitches," he said, "always thinking they know better than a man."

I looked toward the gate, hoping to see Emo or my mother there. "Sit down," said Hyongbu, patting the *maru*, "I'll tell you a story. Do you know the story of the mosquito? You don't know why those little bastards suck our blood, do you? Did your Yankee father ever tell you, Insu-ya?"

"No."

"Then I shall tell you the mosquito story," said Hyongbu.

I tucked my knees under my chin as I sat and looked toward the dark part of the *maru*, where the shadows from the dangling light seemed to flutter as the bulb slowly shifted in a breeze. Hyongbu held his fresh cigarette with trembling fingers. "Well . . . long, long ago there was a little village where I used to live out in the country. A quiet, pretty village by a river with clear water and many fields of rice—it was like Sambongni. In this village lived an old relative of mine. My great-great-grandfather.

"This great-great-grandfather of mine was a famous man. He was even stronger than me or Big Uncle. He could lift ten *kama* of rice with one arm. He could lift an ox over his head.

"He was a famous man, even more famous than your Hyongbu and much, much more famous than your Yankee father. In his whole province there was no woman beautiful enough for him to marry. Oh, there were your Sunis and Sukis, but they wouldn't do at all. What do you think he did, Insu-ya?"

"Did he go to a monastery?"

"No, he went to another village over the mountains! If he became a monk, I never would have been born, would I?" Hyongbu reached over and tapped my temple a few times with the hand that held the cigarette, spilling ash on the floor. "You use your head. So . . . he went far over the mountains into another province, to another village, and found the most beautiful woman there. Ah, a great

beauty—more beautiful than even the most beautiful
women in China. More beautiful than the women of Seoul.
Those long-nose bastards could never touch this woman.
Her face was bright as the moon and her skin was soft as
clouds. My great-great-grandfather wondered why she
hadn't been married off yet. 'What is wrong with your
men?' he asked the village people. 'Why is this woman not
married?' Everyone was quiet, but one villager took him
to the side and told him that she was a demon. 'Ha,' said
my great-great-grandfather. 'She's no demon. Look how
beautiful she is. And what if she is a demon, *ungh*? I'll
marry her anyway and we will be happy.' The villagers all
gave him their blessing and thanked him for taking her
away.

"Now my great-great-grandfather wasn't a stupid man.
He knew about demons and such things. On his way over
the mountain passes he made sure to check if his new wife
had a reflection. He had tried to see her face in the bowl
of water when he married her, but she had bowed too
quickly. You know, don't you? Back then all you had to
do to get married was to bow together with a bowl of
water between you."

"Why did he check for a reflection?"

"Why? Because demons don't have reflections. Or if
they're fox demons they always have the reflection of a
fox." Hyongbu lit another cigarette. "Well, she had a reflection. The water was a little rippled, but he knew the
reflection was as beautiful as she was. My grandfather
brought her back to his village, and they had a three-day
festival to celebrate his marriage. From all around, relatives came to eat and dance and wish them good fortune.

"Ah, it was a happy time. Two cows butchered, three
pigs, ducks, and chickens. Many kinds of *kimchi* and colorful rice cakes. All those delicious banquet foods. After
the celebration everything got quiet and content. Ah, my
grandfather was happy—but not for long.

"Because four days after the new wife was in his village,
a baby was found with its throat all bitten and torn. It was

all dried up. No blood at all. They said a fox demon must
be in the village. They called a *mudang* and chased all the
bad spirits away. The next morning, they found a little boy
all chewed up under his blanket. They were scared. They
put men out in the streets at night to guard the village, but
in the morning the men were all bitten and sucked dry,
too. It was horrible. People started to stay up at night. They
carried lanterns and always slept out on the *maru* together
so everyone could be seen. Then, one night, it stopped.
People could sleep again and not worry about getting
eaten. There was a big funeral for the people who had
died, and another *mudang* was called from far away."
Hyongbu puffed his cigarette for a while.

"Well, for a month, no one died, and then it happened
again. Just the same way. First an infant, then a child, and
then grown-ups. All bitten and chewed and all their blood
sucked out. My grandfather was worried. While his family
all slept on the *maru*, he stayed up and watched. He always
worried because his new wife would have to go to the
bathroom every night in the middle of the night. 'Let me
come with you,' he said. 'The demon might get you while
you're away.' But his wife would always say, 'Don't be
silly. Gentlemen don't follow women to the bathroom.
Anyway, what demon in its right mind would look in a
bathroom in the middle of the night?' She was beautiful,
this woman, but she was a fierce arguer, too. My grandfather let her go alone.

"One night, she was gone for a particularly long time,
and he got so worried that he took the lantern and went
to the outhouse to see if she was all right. He found her
lying on the ground, bleeding and moaning. 'What happened?' he asked. He picked her up and took her back to
the house. She was cut in the thigh—a deep cut. 'What
happened?' he asked her. She said she had slipped and
fallen onto a sharp rock on her way back from the outhouse. My grandfather treated the wound and put her to
bed.

"The next morning, another villager was found dead.

But this time there was more. This man had fought back with a knife, and he had stabbed the demon. They knew it had not died, though, because it had left a little trail of blood as it ran away.

"Now my great-great-grandfather was not a stupid man. He knew there were no sharp rocks near his house. He was suspicious, so on the next night, when his wife limped to the bathroom, he followed her. Carefully and quietly, he crept behind her and watched by moonlight. She made water and came back. That was all. He was so relieved he thought he would shout with joy. He was happy, but the next day, he heard that the demon had stopped. This made my grandfather worry.

"For a whole month he worried. And then it started again. This time the village could not bear it. Most of the people moved away to the houses of their relatives and said that they would not come back until the demon was gone forever.

"By now my grandfather's wife was better, but she was still limping. My grandfather had stayed up so many nights he was looking like an old, old man. He was sick, too. He was a strong man like I told you, but even the strongest men have to sleep sometimes. One night he let his brother stay up, and he slept.

"In the morning, it was horrible. Blood all over the *maru*. All over the walls. The brother had fought fiercely because he was strong, too, but he was dead—all white. His eyes were wide, wide open and there was a snarl on his face. Blood all over the blankets where the family slept—even on the blanket of my grandfather's new wife.

"He was sick now, and even though he wanted to find this demon and kill it—even though he wanted to kill all the people who said that the demon was bad fortune brought by his new wife—he had to rest and sleep. One night, while he slept, he heard a slurping sound. A sound like someone was eating noodles. Very quietly, he opened his eyes and looked. Then he shut them so very quickly!

Ah, it was horrible! It was his wife. His wife was sucking at the throat of his father. She was chewing and slurping and her face was the face of a fox. His wife was the fox demon!"

I shuddered and hid my face between my knees. I closed my eyes. It was cold—the room was cold and it was strangely quiet outside. "Hyongbu?"

"His wife was a fox demon!"

"Hyongbu?" I said again.

He was looking into the far, dark corner of the *maru*. "A demon," he said. "My grandfather wanted to scream, but he was weak now. If the demon knew, it would kill him, too.

"So while his new wife sucked his father's blood, he pretended to sleep. He shivered in a cold sweat and he trembled with fear.

"In the morning they put the father's body away into the room where the brother's body lay. My grandfather tried to act as if he had seen nothing, but his wife noticed. 'You're acting strangely,' she said. 'You must be more sick today.' 'Yes,' he said. 'That's it. That's it.' He wanted to cry. He loved his wife. She was the most beautiful woman in the province. It was hard to believe that she was the fox demon.

"My grandfather did not stay in bed that day. He went out into the backyard and started piling wood. He made large stacks into walls and a door. He made a roof and a small hole in the back wall—just large enough to crawl through. When he was finished, there was a little house of firewood in the backyard.

" 'You must be crazy,' said his wife. 'You're all sick and you build a silly house. What's wrong with you?' My grandfather couldn't bear speaking to her. He pretended he was delirious with fever."

"Hyongbu?" I whispered.

"Night came again. The whole village was empty now. Only grandfather's family was left. They were all pale with fear—thin and dark-eyed. All except the new wife. She was as beautiful as ever. Everyone tried not to sleep, but one by one, one by one, they each collapsed.

"Late, when the lantern flickered almost out, my grandfather heard a rustling beside him. His wife was getting up. He was afraid. He was afraid.

"The new wife stood up, and slowly, very slowly, her body hunched over and curled. Under her skirt, nine red tails crept out onto the floor. When she turned, my grandfather saw her face in the lantern light. She was a fox demon!

"She limped over to my grandfather's sister. She licked her teeth. Her tongue was long and wet and her eyes were devious and hungry. Just as she was leaning down to bite with those long, white teeth, my grandfather sat up and shouted, 'Fox demon! Fox demon, try and get me! I have more blood than that little girl! See if you can get me, *ungh*?'

"The demon spoke in the new wife's voice. 'Go away, husband. Leave me. Let me eat this one and I will let you live and be happy.' 'No,' said my grandfather. 'I am not your husband. I married a woman, not a fox demon. I won't let you suck my sister's blood. Here, eat me instead!'

" 'Leave me,' said the fox demon. 'Please leave me alone tonight and you will be happy.' 'No!' my grandfather shouted. He took the lantern and swung it at the demon. He hit the demon again and again until it was afraid it would catch fire and burn to death. The demon chased my grandfather. He ran out into the backyard and into the firewood house.

"The demon was confused. 'Where are you, husband?' it said. 'Where are you? I promise not to hurt you. I'll just tie you up tonight and you'll be safe.' 'Then come in and get me,' said my grandfather. He crawled out of the little hole and plugged it up. When the fox demon went into the house to get him, he ran to the front and shut it. Then, before the lantern could go out, he threw it into the wood and everything caught fire.

" 'Let me out,' said the demon. 'Let me out. Husband, I love you. If I have the blood of just one more person, I won't be a demon anymore. Please let me out.'

"She had been so kind and they had been so happy together. My grandfather knew that if he let her become human, no one in the village would ever know the truth, and he could have a wife. He cried. The fire grew brighter and the flames rose higher and higher. The fox demon screamed inside the burning firewood house.

" 'Let me out! Oh, please let me out! I want to be human. I've been a fox demon for three hundred years. I'll be a real person and we can live together and have children and be happy. I love you, husband. Please, let me out. I want to be a human being. Please, oh, please. . . .'

"As the fire burned and burned, my grandfather went and stood in front of the door. He wanted to open it, but he knew that he shouldn't. He cried and cried. Finally, he reached for the burning door and tried to pull it open, but it was too hot and he couldn't touch it. 'Please, please let me out!' Just then, the roof of the firewood house collapsed. There was a loud scream, then only the sound of the fire.

"My grandfather fell on the ground and wept until dawn. He was so tired then, and the firewood house was all black ashes. When the sun came up, a tiny insect flew out of the ashes and landed on his arm. It was a strange insect he had never seen before, and it was still warm from the ashes. He was about to brush it off, but then he noticed it was biting him. He put his eye close and watched it as it pulled its beak out of his skin and a drop of blood oozed out. The insect sucked up this drop of blood, too, then flew off with a whining sound, way, way up into the sky. This new insect was the first mosquito."

I looked sideways at Hyongbu. I unfolded my arms from around my knees and let the air dry my sweat. He was staring blankly at his empty cigarette pack. For the longest time we sat there in silence, Hyongbu brooding and me too afraid to speak.

In the dim light of the 40-watt bulb that hung over us, the dark corners of the *maru* were barely visible, as distant and indistinct as the memory of dreams. I sat there, becoming slowly rigid, hard as stone against the images that flickered through my thoughts like the shadows of that dangling light, and I would sit there forever until something broke the silence. I would be a stone on the bank of the cold, clear Han; I would be the water splashing and sparkling in the light; I would be the current, invisible, moving unerringly to the center of the world. I closed my eyes and sat inside my own darkness until I heard a sound from outside. My mother had returned. I could hear her voice, then Emo's, and then Yongsu's and Haesuni's. Suddenly I saw the fleeting panicked expression on Haesuni's face as she dangled over the side of the boat, the gleam of light reflecting on her wide eyes. Then I opened my eyes and found Hyongbu curled up in a half-moon around the aluminum ashtray, asleep on the *maru* amidst the dead ashes of his American cigarettes.

✧

Years later, I learned that they had made a terrible mistake when they moved Gannan's grave. When they exhumed her body, they had found her floating in a pool of clear water, the coffin rotted away but her body as fresh as if she had been asleep. There was an argument about how to take this omen, but since the senior geomancer had read the wind and the water and consulted the astrological charts, they went against the evidence before their eyes, despite Big Uncle's objections, and they fished her out, changed the winding sheets, and took her by cart, then by train, then by cart again to the ancestral mountain near Sambongni. Late in the afternoon they had lifted her new pine coffin off the cart and carried it up the steep slopes, following an animal's path to the site that the geomancer had selected—far enough from the ancestors not to offend them. They'd buried the coffin, said what had to be said, chanted while they tamped down the earth, performed the ceremony afterward. And before they left, Big Uncle made sure the knee-high mound was well-sodded to survive the next rain. But it was all half-hearted. Hers was not an ancestral grave, and it was not on the ancestors' mountain, and there was no one in Sambongni to make the annual journey to trim the grass and add to the settling mound so that it would not disappear into the *earth. After the first monsoon, one of the Country Aunts who happened to be up that way gathering chestnuts had repaired the damage, but after the second and the third monsoon seasons had passed, Gannan's grave had eroded away to nothing. It had become part of the landscape, and no one remembered where it was.*

Years later on a trip to Sambongni I visited the graves of my maternal grandfather and grandmother, and later that afternoon I had hiked over the mountain to find what remained of Gannan's grave mound. Country Aunt pointed out the trail the burial party had taken, and I followed it through the high grass. It was a rabbit's trail, I think. It wound up the slope, following the contours of the earth until it reached a momentary open and flat spot near a few chestnut trees. That was where it might have been. If I could have read the wind and the water and balanced heaven and earth, I would have located her grave there, two-thirds of the way up the hillside, overlooking the shimmering river in the distance. It was a quiet spot, breezy but sheltered from the strong wind, in sunlight most of the day— the sort of spot where I imagined Gannan might have lingered early in the evening to watch the sun go down over the hills. She would have been lonely, and she would have been worried about something, but she would have smiled that faint and nostalgic smile. When the sun went down she would close her eyes and sigh at the hardships of life, and then she would go to sleep.

I believed I could feel her spirit there that day though I never found the faintest trace of her grave. As I hiked back down to Sambongni, I sang Gannan the lullaby she had sung for me so many times.

Down the silvery Milky Way
Through the deep blue night
Sail a hare and a ch'aesu tree
On a ship of white.
With no oars, without a sail
With no chart or plan

Sailing, so soft, they're sailing
Into the Westward Land.

I looked back at the gentle mound of the hill, the same shape as
a grave mound. In my memory, that hill is Gannan's grave.

3

Fire

Insignia

Dear Father,
    This week I read The Count of Monte Cristo. It is
by Alexander Dumas. He also wrote The Man in the
Iron Mask. But I like this one much better. I think Mr.
Dumas is now my favorite writer. How are you? I
hope you have killed many enemies. I hope you do
not get wounded. Next I am going to read The War of
the Worlds by Mr. H.G. Wells.

Your son,
Heinz

*I wrote to my father at least once a month while he was in
Vietnam because my mother told me that the letters made him
very proud and happy. The letters I got back from Vietnam were
brief and feather-light, scrawled in a practically illegible Ger-
manic script on single sheets of translucent blue Air Mail paper.
The letters never said anything about the war, but they encour-
aged my studies, asked after my grades, told me to be good. They
were always signed, "Your Father, Heinz," as if to remind me
that he was my father and not some yellow-haired stranger. It*

*was because of the letters I had written him that, on my eleventh
birthday, in the dead of winter, my father took me to the Stars
and Stripes bookstore in ASCOM.*

*I remember squinting to make out the small Quonset hut
that stood by itself, no other buildings around it to break
the cold wind. I remember walking over the tarmac under
the PX hill, how I could feel my thighs beginning to go
numb as the wind rose and dusted us with a fine and painful
mist of ice crystals. I remember us stepping down a couple
of cement steps between frozen snow drifts scoured a brilliant
white by the wind, and my father pulling open the wire-
reinforced glass door, bracing it against the wind until I stepped
inside, into the sudden blast of dry heat from the clicking diesel
stove; the door slams shut behind us, startling the Korean man
who sits drowsing at the cash register, and we quickly remove
our gloves and our hats, unzipping our green flight jackets to
let the heat in.*

"Bery cold to buy book," says the Korean man.

"Taksan cold," says my father. "Like a witch's tit."

*I know this bookstore, so I quickly move away from the door
and stand in front of the diesel stove, holding the flaps of my
jacket open as if they were fabric wings. When the numbness
leaves me I shiver a few times as the warmth enters my body. I
go over to comic books to wait until my father picks up his usual*
Time, Newsweek, *and* The Army Times.

*But today he is looking in a section where we have never been
before—the expensive section with the leather-bound Bibles in
boxes and clothbound books like the ones in the school library.
When my father buys books they are paperback—fifty cents
apiece if not cheaper—but this one is several dollars, the price
of ten books. It is* Kim, *by Rudyard Kipling—blue cloth binding;
a gold-embossed man running with a torch; the signatures, each
distinct, precisely stacked, sewn and cut between the covers; the
smell of paper and glue.*

*I remember the size of my father's hand as he grasped the
book by the spine and opened it to make the inscription. I remember the size of my smaller, darker hand as I received the*

book and opened it to look at the inscription, barely legible to me:

For my son on his eleventh birthday.

From your father,
Heinz

He never knew that I wouldn't read it until the fourth anniversary of his death, and by then the original would be long lost, but the inscription burned so deep into my memory that when I opened the new paper-bound copy I could see the words projected onto the title page.

My father died believing I had read the book; believing I had made some decision about its contents, his message to me; believing I had forgotten or not cared enough to mention the remarkable coincidences, the ironic resonances. Perhaps when he quoted Kipling to me when I was in high school he was telling me he had gotten over my silence. Perhaps he, himself, had forgotten. But now I remember him in his Russian-style hat, wearing his sheepskin jacket, smoking a cigar, grinning. The wrinkles around his eyes—cut deep from squinting into the Vietnam sun, from peering into the observation glasses at the 38th parallel, at the DMZ between Koreas—they fan out like the delta of a river, and he is smiling so hard, laughing his surprisingly loud and barky laugh, that tears stream from the corners of his cold blue eyes and are squeezed into those channels.

When he saw me for the first time after my birth, when Emo held me out to him as he stepped down from the green U.S. Army bus, he had held me like a piece of wood, a rifle stock at present arms. He had held his son and turned bright red from the shame of having a mixed-blood child—or was it simply that he did not know how to hold an infant? He handed me back to Emo and walked home in a foul mood. Later he erupted at my mother for daring to let him be seen in public with a child presented to him by a Korean.

Again I remember the size of his hand, that bright white palm *twice the size of my face. I had dropped a clump of rice on the floor and picked it up to smear it against the lip of the lacquer table in the customary way, to be cleaned up later, and he had slapped me so hard I had fallen sideways onto the floor. "How dare you waste your food! Do you know how long I work for that rice? Eat it!" Somehow I put the soiled and sticky rice glob into my mouth and chew it, chew it until I need hardly swallow. The side of my face is bright red, later to bruise, and my mother's voice leaps up against him. "He only baby! He not know. Rice dirty! Kaesaeki-ya!" They argue and argue, but I can neither see nor hear them with my vision blurred and my ears ringing with the repercussion of his slap.*

My father's hand arched out of the hot water like a knuckled fish, and he draped it in the dun-colored washcloth so it looked like the wet, textured hide of a land animal. It came up with a slurping sound as the water drained out, leaving a sucking pocket of air—*shuuuuurp!* "Badogaaaa!" he said. "Yongchoraaa!" and I leaned back and away from him in the round bathtub, laughing with fear and amusement. My father put the washcloth away, then ducked his head under the hot water and emerged again, sputtering.

"You're a big boy now," he said to me. "You used to be afraid of Yongchora and Badoga, but now you're a big boy. Six years old. It's time for you to go to school and learn some English." He pulled me to his chest, which was matted with clumps of dark, reddish hair. "What do you say?"

"I no go school," I said. "I go school dey hit."

"Only if you're bad."

"I no bad. Good."

"Then you've got no problem. You don't want to grow up a heathen, do you?"

"*Headen?*"

My father lifted me high above his head, where the air

was steamy hot, then unexpectedly cold. Drops of condensation from the ceiling dripped on my back and pierced
my flesh.

"Next week you go to Sunday school, my little Booby."

I did not know what he was talking about. When he
put me down and stood up, towering out of the water like
a golden-haired giant, I cowered back against the lip of the
round tub.

Sunday school. I didn't know those words, but now
for the first time in the many times I had bathed in the
Japanese-style tub, I saw that it was the exact shape of the
iron pots in which Emo cooked our rice.

My father splashed out onto the tiles and began to dry
himself with his too-small towel. "Next week, rain or
shine," he said. "We're going to Sunday school, my little
man."

He had appeared unexpectedly that day, still sweaty
and disheveled from field maneuvers, with a whole case
of C-rations. I had leapt up at him, shouting "Aboji, aboji!"
grabbing onto his sleeves and counting his stripes to see if
he had gotten any more. He had asked me where Mahmi
was, and I had answered as I had been told: "Mahmi not
home." Not asking where she might have gone, he had
stoked the fire himself and prepared the hot bath.

When we emerged from the steaming room, wrapped
in our towels, we saw Emo down in the kitchen, wiping
her forehead on the dishtowel she carried.

"Ask Emo when Mommy will be home," my father said
to me.

I translated for him and gave Emo's reply: "Emo say
Mahmi come back eat nighttime."

"Where is she?"

I knew my mother was probably at the NCO Club or
at the PX buying things for the black market. "Mahmi go
friend," I said.

"Ask Emo."

"Emo," I said in Korean, "where did Mahmi go?"

Emo said quickly, "She's going to the club where she

always goes, and then to Paekmajang. Tell your father she's gone to bring Country Aunt home with her." Country Aunt had gone out a little earlier to the market.

"Emo say Mahmi go get Country Emo. They come nighttime eat."

"Well, Booby, then you and me are going to ASCOM for lunch. How about that?"

"Okay!" I said.

"Tell Emo we'll be back by dinnertime. And you go put on some nice clothes."

"Emo," I said, "Aboji is taking me to the army post to eat lunch. We'll come back for dinner. Can you give me good clothes?"

Emo led me to the room and dressed me in the *Lederhosen* my grandmother had sent from Germany. Instead of my Korean rubber shoes, she made me wear brown leather shoes with clean white socks, and instead of my usual white T-shirt, she buttoned me into a short-sleeved shirt with a constricting collar. When she had me all dressed up, Emo combed my wet hair and flipped it to one side, parting it on the left the way my father preferred. "When you go through the gate, remember to ask one of the ladies in line to tell Mahmi to come home, *ungh*? Mahmi didn't know your father was coming today. On days he comes, she's supposed to be home."

"*Ungh*, Emo."

"Don't forget. It's an important matter."

"I won't forget."

Emo let me clomp across the *maru* in my leather shoes. I ran to my father and followed him out to the road to catch a taxi. We didn't have to wait very long for the dented blue cab to appear. It was the same one that had brought him to the house.

"ASCOM, main gate," my father said to the driver as we got into the back.

The skinny driver looked into the rearview mirror and saluted. "We go numbah one, sah-jing," he said, and drove off down the dirt road. I waved to Emo through the rear window and watched with wonder how quickly the rice paddies by the embankment receded from us. When we drew near the Catholic church that bordered the main road the taxi suddenly stopped bouncing—we had reached the blacktop to Inchon.

"Were you good while I was in the field?" said my father.

I nodded quickly. "I *too* good."

"Not *too* good. *Very* good."

"I *very* good."

"I *was* very good."

"I *was* very good," I said loudly.

"Boy-san undastan bery good," said the taxi driver, looking back at us. "Soon sound like GI—no shit."

"That's right," said my father.

"I *talk* very good," I said to impress them.

My father and the taxi driver laughed. We continued the English lesson, the driver joining in to amuse us, until we reached the ASCOM gate where a dozen women were lined up waiting for GIs to take them in. This was where I had seen Gannan each time my mother brought me to ASCOM. Sometimes Gannan would still be waiting there in the hot sun, calling out to the passing GIs, when we came back hours later. If she had married a sergeant, she could have gone to the front of the line and the MP would have let her in without a word.

"Let's go," said my father, picking me up out of the backseat. "Where do you want to eat? You're getting heavy."

"Snack Bar," I said.

"The Snack Bar it is." He put me down, paid the driver, and led me toward the gate.

A woman in line called, "Sah-jing, I give you one good time. You take me inside?" I didn't recognize her. She must have been new—none of the other women ever said anything to my father because they knew he was married to a Korean. Another woman, a friend of Gannan's, grabbed the new woman's arm and whispered something to her. "Sorry, sah-jing," said the new woman, smiling. My father ignored all of this, but I waved at the women I knew and they all said hello to me. One of Gannan's friends gave me a sympathetic look and patted my head.

"*Ajuma,*" I said, "when you go in, tell my mother my father is here. Tell her to go home before dinnertime."

"All right," she said. "You go in and have fun with your father. I'll tell your mother."

I thanked her and ran in through the gate where my father waited with a displeased look. One of the things that always made him angry was when Mahmi stopped to talk to the other women.

"Hey, Insu," called the Korean MP, speaking half Korean and half English, "your *aboji* doesn't look too happy. Ask him if he wants to buy a good watch."

"Aboji, you want buy watchee? MP ask you."

"What kind?"

"Timex," said the MP, lifting his right arm. "Good watchee. I sell you five dallah. See, steel watcheeban look nice."

My father examined the watch and said, "Three dollars."

The MP was supposed to argue with him, but he surprised him instead by saying, "Okay, suree dallah."

"Fine," said my father. He pulled out his old wallet and handed the MP three MPC dollars. The MP unsnapped the watch and pulled it off, giving it to my father with a big smile and a bow.

"This watchee go long time," said the MP. "You makee watcheeban bigger and you wear. You watchee you give Insu when he know how time tell, okay?"

"Sure," said my father. "Heinz, you get my old watch when you start school. How about that?"

"Okay."

As we left, I turned to look back toward the gate. The MP waved to me. "I like new watchee," I said. "I can have old watchee today?"

"Not *watchee.* Say *watch.*"

"Watchy."

"Watch. You stop right after the *ch."*

"Waatch."

"Good. Ten times now, after me. *Watch, watch. . . ."*

Even when I could say it properly, he wouldn't give me the old watch. He would probably give it to Hyongbu or his houseboy in Camp Casey, and when I started school, Mahmi would have to buy me one herself.

My father and I went first to the NCO Club, which was just inside the gate. He bought me a can of Coke and had a beer while he cooled off in the air-conditioned bar, sitting on the same stool the yellow-haired GI had been sitting on before he had met Gannan. We could have eaten there, too, but my father didn't like this NCO Club very much. Mahmi knew too many people there; she would talk to all the waitresses and see the manager about some business. Or she would play slot machines for hours. She didn't play very long when my father was with her, but he probably knew.

While my father drank his beer, I played with the can opener that was chained to the counter. If I pressed it properly I could make the can go *crack crack* and leave sharp, triangular teeth in a circle around the rim of the can. When I was done, the top of my Coke can looked like a face with a sharp-toothed smile along the bottom.

"Careful," said my father.

I drank the rest of the bubbly Coke through its dangerous smile. I would rather have drunk it outside on the grass like I did when Mahmi brought me to ASCOM, but my father liked to keep me near him. He only played slot machines with the change he had in his pocket and cursed when he lost. He hardly talked to anyone except other GIs he knew, and there weren't many of those in ASCOM because he was from Camp Casey. I wondered if he ever sang and danced like the Koreans. Every time Hyongbu drank Johnnie Walker or *makolli,* he would start to talk loudly and sing even if he was by himself, but my father sat quietly.

Now I remembered Rubberhand's mother singing the sad song on the night when Gannan died. I didn't remember any of the words, but I could almost hear it again, with the sound of the wind and rain, as the air conditioner buzzed in the background. I felt suddenly alone and very cold in the dark NCO Club bar.

"Aboji," I said.

"Hmmm?" My father looked down at me from his awful height, more frightening than comforting.

"Aboji," I said again. My mouth twisted into a funny shape and my eyes filled with tears. "Gannan die!" I said, bursting into tears. My father put me on his lap and held me while I cried.

"*Genug, mein Heinzchen, genug, genug,*" he said after a while. "*Wir mussen nicht*—we shouldn't get too sad." He rocked me back and forth, patting my back as if to make me burp. When I had calmed enough, my father made me tell him everything I could in the English words I knew, but it took a long time before I felt any better because, when I was done, he didn't have the proper words to comfort me.

Later, on our way to the Snack Bar, my father told me a story about how his grandmother had decided to die one evening before leaving her home in Czechoslovakia. She had simply gone upstairs to bed on the night before and died in her sleep.

"You burn you granma clothes, Aboji?"

"No. We were poor. We wore them and gave them to people."

"Ghost no come back?"

"No. Well, maybe it did, but we all had to leave the house to go to Germany."

"Why you go German?"

"Some bad people chased us out of our home." He was silent for a while.

We crested the hill and climbed up the stairs to where the PX, Foodland, the Snack Bar, and the Post Theatre were all lined up along the sidewalk. Here, many GIs trafficked back and forth between the PX and the Snack Bar. Korean shoeshine boys in their AAFES uniforms called out to them to buy magazines, newspapers, and *Playboy* calendars, or to get special spit shines. We passed through the business and went into the Snack Bar, and each time my father saluted or returned a salute along the way, I quickly imitated him. My father stopped in the Snack Bar foyer and bought a *Stars and Stripes*.

"Shoeshine?" said the Korean man.

"No."

"For boy-san maybe? He look just like you."

My father looked down at me. "How would you like a shoeshine?" he asked with a smile.

I nodded. The man lifted me up onto the shoeshine seat, and because my legs were too short to reach the foot rests, he pulled my shoes off. My father sat in the other seat and read the paper while I watched the man shine my shoes with rapid motions that reminded me of a wet dog shaking itself dry.

I could smell my father's perspiration, which had soaked the sides and back of his summer uniform shirt. His yellow-smell wasn't as strong as usual. Sometimes I could smell him in the room days after he went back to Camp Casey.

"Aboji," I said.

"Hmm?"

"Why you not come when Gannan dead?"

"I didn't know," he said. "I was up in the hills near the DMZ. I would have gotten emergency leave if I had known."

"What *emergen see?*"

"Emergency *leave.* I ask my CO if I can go home because a relative is sick or there's a funeral. Then he lets me go for a few days."

"Okay." I went back to watching the shoeshine boy buffing my shoes. My father folded the paper in half and read the back part with a frown.

I stepped cautiously down in my newly shined shoes while my father paid and tipped the shoeshine boy, and during my meal of hamburger and Coke, I was careful not to drip anything. My father ate a bowl of chili with lots of crackers and a huge glass of 7-Up.

In one corner of the Snack Bar a jukebox played the same two country & western songs over and over while in the other corner, two pinball machines made a clamorous racket as the GIs knocked them about and cursed at them. One Black GI stayed on a machine all by himself, tapping the sides to the music. When I became a GI I would do these things, too, until I was a sergeant like my father.

"What do you want to do now?" said my father.

"Ice cream."

"How about ice cream, then we go home?"

"Okay."

As we left the Snack Bar with our ice-cream cones, I saw a taxi coming from the direction of the Lower Four Club. It had stopped for a moment to let two GIs cross the street to the Post Office. The driver had taken off his driver's hat and was turned around, getting a light for his cigarette. In the backseat, next to the woman who held the lighter, sat my mother.

"Wait here," said my father. "I'll go get the cab to call us one." He tapped my shoulder and turned to go down the stairs. He hadn't seen Mahmi yet, but I knew that if he did, something bad would happen. I had heard him yelling at her for going on post to the clubs, and I knew how much she tried to keep it a secret. Mahmi had explained to me many times about how my father wasn't supposed to know about how she bought things and then sold them to the black market people.

My heart pounded fiercely as my father took the first steps toward the street. If he saw Mahmi they would argue all night and then she would be unhappy for a long time. I did not want her to be sad the way Gannan had been.

"*Aboji!*" I called.

"What is it?"

When he turned to look at me, I said, "I show some-sing," and turning to a tall red-haired GI who had just come out of the Snack Bar with his friends, I did the thing Hyongbu had taught me many times. "Hwuk you!" I shouted. "Hwuk you, muddahwukka! Hwuk you! Eat my shet!" I waved my ice cream in one hand and thrust the middle finger of my other hand into his crotch. I heard the GIs laughing and a loud "Hey!" from my father behind me. Then, before I quite knew what had happened, I was lifted into the air, my ice cream splattering on the side-walk, and I felt a terrible, hot pain on my backside again and again. I heard the loud slaps of my father's giant palm against the thick leather seat of my pants and his tremen-dous voice, saying, "Don't you *ever* do that again, you son of a bitch!" and just before my vision blurred as I burst out crying over my father's shoulder, I saw Mahmi's taxi driving off down the street.

❖

I had turned six in January, and I would be going to the American school in September, but my father thought I needed to learn proper manners after what I had done in ASCOM. The next time he came home, he took me to the Catholic church about a kilometer from our house and enrolled me in a class of children my size. The English-speaking nun told him it was not a good idea to put me in a class with children who were older than me, but she could not change his mind.

"You're Francis's husband," she said.

"Francis?" said my father.

"Francis Hoa Sen. That's her name, isn't it?"

"I call her Lee, Sister."

"Her first son would be old enough for this class, but Insu will have problems."

"It's *Heinz*," said my father. "He's my wife's *only* son. He can handle the class. He's smart. He's bigger than most of those kids."

"Well, I suppose we could give it a try," said the nun. "And let the Good Lord decide for what he *is* or *isn't* ready. Have your wife speak to Sister Margaret before she brings him to his first class."

My mother bought me canvas school slippers and a

blue plastic pencil box and she walked me to school the next Sunday. She left me at the gate with the nun as if she would never see me again. The nun made Mahmi uncomfortable—the big American MPs with their rifles and pistols didn't scare her, but the woman in the black habit seemed to frighten her, and I felt the same strange fear in my heart. Mahmi left after a bow and a few quiet pleasantries, and I was alone with the nun, who guided me inside with a light touch behind my shoulders.

"In there," said the nun. "Sit in the middle where there's room."

I entered the classroom, changed into my slippers, and sat down where I found a space on the floor among the other children. Everyone just stared at first. They didn't begin to whisper until the nun came in and started the class, but when they learned that I didn't know any songs and couldn't read the page numbers in my prayer book, they talked loudly enough for me to hear: "Stupid." "Look, he's holding his book upside down." "He's a half-wit if he can't read yet. Something's wrong with his head, like Rubberhand." "His father's an American soldier. I saw him. He's big and scary like a long-nose goblin. His hair's all yellow and he has fur on his arms."

No one would play with me during recess, so I went down to the rice paddies and sailed twig boats by myself until I saw everyone leave the school. Then I went home.

I didn't tell anyone about missing school because I knew that when they found out, they would send me every day. It was bad enough when the next Sunday came. I thought of pretending to be sick or throwing up the way Rubberhand had taught me, but Mahmi was going to walk me to school again. When she asked me if school was fun, I told her it wasn't.

"You'll make friends," she said.

I went quietly most of the way, swinging my slipper bag and kicking pebbles with my new black canvas shoes.

"Your father says you should learn a lot because you'll be behind the American children when you go to the American school this fall. You'll be older than the others. You should know more."

"I have to?"

"Yes. American children start school when they're five years old."

I held her hand until we got to the gate of the Catholic church, then I let go and quickly ran inside without looking back because I was afraid to see the expression on her face.

That day I held my book the right way, but still, no one spoke to me. After the songs and the prayer, a pug-nosed boy and a fat-faced boy started slapping at each other with their prayer books. When they saw me watching they turned to me, instead, and took turns slapping their books across my face.

"*Ya*, why hit me?"

The pug-nosed boy stopped, but the fat-faced boy slapped me again. "Hello *saeki-ya*!" he said.

My hand trembled on my prayer book. I started to feel very hot where he had hit me in the face, and I tried to say something back to him to make him angry, but nothing came out. The heat in my face moved down and made something sizzle in my throat.

"Hello," he said again.

"Hello," said the pug-nosed boy. "Hello, give me cho-co-late."

Suddenly, the whole room was filled with laughing faces and open mouths I had not seen before. "Hello, Hello, Hello," they said. "Hello, give me gum. Hello, give me cho-co-late. Hello, wipe my ass. Hello. Hello." I felt suddenly distant from the room; the voices and the faces pulled back, incredibly far away, and the mouths moved very slowly, slurring their syllables into sounds that had lost their meaning. The fat-faced boy who had hit me was pulling his book back, in a syrupy motion, to hit me in the face again, but as I watched, my own trembling hand snapped out with blinding speed and my prayer book hit him squarely across the nose. The fat-faced boy looked confused for a second, but then he noticed the blood that gushed from his nose. He screamed. The laughing suddenly stopped. A girl began to cry as if she were the one I had hit. Then the sister came in and turned pale when she saw the blood on the wooden floor. "Who did it?" she said, rushing to the fat-faced boy. Everyone pointed at me before I could explain.

The nun wadded up two pieces of tissue paper and stuffed them into the fat-faced boy's nostrils, and while he sat there crying, she grabbed me by the arm and dragged me outside to where all our shoes were lined up.

"Why did you hit him?" she said.

I was too confused to answer. I could only frown and look away, back into the room at the floor where the blood was pooled.

"Who started it?"

I looked down at the blood on my slippers.

"Go home!" said the nun. "I'll talk to your mother and father later."

I changed shoes and ran outside the church gate, sobbing. I took my slipper bag and slammed it against a telephone pole until the pencil box shattered inside. I kicked stones until my toes hurt and I tore a hole through my black canvas shoes. By the time I stood on top of the embankment overlooking the rice paddies, my sobbing had turned to sniffles. I wiped my nose on the length of my forearm and coughed up a thick blob of mucus. When I remembered the nun's hateful face, the terrible sizzling came back in my throat and it did not go away until I had flung my slipper bag far out into a flooded paddy.

"Insu-ya," my mother said that evening after my father had left for Camp Casey. "You don't have to go to the Catholic church school anymore."

"Was it because I was bad? Will Aboji be angry with me?"

"No. Your father said you have to start learning American writing. You can rest and play. You'll be going to the American school soon."

That night, when we were all asleep on the floor on our sleeping mats, I woke for a moment, feeling afraid, as if I were some stranger my mother and father would send away. I reached across the mat and touched my mother's warm hand. She closed her fingers around my cold palm, and I slept.

✧

It was cool the morning my father left for Vietnam. The sparrows made me open my eyes, and I was lying on my side, looking toward the center of the room where the others were still unconscious. I had been crying. The sleeping mat was still damp in front of my face.

There was a shadow in front of the curtainless window, and I looked, moving only my eyes, to see the sparrow sitting on the window ledge, silhouetted against the bright white light of morning. As it chirped and swiveled its small head, its eyes gleamed, and its beak seemed to cut the air like a freshly sharpened knife. I felt a sudden pain in my heart, but I remained silent and still for a moment, my eyes closed into slits as I felt the rigidness return to my throat with a momentary flash of the evil dream from which I had awakened. Already, the dream had evaporated into nothing more than a few fleeting images, and those, too, would be gone when I got up. My sweat had dried quicker than my tears, the woodlike stiffness left me, and the squeaking I heard now, as the sparrow darted into the air, was just a branch in the wind. I tried to remember the face I had seen—that important face—but I only saw my own reflection now, familiar and strange in my mind's eye.

I went out into the garden before anyone else was up, and in the dew-covered foliage, on top of the damp boulder, I sat and waited for a vision of the Japanese Colonel or perhaps a glimpse of Gannan out of the corner of my eye. But there was nothing, only the chirping of sparrows that made me look toward the magpie's grave and the dark, weathered wood of the small demon post that still stood under the chestnut tree. For a long time I tried to remember my dream, to recapture the face that looked like me, but with each passing moment it became more and more difficult until I was left with nothing but an uneasy feeling.

It was still early, and the air was still cool when the wounded veterans came. I was pissing in the garden when the doorbell rang, and before anyone went to answer, a man stooped through the little door in the gate and stumbled inside. He seemed to be hugging himself inside his shirt. He had no arms.

While I watched, another man came in on crutches, then another. One of them was missing a whole leg; one leg of his pants was folded up and pinned so it flapped like a tiny flag under his hip. The other man had a glossy stump where his right hand had been and his left leg was missing below the knee.

They gathered by the gate and started hobbling up the hill to the house. Emo came out and shouted, "Who is it!" But the men did not stop; they continued up the hill until they were standing in front of the house.

"*Ajumoni*," said the man with no arms, "please give us some charity."

"We don't have money!" said Emo. "Come some other time."

I came down from the garden to get a better look. The man without arms balanced himself first on one foot, then on the other. "Please give us some charity," he chanted.

The man with no hands looked around the house and said loudly, "What a rich house. Look at this. What a rich house."

"Please give us some charity." The man with no leg hopped toward the *maru*.

Emo quickly stood in the way. Mahmi came out and saw them. "What is it?" she asked Emo.

"These people want some money."

The men moved closer to the *maru*. "Please give us some charity."

"We don't have money," said Mahmi. She reached into her purse and pulled out a 100-*won* note. "This is all we have. Take it." She looked carefully at the men, then gave the money to the man with no leg.

The man with the stump was also missing three fingers from his left hand. "One hundred *won*!" he said. "*Ajumoni*, if you can't give us money, at least give us some cigarettes! You're smoking an American cigarette." He made scissors motions with his two fingers. "Smells good."

"Please give us some charity."

They edged closer to the *maru*. Emo stood in their way. "We gave you money! Please leave!" she said.

"Please give us some charity."

Mahmi gave her pack of Salems to the man with no leg. "Do you have matches?" he said.

As Mahmi looked in her purse, my father came down from the *maru* in his U.S. Army uniform, frowning. His short yellow hair sparkled in the sunlight.

The wounded veterans staggered away and stood huddled under the chestnut tree, as if they were trying to make one whole man.

"What's going on?" said my father.

Mahmi explained in English. My father took the old leather wallet out of his pocket and pulled out a 500-*won* note. He put on his low-quarter shoes and went to the veterans. He hesitated before he gave the money to the man with no leg.

"Please give us some charity," said the man with no arms, and then they all bowed in unison and said, "Thank you, thank you."

"This is pathetic," said my father. "That man only has two fingers. The other guy probably can't even feed himself."

The wounded veterans didn't speak English. They nodded and smiled. The man with no leg found matches in his own pocket. Leaning on his crutches, he lit a Salem and carefully held it out beside him. The man with the stump took the cigarette gently between his two fingers and pressed it to his lips. "Good, good," he said. "Haven't smoked an American cigarette in a long time." The man with no leg lit another cigarette and shared it with the man with no arms. He smoked, then held the Salem so the man with no arms could lean forward and awkwardly suck at the filter.

The wounded veterans puffed into the fresh morning air and looked around, as if they had just arrived. They talked among themselves while we watched.

"Please leave now," Emo said after a few minutes.

The veterans bowed. "Thank you, thank you," they said. "Good house. Good people. The boy looks like he'll be a strong man."

I hid behind my father, wrapping my arms around his waist.

"Good-bye," they said. They hobbled down to the gate. First, the man with no arms skipped through, then the others followed, banging their crutches against the gate frame.

The gate closed. Emo went back into the house. My mother and my father waited a moment, then walked down to the gate with me following behind. My father patted me on the head. "See you again next week," he said. "Be good. I don't want any more nonsense from you, understand?"

I nodded, gave him a reluctant smile, and said good-bye.

When they had gone, I locked the gate. I ran and stood under the chestnut tree and, pulling my arms through the short sleeves, I hugged myself inside my T-shirt and balanced first on one foot, then the other. "Please give us some charity," I chanted in a husky voice.

"*Ya!*" Emo shouted from inside the house. "Don't do that!"

The shirt felt like a warm blanket around me. I skipped up to the garden and leaned forward like a bird, trying to see if anything had grown. Nothing.

That evening, Mahmi told me that my father had left for Vietnam, and that he wouldn't be there to take me to my first day of American school.

There was no one in Samnung for me to play with. One of my only friends was Cholsu, the son of our neighbor, and he only played with me because the other children did not like him. Cholsu was a bully, and he had picked on me constantly, from the first day we had met at the crumbled wall between our houses, until I fought back one day and beat him. After that, he would only play-fight me and taunted me with the fact that he went to school and I didn't. He was three years older than me, quicker in mind and body, but I was clearly bigger and stronger.

Three days after my last day of Catholic school, Cholsu came and gave his usual call from outside the gate. "Insu-ya, play!"

"What do you want to do today?" he asked when I let him in.

"Don't know."

"How about a reading lesson?" he said. "You might be bigger than me, but I'm older and smarter. Sugi told me she had a stupid boy in her class. It's you, *ungh*?"

I didn't want to tell him, but my face gave me away.

"You may be a big Yankee-brat, but you're stupid. Sugi said you can't even read." With a stick, he drew a character on the ground. "See, this is 'shit.' " He drew another. "This is 'dog.' It's you—'shit-dog.' Understand?"

Cholsu was calling me a mongrel dog—the ownerless kind that ran through the villages, eating garbage and even their own shit when food was scarce. I erased the characters with my foot. "I can talk American."

"So what? You don't even know how to talk respectably to adults. My mother thinks you're an idiot. You can't even say *neh*." He picked a ladybug off a branch and smashed it between his fingers. "See this," he said, showing me the yellow mess. "Smell it."

I was upset, but still curious. It smelled like intense body odor. I made a face.

"This is yellow-smell. Yankees like your father smell like this." He wiped the mess on my shirt and ran away before I could hit him. I was slow, and I knew I could never catch him, but I ran after him, chasing him all over the neighborhood as he laughed at me, waited, and darted off just before I could reach him. Finally, tired, breathless and angry, I stopped and caught my breath while he taunted me with a song.

> Chimpanzee's asshole is red
> Red as an apple
> Apple tastes good
> Good as a banana
> Banana is long
> Long like a freight train
> Freight train goes fast
> Fast as an aeroplane
> Aeroplane flies high
> High as Paekdu Mountain!

He sang it again and again, but he changed the first line to "Insu's asshole is red."

I went back home, and he followed just far enough away so that I couldn't catch him. I closed our gate on his face.

"Shit-dog," he said through the door.

I trudged up to where the rock garden had been, and there, under the trees, I sat with my back to a boulder and tried to calm my breathing. I wanted to kill Cholsu—I knew it suddenly—and when the thought entered my mind my breathing grew faster and faster until I was panting and covered in a cold sweat. My chest heaved up and down and a thin line of mucus leaked from my nose. I saw a purple ring around my vision, like afterimages of the sun, and when I tried to rub my eyes and blink them away, the rings grew brighter and wider until suddenly my vision went entirely white.

"Hello," said the ghost of the Japanese Colonel. He had never spoken to me before, and his eyes had never been quite so sad.

"Hello," I said.

"This is a beautiful place," said the ghost of the Japanese Colonel. "This is not a place you should be afraid of."

"I'm not afraid," I said.

"Good."

When I opened my eyes, he was gone and I was lying on my side in front of the boulder. I felt like I had just awakened from a long and restful sleep. I lay there for a while, as if I were on my sleeping mat, rolling onto my back to look up at the darkening blue of the sky.

A few long minutes later, I went back outside to stand on the pathway overlooking the rice paddies and watch the farmers repairing their irrigation ditches. In the flooded paddies, children were catching frogs and sailing wood-and-paper boats.

Cholsu saw me. He came up the trail with a large pregnant frog dangling in his grip. "I'm going to smash it till it's stretch-dead," he said. He lifted the long, limp frog and gripped it more tightly by its rubbery hind legs. It twitched weakly. "Where's a rock?"

I pointed one out—large and half-buried.

"Why don't you have any frogs, *ungh*?"

"I was inside," I said.

"Stupid." Cholsu stood a little to the left and swung the frog upward. I did not look. I heard a thick, wet splat, and when I opened my eyes, all that was left in Cholsu's hand were the two hind legs attached to shredded hips and little bits of entrail. The rest of the frog was a thick mess of gore splattered all over the rock. The only things I could recognize were the black, gelatinous eggs. "It's stretch-dead," said Cholsu. "Come on, let's go catch frogs."

"I don't want to."

"Son of a bitch," he said. He impaled the frog legs onto a loop of wire he wore on his hip and went back down to the rice paddy, leaving me to wonder why he had come up in the first place.

Flies droned around the rock.

I went down to catch frogs the next day, enticing them with the tips of wild wheat stalks. But when I caught them I always let them go again so that I could watch them execute their beautiful scissors kicks with their mottled green legs the color of my father's uniform.

✧

Late in the summer, Cholsu's mother cried every night— so loudly that we could hear her from our house. Mahmi told me that Cholsu had been hit by a taxi. At first it had seemed he might recover, but he had died unexpectedly in the hospital. They said it was from internal injuries.

For the rest of the summer, I avoided walking in front of Cholsu's house because I had not been sad at the news of his death. At night I stayed inside and stopped looking out of the window because I was afraid I might see his ghost.

Toward the end of August, my mother suddenly decided one night that we would move out of the Japanese Colonel's house.

"Are we going to Vietnam, too, Mahmi?"

"No, Insu-ya. We're moving to a smaller house on the other side of town. It's a house in Tatagumi in the neighborhood where you were born."

"Will it be scary there at night?"

"No. There won't be any big trees in the yard, so no ghosts will be able to hide in them. It will be quiet. You'll go to the American school and make friends."

I left all my secret things under the trees and the boulders where the rock garden used to be. Before we left, I stood in front of Cholsu's house for a while. I visited the place where he had smashed the frog on the rock. But I found no traces of the frog. I felt no trace of grief.

I remember a numbness came over me when we left the house of the Japanese Colonel, as if I had left part of my own spirit behind among the trees with my mementos of Gannan, which I could not bear to bring with me. Late one afternoon the ghost of the Japanese Colonel had appeared to me among the boulders in the old rock garden. He had gazed upon me, especially forlorn, anticipating a loneliness greater than what he already endured. I had expected to see Gannan as I waited there cross-legged on the cool, abrasive stone with the tiny demon post in my hand, but it was the Japanese Colonel who came. He looked at me, his eyes shimmering, the leaves behind him quivering with anticipation of something dire, and he had leaned forward, reaching out his left hand to touch me—I realize now—for the first time. Suddenly I could no longer see him, but I felt my back straighten, and then I had the oddest sensation—more like a knowledge than a sensation—that he had thrust his fingertip into my skull and run it all the way around the crown of my head. My eyes were closed—I knew. But somehow the top of my head had vanished, as if my skull were the cylinder of an open can, and I could see the blue sky receding to infinity directly above me. My body was hollow. It was empty, although it held my shape, and into the contoured vessel the sky came pouring in like a bright blue liquid, and I felt that I had no outside and no inside, that the sky *within me and the air outside me were the same substance and my self but a thin veneer that floated between them like some filmy membrane in water. I was breathing in the liquid sky through the top of my open head, and the air was cold with the freshness that lingers after a hard rain. I sat there for the longest time until, degree by degree, I realized that I was seeing again through my eyes. The afternoon light had dimmed into a reddish gold and the air was cool against my too-sensitive flesh. When I stood up I collapsed once before the life came back into my legs and I could walk again.*

The Japanese Colonel was gone. The demon post was gone, and I never paused to wonder how it had disappeared. I would never see the House of the Japanese Colonel again. Never—not even in my dreams.

I believed I would learn something about my father's world at the American school. I believed there was something mysterious about the pale-skinned children with the yellow hair and the blue and green eyes, whose tongues were more suited than mine to their slippery English words. I believed there was something grand and magical about America because those who came back would march in rank, their arms interlinked over each other's shoulders, chanting, "Hey! Hey! Get out of my way! I just came back from the U! S! A!" I was thirsty to drink in the source of that mystery, but like the others who were like me, I would come away more parched than before.

I remember, on that first morning, how the bus driver tipped his hat, ground the gearshift forward and spat out of his little window, how, with a hiss of released brakes, the flat-faced Army bus lurched away from the curb. "Hey, papa-san, you better haul ass!" a GI called from the back where we sat, "we only got till oh-eight-hundred!" I remember how my stomach had felt funny from getting up so early, how I felt empty inside from not having slept enough. My mother had tried to fill up that emptiness by making me eat ramyon, but everything had gotten mixed up— the ramyon noodles, the kimchi juice, and milk had curdled in my stomach, giving me that imminent feeling of having to throw up.

"Insu-ya, would you like some gum?" my mother had asked me, and I had looked around, through the cigarette smoke, at the people on the bus—in the front half sat the white GIs going to Yongsan, most of them braced against the windows or leaning their heads against the backs of the green seats. Some were awake, reading paperback westerns or The Stars & Stripes; and a few talked to each other but couldn't be heard through the loud rattling and rumbling of the bus.

In the back half of the bus sat four Korean women with their children whom they were taking to school, two KATUSAs, a red-haired man in civilian clothes, and all the Black GIs. I remember my mother and I were sitting across from a fat Korean woman in a black muumuu who snorted and tossed her hair every few moments, exhaling vast clouds of cigarette smoke. All the women on the bus were smoking, and my mother was looking through her clutch purse for her own cigarettes. "Here," she said, and I took the stick of gum she offered me and put it in my mouth, but I couldn't chew it more than a few times because it was a Juicy Fruit—too thick for the emptiness and sickness boiling within me. I remember what I wanted was a Spearmint, from a white pack, that would taste light and cold, but my mother usually carried the yellow gum or the green Doublemint gum. I looked over my shoulder at the wide back seat that stretched across the whole back of the bus, at the Black GIs who sat there playing cards, laughing and tossing money into a U.S. Army cap which one of them would snatch and put on his head from time to time, letting the money spill over his face and onto the floor so that his friends would have to scramble to pick it up, loudly joking the whole time. I remember, when no one was looking, I turned around and spat my mouthful of gum and juice on the floor under the seat in front of me, and it was then that I noticed my mother talking to the woman in the black muumuu. I leaned forward and looked across my mother's body and saw that someone was sitting beside the fat woman, but all I could make out were a pair of green-stockinged legs sticking straight out like pine needles.

✧

"Your son is very handsome," said the fat woman in the muumuu. "How old is he?"

"Six," said Mahmi.

"In American age?"

"Yes."

"My son is eight in Korean age, but I'm just making him six in American age and putting him in first grade. James, say hello to the *ajuma*."

"Oh, he looks smart," said Mahmi. "Do you speak English, James?"

"I do a little bit," he said in Korean. He looked at me for a moment before his dark face disappeared behind his mother again.

I pressed myself back against the seat and scribbled on the fogged window. Each time I drew a line, I looked through it. The bus passed by a group of women on their way to market with huge metal basins of vegetables balanced on their heads.

Someone tapped me on the shoulder. "Hey, tiger, help me open the window." I turned and saw a giant black hand resting against the back of the seat. "Just push that little thing down and pull the window up." The hand moved and pointed. I tried to find the spot where the darker skin turned into the pale skin of the palm, but it was like trying to decide exactly when daylight began. I nodded up at the GI and pushed the lever down. "Two clicks up," he said, touching one of the metal stops on his side of the window. I pulled up on my half until it clicked twice, then sat back to breathe the fresh morning air. "Right on," said the GI. "We got some fuckin' oxygen back here now. Who's dealin'?"

I felt much better breathing the cold air. Though a steady stream of cigarette smoke was sucked out through the open window, I didn't have to inhale the heavy human smells inside the bus anymore.

The bus passed the tile factory and the electrical plant just outside Pupyong as the bus approached Sosa. I leaned my head against the aluminum frame of the window and tried to sleep, but every time the bus went over a bump, my temple banged against the metal. It was uncomfortable until my head went numb and the banging became a familiar rhythm. I slept until we reached Yong Dong P'o, where the stops were frequent.

By the time we crossed the Han River bridge and passed the statue of the heroic paratrooper, the aisles of the bus were full of standing passengers. Soon, we reached the back entrance to the Yongsan Army post, which was like a park in the middle of the busy city. The bus stopped at the gatehouse and an MP came aboard to make sure everyone was authorized to go on post. The GIs in uniform just ignored him, but all the Korean women and the one man in civilian clothes had to show their ID cards. In a minute the MP left and the bus went on.

All the loud traffic and the crowds of people vanished when we passed beyond the Yongsan gate. I had been there before, but I didn't remember how quiet or how beautiful it was. The trees that lined the road were taller than any trees I had seen outside and the buildings looked firmer and more rooted to the earth. Even the air was different—it was soothing and clean. The Yongsan Army post seemed even emptier than ASCOM.

We arrived across the street from the Seoul American Elementary School half an hour early. The woman in the black muumuu took her son by the hand and stood up to squeeze herself out between the GIs in the aisle. "Aren't you getting off, too?" she asked my mother.

"I'm taking him to get something to eat," said Mahmi.

"Will you be here until school ends today?"

"Yes."

"Then let's meet later at lunchtime."

"Yes, I'll see you later then. Good-bye." The GIs pressed themselves against the seats and even stepped in between occupied seats to let her pass. A few of the white GIs gave James a disapproving glance as he followed her out.

The seat left by the fat woman was empty until a short, yellow-haired GI and an Air Force corporal sat down in it. "What a fuckin' whale," said the yellow-haired GI. "Mama whale and baby coon." The corporal just looked at him, slumped back, and closed his eyes.

I realized I was no longer sick, but quite hungry. I hoped Mahmi would buy me a hamburger so that I would feel full and not be afraid of the cream-colored brick buildings I had seen through the window.

"Mahmi, where are we going?"

"I'll take you to the bus terminal and buy you something to eat so you won't be hungry before lunchtime. Do you have your lunch ticket?"

"*Ungh.*" I made sure it was in my front pocket.

The bus went up a long hill, then down again until it reached another gate. It waited there until the traffic stopped on the road outside, then crossed over to the entrance to the other half of the Yongsan Army post. At that gate another MP came aboard and checked ID cards again. I showed him my card, though I really didn't need to. He smiled and snapped me a mock salute as he left.

At the main bus terminal, the bus pulled into its space behind a yellow metal stall and seemed to relax with a great hiss. The driver opened the door and stepped out, wiping his forehead under his hat. Everyone got up, but

Mahmi stayed seated until the bus was nearly empty and we were the last ones out.

My mother took me to the refreshment stand, which had just opened, and bought me a doughnut, a hot dog, and a red-white-and-blue can of Pepsi-Cola, a drink I had never seen in ASCOM. She got a coffee and a hot dog for herself, paying with a multicolored handful of the small MPC bills. I had once seen a real greenback dollar bill, which was supposed to be worth much more than an MPC dollar, but the man's face on it had seemed solemn and mean compared to the beautiful princess woman on the MPC bill.

I ate the doughnut slowly. "We have to go in a little while," said Mahmi. She led me outside the terminal, though I tried to stall by loading a bright mess of ketchup and mustard onto my hot dog.

We caught an Arirang taxi and arrived at the school just before eight o'clock, while all the older children were in line waiting for the building to open. I stood in front of the main building on the sidewalk next to the school sign, hastily finishing my food, watching the taxicab leave, as I knew my mother would in a few moments. The hot dog turned into an uncomfortable lump in my stomach.

"Mahmi, are you going to stay with me?"

"I have to leave after I take you to your teacher."

"Then when am I going home?"

"After school, I'll wait for you by the bus stop over there." She pointed to a maple tree at the side of the road. "I'll be under there with the other mothers."

We walked around the main building, up a walkway to a long and wide building that overlooked the immense playground to our left. The building grew larger and larger. The air smelled different when we went inside, and it was unbearably warm.

The teacher met us at the door of the classroom. She said hello and talked to my mother while I stared at the coat hooks in the wide hallway. "Thank you," said Mahmi, very politely. The teacher said something in smooth English that made my mother sound like she was speaking the wrong language. "Insu-ya, study well and listen to the teacher," Mahmi said to me in Korean. "Come to the bus stop when school is over."

I nodded. With a disapproving glance at my mother, the teacher took me by the shoulders and led me into the classroom. When I turned to look at the door, Mahmi was gone. I wanted to turn and run out after her, but the teacher held my shoulders tightly and pushed me away from the door. When I struggled, her fingernails dug into my flesh.

"I'm Mrs. McPhee. What's your name?"

I looked up at her long enough to see the downward wrinkles around her mouth, the loose flesh of her neck, and the few brown hairs that poked out of her chin. Her nostrils were hairy and frighteningly dark. I bowed my head down and stared at her black buckle shoes. I thought I would never see my mother again.

"What's your name?"

"Insu."

"Is that your American name?"

"No."

"Well, we'll use your American name here. We don't speak Korean, understand? Tell me your American name." She guided me to a desk in the middle part of the room.

I continued to stare at her shoes because I didn't want to look around me. This must have been how Gannan felt when she first met the yellow-haired GI bastard at the NCO Club.

"What's your name, young man? Answer me."

"Heinz," I said finally. It sounded strange to me, more like "Ha-inju." I had only said it a few times to myself, and from my mouth, it didn't sound the way it did when my father called me.

Mrs. McPhee looked at a stiff white piece of paper in her hand and read off my name. "*Heinz.* That's a German name, isn't it?"

I looked at her.

"And how old are you?"

"Sixu."

"That's *six*. Not *sixu*—six. Heinz, this is going to be your desk from now on. Make sure you remember which one it is because you have to sit here after recess. After recess we'll make name tags. Okey-dokey." Mrs. McPhee pulled the chair out for me and sat me down by pushing on the top of my head, and she leaned her weight on me as she walked away as if she were pushing herself off from some piece of furniture.

With my eyes forced downward, I noticed that the linoleum tiles on the floor were all gray except in the places that had been repaired. One tile under my desk was black with white wisps of cloud and I carefully memorized it until I could see all the different pictures inside. My neck became sore from looking down for so long, but I kept my head bent, not even daring to glance up until the teacher called our names and made us stand up one at a time.

I examined the other students then—for the first time —as I took my turn and stood in terror, visible to everyone in the room, waiting for her to call the next name. I had never seen so many different colors of hair in one place. The boy who sat at my left had hair so white I thought he must have been scared out of his wits by a ghost, and his gray eyes blinked and rolled side to side under fantastically long eyelashes; he was surely a goblin brat. In front of me sat a dark-haired boy with soft brown animal fur growing over the back of his neck, and to my right sat a yellow-haired girl who had no front teeth; she smiled and stood up when her name was called, and before she sat down again, I noticed the wonderful golden hair that covered her arms like a patch of ripe buckwheat bending in the wind.

"Sit down, Heinz," said Mrs. McPhee.

I sat down and glanced around the room. A red-haired boy sat at the front of the class and a black-haired Korean girl sat in the back, but I didn't see any of the blue hair or green hair that Hyongbu had told me I would see.

✧

Mahmi had told me I would learn to read and write like an American, but Mrs. McPhee had us sing a song about her country and swear to be loyal to the garish flag. The day went very slowly, and I fought sleep the whole time I was in the classroom.

During the morning recess time, I stood by myself and watched the other children playing together. All the American kids called each other by name, as if they had all known each other for a long time, and they ran around or dangled from the monkey bars together. They played at who could swing the highest on the swings or lifted each other high into the air on the teeter-totters. The girls played hopscotch and four-square games marked out on the sidewalk.

I stood alone by the water fountain, and to look like I was doing something, I took drink after drink of water while my heart grew heavier, pulling me down with its weight. I avoided the children who were chattering around Mrs. McPhee, and I walked back and forth along a bare wall to keep from crying. Each time I paused I would think of my mother and my Korean friends. I didn't want to be in the hot classroom copying letters from the board, and I didn't want to play with the Americans with their strange hair. I wanted to go out to the rice paddies and sail my wooden boat, to run through the back alleys with my friends, to get into a neighborhood rock fight, to taunt and run from savage alley dogs. Even ASCOM was better than this, because there I could go where I wanted while Mahmi played slot machines. I could leap into Dumpsters to look for food and magazines, or run through the empty baseball field and find broken bats and lost balls. In ASCOM the GIs would talk to me and give me things, but here there was nothing to do but be by myself. I wondered where James had gone.

When the bell finally rang, I wiped my nose and plod-
ded up to the classroom. It was comforting to sit in my
familiar seat near the dark tile again. I felt less lonely when
I had my fat red pencil and ugly newsprint paper in front
of me, but I was impatient for school to end.

Mrs. McPhee gathered us together again after the bathroom break. The lunch bell had rung just in time for me
to go to the bathroom without wetting my pants, and I
reminded myself never to drink so much water again during recess.

With all the other first-grade classes, we walked in a
double boy-girl line to the cafeteria across the street. I had
to hold hands with a gangly straw-haired girl who kept
rubbing her nose with the cuff of her blouse. I remembered
that the Korean schoolchildren always sang when they
walked in lines so I expected Mrs. McPhee to teach us a
lunchtime song, but she didn't seem to care; she was more
concerned with keeping us quiet and making sure we all
had our lunch tickets.

For the first time since the bus ride, I saw James. He
was in line behind me with his purple SAES lunch ticket
pinned to the pocket of his shirt. I saw only a few other
Black children; and though there were some who looked
part Korean, it seemed that most of the first graders
had unusually pale skin. I wondered if it was true that
Americans bathed every day and ate only white bread
and milk. That would explain their paleness, I thought,
but then the idea of having only white bread and milk for
lunch made me feel sick again, and I hoped the rumors
weren't true. After all, Americans did eat hot dogs and
hamburgers, too, and since they all made such a big deal
about dessert, maybe we would have chocolate ice cream
for lunch.

All the tables had already been set up with trays, silverware, and napkins. We simply gave our lunch tickets
to the man who was dressed like a doctor, and then sat
down on the chairs, which were a bit too high for us. The
foods were arranged in little compartments on our trays:

green beans, corn, and bland spaghetti; an ugly U.S. Army cup full of milk sat in a round depression at the top.

I ate everything on the tray as Mrs. McPhee had instructed us, and after I drank the last of my milk, I threw up into the big compartment that had held the spaghetti. For a moment I didn't know what had happened because the food had come up so naturally. I didn't feel sick the way I had on the bus. Perhaps my stomach just didn't want the lunch food to be inside it; I couldn't see any of the hot dog with the other things. I looked around, then sat quietly until lunch was over. The other children at the table didn't seem to have noticed what I had done because I had been so quiet, but when Mrs. McPhee walked by, she asked me why I had mixed my milk and spaghetti into such a mess.

"I . . . no eat," I said.

"Well, young man, you should have respect for your food. I don't want to see you doing this sort of thing again. Do you hear me?"

"Yesu."

"Good. Now get in line for your dessert. This is the last time you'll get it without finishing your meal."

I was surprised and very happy to get the wide orange popsicle, and I ate it slowly, letting each cold piece melt in my mouth to take the sour milk taste away.

Lunch recess was not as bad as morning recess because James remembered me. We were the first to the swings, so we swung as high as we could standing up, shouting in joy and yelling curses in Korean at the American children who couldn't understand us.

When the playground teacher noticed us, she first asked us to get off, then tried to show us how to swing safely sitting down because it was not proper to stand up in the swings at the American school. But she was much too slow, and when she saw that she wasn't very good at it, she asked James if he could show me. "My husband usually pushes me," she said as she left.

"Why would her husband push her?" I asked James.

"Maybe he doesn't like her."

The recess went quickly. Though the day grew hot, James and I stayed cool on our swings. When the bell rang we each took a drink of water and went back toward the first-grade building.

"There's a boy in our class who looks like a goblin brat," I said. "His eyes are a funny color."

"American goblins aren't even scary," said James.

"Do you think he's really a goblin brat?"

"Don't know. You have to see them at nighttime to tell." James ran into his class line and bumped into a fat yellow-haired boy. "*Ya*, you son of a bitch," he said to him in Korean.

"I'm gonna tell on you for talking gook-talk," said the yellow-haired boy.

James stepped back and ignored him. When the lines moved into the building, he straggled behind for a moment before running in.

After school I met James by the swings and walked to the bus stop with him. The American children who lived on post walked home or waited in front of the school building to get their buses, but the children from Pupyong and Inchon, because they had no school bus, all gathered at the Army bus stop. There were many more schoolchildren than I remembered seeing in the morning.

I saw our mothers sitting together with the other mothers near the bus stop, under the maple tree that spread its leaves over them like open hands. James and I both took our folded papers out of our back pockets and ran to them. "Mahmi!" I called. James called his mother *om-ma* in Korean. We unfolded our papers, which said exactly the same thing, and gave them to our mothers in exchange for ice-cold cans of Coca-Cola they had bought for us. I drank mine so quickly the foam rose up to my throat.

"What does this say?" said James's mother.

Mahmi read the papers and translated for her.

Dear Mom and Dad,
    Today was my first day at Seoul American Elementary School. We learned how to print our names. We had spaghetti for lunch.

Love,
Name

"He sure wrote well," said James's mother, patting him on the head. "These American schools make them write the oddest things. What does this 'name of love' mean? Is it some Christian thing?"

"I wouldn't know," said Mahmi. "How was school?" she asked us.

James and I talked excitedly about lunch and recess and all the strange people we had seen. Our mothers listened quietly and asked many questions when we were through.

The afternoon bus to ASCOM was nearly empty. James and I were so hot and tired we stretched out, taking whole seats to ourselves, and slept while our mothers smoked and talked together.

James and his mother got off at the first stop in Pupyong, but Mahmi and I stayed on the bus until it made its final stop in front of the Service Club on top of the hill on post. We crossed the street and went down to the Lower Four Club, where Gannan had been a waitress for a while. I ordered a hamburger, French fries, and a Coke, and I ate while Mahmi went in the back to play three dollars in the nickel slot machines.

By the time I went home, it seemed all the school memories were just a dream from some other day, and I didn't think I would ever have to go back.

❖

Since we had left the house in Samnung, we had moved to Tatagumi, a neighborhood closer to ASCOM. We lived down a narrow alley, just past the local carpenter's shop, in a small house with no garden and no trees. In the tiny yard of packed dirt between the walls and the *maru* at the entrance there was only a small shed, the outhouse, and a brick-paved space for storage jars.

The house had only two rooms and a kitchen, and it seemed terribly small, as if we had been confined to a back corner of the Japanese Colonel's house for punishment. Mahmi said we had moved because this house was cheaper, but I knew that she was also afraid. After Gannan's death, everyone had begun to believe the bad stories again.

On the day we moved in, the carpenter had just finished two wardrobe cabinets, and he had stood them outside his shop to let the varnish dry. As the three sweaty wagon men pulled their loads into the alley the carpenter had come out to stop them and Hyongbu had to help spray the alley with water to keep the dust down before they could continue. Mahmi was in ASCOM and everyone else was already in the new house, so I got down from the wagon I was riding to wait as the carpenter argued with the wagon men and Hyongbu suggested a round of *makkoli* after the moving was done.

One of the wagon men went into the carpenter's shop to get a drink of water and came out again in a hurry. "What are you, a cabinet maker or a coffin maker?" he asked.

The carpenter splashed another gourd full of water and wiped his forehead. "A box is a box," he said. "One you put your clothes in. The other you put your body in."

"Yeah, what's the difference?" said another wagon man. They laughed together as they finished spraying the water.

"*Ya*, are you moving in?" someone said from behind me. "If you don't belong in this neighborhood, you have to fight me."

Something bounced off the fat automobile tire of the wagon, and I turned, following the stone's path backward, to see a yellow-haired boy standing at the gate of his house. That is how I had met Jani.

✧

"How was the American school?" Jani said when I caught up with him late in the afternoon. "Do you think you'll have field days and class foot races like we do in Korean school?"

I told him about my first day of school as we walked up the street toward the train station. Before I had even finished describing all the strange people, the terrible food, and the boring lessons, we had reached the rice paddies at the edge of town. We crossed the railroad tracks and sat on the far embankment to watch the traffic along the upper road to Inchon.

"So you met a white-haired guy and a Black guy all in the same day," said Jani. "Do they smell funny like the American soldiers? I've never smelled American kids before."

"No," I said, trying hard to remember the smells. "James is half Korean so he doesn't smell. The white-haired goblin brat smelled like a baby."

"A baby?"

"Ungh."

"That's funny. Is the Black guy stupid with curly hair like this?" He twirled his finger around and around.

"He talks American better than me. His hair doesn't curl so much."

Jani got up and threw a rock into the rice paddy beneath us. "Can he fight?"

"Don't know."

"Find out sometime. My mother told me Black soldiers carry razors around and cut people when they get in fights. Maybe he'll show you how to use a razor. Do you like this Black guy?"

"Don't know yet."

Jani sang, "Negro men from Africa may as well not wash their faces." Then he sang the other song about Black people which everybody knew.

Negro men from Africa are all so very kind,
They give away their cho-co-late to every passer-by.

We sang this together a couple of times.

"When will you get to go to the American school with me?" I asked.

"I don't know. My mother said she could send me to American school when she married a GI, but she hasn't found one yet. She wants to find one who has yellow hair so it will look like he's my father."

"What happened to your real father?"

"He's dead."

"How?"

"He got killed in Vietnam."

"Shot?"

Jani nodded. "When I join the American Army I'll go to Vietnam and kill the bastard who did it."

"I'll go with you. My father's there, and I can help him."

"Ungh, that would be good. Was it hard talking American all day?"

"My mouth hurts. But there were lots of kids who talk Korean at recess. We have three recess times."

"You ride the Army bus?"

I told him how much fun it was with all the Black GIs playing in the backseat. I didn't tell him how afraid I had been.

"I hope my mother finds me a father soon. I want to go to the American school."

"Don't let her get married to the yellow-hair who was Gannan's boyfriend."

"Why not?"

"He's a bastard and I have to kill him," I said.

We saw the dinnertime U.S. Army bus coming down the road toward Pupyong. It was time to go home. As we crossed the tracks again, we met a gang of boys led by someone Jani knew from school. I wanted to run, but Jani waved and called out to them.

"Don't go yet!" called Jani's friend. "The first evening train is coming in a minute."

The older boys put long nails on the tracks to be flattened by the train so they could sharpen them into knives. We waited a little ways down the embankment, and when the train passed we all made the most horrible and obscene gestures we knew. I did the thing Hyongbu had shown me by the river at Big Uncle's village and everyone thought it was funny, but one of the boys turned around with his pants down and shat so the people on the train could see, and that was considered the best. We had great fun, and afterward, while the others went up to look for their flattened nails, Jani and I went back to Tatagumi.

It wasn't until I saw the Air Force corporal read the ten o'clock news on AFKN TV that I began to worry about the next school day.

✧

After riding up with me and waiting for me every day for a hundred days, my mother stopped bringing me to school. I was frightened at first, but James said that I would never grow up if I missed my mother so much. "Let's be brothers from now on," he said. He taught me a secret way of speaking Korean that no one else would understand, and after I could manage the trick of adding the nonsense syllables in the right places, he swore an oath with me never to betray each other. We wrote our initials together on the condensation inside the bus window, then rubbed them out. "There," he said. "Now we have a secret that's invisible to everyone else. If we betray each other we'll disappear just like the letters." We sat and looked carefully at the glass, but couldn't see even a smudge.

"Let's go to the bus station today before school," I said. "I have money to buy something good to eat."

"All right," said James. He bit his lip for a moment. "We have to sit at the back of the bus so no one will see us," he said in the secret language.

"Why?"

"They'll tell on us because your mother's not riding with us anymore."

We staggered to the back of the bus, keeping our balance by holding on to each seat as we passed. We sat in opposite corners of the backseat, which was empty that day, and when we reached the school bus stop ten minutes later, we pretended to be asleep. The other children got out without noticing us and the GIs didn't say anything. I listened to my pounding heart until the bus lurched forward and hid the sound with its rumbling. I peeked at James for a moment, then closed my eyes again and stayed tightly curled for the long time it took to reach the main terminal.

We stayed hidden until the bus driver and all the GIs had gone out. Even the MP who checked the bus at the gate hadn't noticed us. We jumped out of our seats and ran out to the terminal snack bar, dodging back and forth between the yellow pylons of the empty bus stalls.

I had thought of buying hot dogs as usual, but James said Eskimo Pies would be better.

"Eskimo Pies?" said the Korean man behind the counter. "You kids can't have them until you've eaten something better for you."

"Then we'll have hot dogs," I said.

"Where's your mother today?"

"I'm coming alone now, *ajoshi*."

"It's about time," said the Snackbar *ajoshi*. He put the hot dogs on the counter and took the money. He looked down at James. "I haven't seen *your* mother in a real long time. You're older, *ungh*?"

"Yes, sir," said James.

The Snackbar *ajoshi* pointed to the paper cook's hat he was wearing with his apron. "You boys want some hats like this?"

"Can you really give us some?" we said. "Yes, sir! Give us one!"

He tossed us each a hat and told us to go to school.

We put the hats on, and some of the GIs in the terminal laughed. "Fuckin' mini chefs," said an MP.

A tall Black GI bought some doughnuts and coffee after us. "Can I buy one of them hats, too?" he said.

The Snackbar *ajoshi* smiled shyly and bowed a little. "No, no," he said in English. "Dirry hat. I give baby-san presento."

The GI flashed a smile. "Just pullin' your leg, papa-san. No sweat, man."

We ate quickly and bought Eskimo Pies before we left. James grabbed two fistfuls of wooden stirring sticks and hid them in his back pockets while the Snackbar man wasn't looking. "Do you know the way to school?" he asked.

I looked back at the gray terminal buildings and scratched my head with my free hand. "*Ungh*," I said after a moment. "We just follow the bus road."

We walked quickly past the green brick buildings and turned right after the Service Club. When we reached the gate, we waited for the traffic to clear, then ran across to the other gate. I took out my thin wallet and showed my ID card to the KATUSA MP.

"What are you two doing here?"

"We're going to school," said James.

"Give me a bite of your ice cakes."

James and I looked at each other.

The MP glared down at us until we offered him the Eskimo Pies and he had taken two large bites, staining his white scarf with chocolate. "School?" he said. "You fellows are late. You'd better hurry and get there before there's trouble."

We ran up the hill until we were breathless, then sat down and finished what was left of the Eskimo Pies. "That son of a bitch," said James.

"How late do you think we are?"

James looked at his Timex and counted slowly. "I forgot to wind my watch. The needles haven't moved."

"We always come early, anyway."

In a sheltered clump of woods on the way down to school, James produced the fistfuls of stirring sticks he had hidden in his back pockets. "Here," he said, giving me half of them, "let's make something." We sharpened the slender sticks against a boulder by rubbing them back and forth against the rough stone, and when they were all identically pointed, we took turns sticking them into the spongy earth until we had a small corral.

"Now what if an animal comes?" said James.

"A small one would fit inside," I said, "but it would just jump out again."

"I want the animal to stay inside. Do you think it would come in if it was warm?"

"Warm?" I said.

"My uncle told me Indians can make fire by rubbing two sticks together really fast. Let's make a fire inside the fence."

We had several sticks left, so I held one tightly while James took another and rubbed it against mine. Nothing happened. "Do it faster," I said.

James took a deep breath and started to rub faster and faster, pressing down so hard that I had to lay my hand against a rock for support. He bore down with his weight, his cheeks flushing, then going darker with the effort. After a few moments he let out a long breath of air and collapsed in exhaustion. The sticks were warm, but there was no fire.

"Maybe it's not the right kind of sticks," I said.

James's stirring stick was splintered now, so he took one of mine and got up when he had caught his breath. "Let's go," he said. "We can bring bigger sticks next time."

On the way out of the woods we found a bush ripe with berries. We picked and ate them until our hands and lips were stained dark with juice, and we didn't get to school until after the fourth graders went in after their recess. It was nearly lunchtime.

"We're in trouble," I said, wiping my hands on my pants.

"What if we just sneak in after lunch recess?"

I thought about it, but I wanted to eat lunch. "I'm hungry now. Aren't you hungry?"

"*Ungh*," said James. "Let's go. What can the teacher do?"

People seemed to be watching us from the silent school building as we approached. We stood quietly for a long time in front of the second- and third-grade building where James had had to go ever since they had found out how old he really was.

"Meet me at lunch recess," whispered James. He walked up the stairs, opened the glass door, and disappeared inside.

I tried not to make any noise on my way to the first-grade building, but the grass crackled loudly under my shoes. I opened the door very slowly, just wide enough to step through. As I opened the second door, the first hissed and slammed shut. I jumped, shuddering for a moment before I slipped through the second door and stood at the end of the blue-gray corridor where all the coat hooks pointed at me. I thought I could hear Mrs. McPhee talking to the class about how she would punish me.

I wanted to run away, but I walked carefully down the hall and waited just outside the open classroom door for my heart to stop thudding against the inside of my chest. I peeked into the room.

Every noise stopped when the class saw me. Mrs. McPhee put down her chalk and stared at me for a moment before she said, "Well, *hello*. And whose dirty little face might *this* be under that funny little hat? Come in, young man."

I stood next to the blackboard by the door and looked down at my dirty shoes. A large stain of chocolate and cream blotted the top of my left sock.

"It's practically lunchtime," said Mrs. McPhee, looking up at the electric clock. "Where have you been all morning?"

"I fall asleep on bus," I said.

"Well, go to your seat, young man. We'll deal with this later. Make sure you get washed up before lunch. And take your hat off when you're indoors."

"Yesu, Ma'am." I wiped my nose and went to my seat.

Just before lunch, the Principal came to our class and

gave an important talk about how we should never speak
Korean at school, although he knew it was perfectly all
right to speak it "on the economy." In case we hadn't understood, he added, "From today on it is against the rules
to speak Korean during school hours." The American children thought this was funny, and they all laughed, but the
rest of us were sullen on the way to the cafeteria. The
teachers hovered around us to listen in case we whispered
to each other in Korean.

James and I did what we did every day after lunch: we
swung as high as we could on the swings and then, when
the playground teacher wasn't looking, we let go and flew
into the air. We would land in a crouch and leap up like
monkeys. At times it seemed that we would fly forever,
but when we stood on our feet again it would seem that
we hadn't flown at all.

After school, James said his teacher hadn't punished
him, but had only asked for a note from his mother.

"What did you tell her?"

"That I fell asleep on the bus," he said.

"How can your mother write you a note about it? She
doesn't even know."

"I don't know. American mothers can write notes about
anything."

We decided it was safe enough to miss more school. So
we wouldn't have to bother with notes, we planned to
miss whole days from now on. As we walked toward the
water fountain, the playground teacher stopped us and
told us to stop speaking Korean.

"We not talking Korean," said James.

"I distinctly heard you two just a moment ago."

I wiped my nose and looked up at her. "We say Korean
word not in American," I said. "We not know too much
American."

"This can't go on," said the teacher. "If I have to tell
you young men again, I'm going to have to have a word
with your teachers."

"Okay," we said.

"And if you hear any of your friends speaking Korean, I want you to report them to me. Is that clear?"

"Yesu, Ma'am," we said. We ran to the far side of the playground where all the half-Korean boys had gathered with the Korean boys. There, where no one could hear us and no one dared tell on us, we all shouted and cursed loudly in Korean.

"What's 'this tinkly'?" said James.

"I don't know."

"Who said it?" asked Jongsu, the oldest Korean boy.

"The playground teacher said it to us."

" 'Tinkly' is what Americans call pissing. Were you guys pissing?"

"No," I said.

James scratched his head. "All we did was talk some Korean and she said, 'I this tinkly hear you two.' "

"That bitch," said Jongsu. "She means Korean words sound like piss. I want to kill her." Jongsu was twelve, and everyone knew it except for his teachers. He had been in fifth grade in Korean school, but after his mother married a GI she had put him in third grade because his English was bad. "Some of you may only be half Korean, but be careful," he said. "You don't want to be like those white long-nose bastards. Even their dirt is white."

We looked toward the other side of the playground where they were playing a game called kootie tag.

"If any one of those kids touches you, come to me. Then I'll show them a thing or two. Understand?"

The whole crowd nodded. Jongsu was the best fighter in the first three grades. We all had to give him our candy and gum if we had any. He had already been in trouble for beating up an American fourth-grader. He always shoved the younger American kids around, but he was good to me and James because his father and James's father were Soul Brothers.

"The playground teacher's coming!" Paulie Tucker came running to us, waving his arms.

"Let's disappear," said Jongsu. He gave Paulie a stick

of gum while we waited for the playground teacher to come closer. The sun glinted on her glasses and her brass playground bell flashed like gold as it dangled in her hand. There was no way she could sneak up on us, so she walked confidently. We waited, and just before she was close enough to say something, we all ran in different directions, in between the Americans and through a game of kick ball. Jongsu met James and me at the faded hopscotch squares which the girls never used.

"Let's play," said James.

We found flat rocks near the swings and came back. Jongsu squatted down and was quiet for a moment. "I'm going to America next year," he said.

"Really?"

"My father got orders for Fort Sill in Okolohomo."

"It'll be fun," said James.

"But my mother doesn't know what to do. She says there aren't any Koreans in Okolohomo. I won't have anyone to talk to and I'll only be able to eat bread. Will you guys write to me?"

"I can't write Korean, but my American writing is all right," I said. "I'll write you."

"I will, too," said James. "My father will know your address."

"Will you send me good things to eat?" Jongsu frowned and looked away. When he turned back, he was smiling. "I'm not going yet," he said, slapping our shoulders. "Hurry. You skip first, Insu."

The bell soon rang. We threw our hopscotch rocks into the middle of the playground as we went back to our classes. Jongsu slipped us pieces of spicy Dentyne gum.

Before class started, Mrs. McPhee sent the hairy boy back to the corner to finish up his ten minutes in the corner for using foul language, then she reminded us again not to speak Korean. "This is an American school. You are here to learn English. To learn English more quickly, you *must* stop speaking Korean."

I wondered why she said this to the whole class when only four of us could speak Korean. While she talked, everyone took turns looking at us. I pretended to read the wall chart of African animals.

Mrs. McPhee started the math lesson by taking down the jar of water she kept on top of the supply shelf and marking the level with a grease pencil. Now there were six marks on the jar, two of them farther apart than the others because one of them was made after the weekend. She said that the marks showed evaporation, which was what happened to water when the sun shined on it. But the sun never touched the jar while it sat on the cabinet. I was sure she just took a sip every day after school, and her story about evaporation was just another American lie, like when she said the sun was a thousand times bigger than the moon.

Before the end of class, Mrs. McPhee wrote a note to the hairy boy's mother and one to my mother, and she explained how I had to bring back a note tomorrow. She pinned her note to my shirt so I wouldn't lose it. "We can't have you falling asleep on the bus again," she said. "God knows where you might wind up. Kimpo Airbase or somewhere."

The girl with the yellow hair swung her feet back and forth under her desk and giggled at the note on my shirt. I looked down at the square of paper, then up at Mrs. McPhee.

"Now don't you lose it."

The yellow-haired girl giggled again. The white-haired boy made a face at her and pointed at her with a nose-picking on his fingertip. "I'm telling," she said. The white-haired boy put his finger in his mouth just before Mrs. McPhee saw him.

"What's this?" said Mrs. McPhee. "You shouldn't be sucking *any* of your fingers, Keith. Now that we finally got you to stop sucking your thumb, we can't just move on to other fingers."

I kicked one of the yellow-haired girl's shoes. She stuck her tongue out at me through the gap in her front teeth. The hairy boy in the corner turned around and faced the class. "Penis!" he said.

Mrs. McPhee turned suddenly red. "My *goodness*, who said that?" She turned around. "Did you say that, Greg?"

"My dad showed me," said the hairy boy, with a big smile. "It's like a birdie."

"Well, we can't go around saying such things. It's downright *vulgar*." She went to her desk and picked up a ruler. "When I was your age I would have had my little fanny paddled for that. I'm going to have a word with your parents at once." She shook the ruler a few times and led the hairy boy to the front of the classroom. "Now tell everyone you're sorry."

The hairy boy only looked down at the floor the way I did when I got into trouble.

"Come on, young man. You should be ashamed of yourself." When he wouldn't talk, Mrs. McPhee smacked him across the palms three times with the ruler, then sat him down and apologized for him.

After school, I asked James what "penis" meant.

"Peanuts?"

I shook my head. "The hairy boy got in *big* trouble for saying it. He said his father showed him and it was like a little bird."

"Could it be a sparrow?"

We asked Tony, who was in sixth grade. We stood under the maple tree and called up, "Hey, older brother, what's 'penis'?"

One of the older girls at the bus stop threw a rock at us. Tony laughed and shook the branch he was straddling. "You filthy bastards," he said in Korean, "it's your pepper." Then he stuck his hand down the front of his pants, and making a large bulge, he said loudly in English, "It's your *dick*!"

I still didn't understand how it could be like a bird, but

it was the most wonderful American word we had learned. James and I said it several times for practice, then ran around saying it to people who didn't know what it meant. It was good to be brothers with James, but after the end of the school year, I would never see him again.

They punished us for speaking our first language. My teacher only scolded us and stood us in the corner, but some would slap our lips, sometimes breaking our skin so we tasted the metallic tang of the blood in our forbidden words.

I learned that my mother's days of accompanying me to school were not all out of devotion to me, but for her black market business as well. On holidays she often took me to Yongsan on the school-hour bus and spent the morning and afternoon shopping in the PX, then at the Commissary, which I discovered was just across the street from my school. She would buy a shopping cart load of American goods—mostly rationed items like coffee, powdered milk, baby formula, cigarettes—and then she would take an Arirang taxi out to a market in Seoul and sell everything to a Yankee goods vendor at the Hollywood market near Pagoda Park.

On those days I absorbed the fantastic chaos of Seoul, ate boiled squid with red pepper paste at street vendors, drank cold cans of Coca-Cola with black marketeers and petty criminals. I discovered that my mother knew all the taxi and bus drivers. They treated her like a relative because she always charmed them and often gave them tips they did not expect. And because they all called her "Insu's mother" in the Korean fashion, it was not long before they all knew and recognized me.

My mother seemed much happier without my father. She was more beautiful, as if she were younger, and though she sometimes looked worried, that expression would quickly pass as she concerned herself with something immediate. She could play cards and gamble as she pleased, and on any given day our house was host to some friend, creditor, or black marketeer. I came to know all the waitresses at the military clubs in ASCOM, the prostitutes and husband-seekers who lined up outside the gates for escorts, the unsponsored wives who rode the Army bus routes with us. That year I learned far more about my mother than about my father.

From the weekend and holiday travels with my mother I memorized all the U.S. Army bus routes and timetables. I learned the location of restaurants, tea rooms, and important market stalls just outside the Army post, and on the side of the base where I went to school, I knew the shortest route to every back gate. I learned very little in school, but without knowing it, my mother had taught me how to get by, without her, in my father's world.

✧

The day of my father's return from his first tour of duty in Vietnam, Mahmi and I waited at the U.S. military airport at Kimpo for seven hours. We had arrived early in the morning. We had taken an Arirang taxi from Pupyong to Kimpo airbase, expecting to wait only an hour or two for his out-processing after he came off the flight, but the plane was late and our wait became a daylong vigil. I did not know what my mother was thinking, whether she was imagining the flight shot out of the sky, or whether she doubted the Korea House translator's reading of my father's letter and imagined we had come on the wrong day. If we were not there to meet him, there was no way my father would be able to find us unless he wrote to her again from his new post in Korea. As the day drew on and the pleasant warmth of morning became the blinding heat of noon, and then as the shadows lengthened where we waited outside, in the shade of a deuce-and-a-half truck, I tried to remember my father's face. He had only been gone for a year, but without a picture I could only imagine him in the vaguest way. The short yellow hair, the square face, the plumped skin, the slightly downturned eyes, the sharp beak nose.

I remembered my father as an MP in the First Cavalry Division. On his shoulder he wore the shield-shaped golden patch with the diagonal black stripe and the horse-head silhouette. He would dab my cheeks with shaving cream while I crept around him and splashed the dirty water in the wash basin. When I learned to talk, I said "*Aboji myondo*" each time he shaved, and he tried to teach me the English: "Daddy, shave." I could never make the strange words, but I learned games quickly. I would imitate his shaving by using a dull knife, or play cowboy, making him snort and rear up to make the horse noise while I clung to his back. I would stop him, patting his short, yellow bristles, and motion for him to graze on the dry leaves I had strewn on the floor. I learned how to unlace his low-quarter shoes so I could use one lace as reins and the other as a whip. We would play until the sweat poured from his body, filling the room with his strange animal smell. I remembered the smell of yellow Dial soap, the gritty texture of Colgate tooth powder, the cold sting of Mennen Skin Bracer, the warm and wet lather of Old Spice shaving soap brushed on my face with the two-tone bristles of a shaving brush. I remembered the odd musk of the foot powder he rubbed between his toes and dumped into his green wool socks and into his black combat boots, the sweet mildewy smell of the damp leather, the pleasant bite of Black Kiwi shoe polish. I could remember all these things, but I could not picture his face. I could see his gap-toothed smile when he removed his false teeth. I could see the blue and green flash of his eyes, the plumpness of the back of his hand when he grasped a pen to write, but I could not remember his face. I had only pieces of my father.

"Mahmi," I said. "Do you think Daeri's face has changed?"

"His skin might be a bit burnt," she said. "Maybe he's lost a little flesh because of his hard life in Vietnam, but why would he look any different?"

"I don't know. What if I don't recognize him?"

"You'll recognize him."

"Do you think he'll remember me?"

"Of course! He's been thinking only of you for that whole year. You're his son." Though she tried to keep pale, Mahmi's skin was burnt quite dark by the summer sun. In her beehive hair and her white polyester *wanpisu*, she was darker than me. Her skin was dark even for a Korean, and sometimes people said she had the skin of a *sangnom*, a commoner. "Do you remember the last time you saw him?" she asked.

"It was with the beggars," I said. "He gave them money and he said I shouldn't make fun."

"That's right." Mahmi looked suddenly worried, and I knew she was thinking of the wounded veterans with pieces of their bodies missing.

"Why didn't he tell me he was going?" I said. Then I saw my father in the distance through the waves of heat rippling over the tarmac, and he looked smaller than I remembered. Other yellow-haired soldiers had come out before him, and I had been afraid to confuse one of them for him, but there was no mistaking when my father emerged from the terminal building—the fresh-cropped crew cut that made his hair bristle straight up like a brush, the fleshy square shape of his face. He was leaner and darker, burnt by the tropical sun and wasted by bouts of malaria. He was wearing his short-sleeved summer khakis, with his bars of decorations and the coiled blue Infantry braid around one shoulder, but he walked differently—methodically, with a step more cautious than I remembered, a step more suited for someone in camouflage fatigues. His ice-blue eyes had a distant look to them—or had they sunk subtly back in their sockets?

Mahmi did not immediately run to him as I had expected. She gave me a quick glance, and I charged forward, sprinting until I grew suddenly self-conscious just in front of my father and came to an awkward stop to look sheepishly up at him. He stepped up to me and lifted me into his hug. He patted and rubbed the top of my head as he let me down on my mother's approach. When she reached him he kissed her. That was the first and only time I saw them kiss.

We rode back to Pupyong in another Arirang taxi. I sat in the front seat with the window open so I didn't hear what they talked about in the back. We drove off the good pavement of the airbase and out into the winding dirt road through the several villages that skirted the other army posts along the bus route to ASCOM. I sat sweating in the vinyl seat, watching the meter click up nickel by nickel as we rattled on in the heat.

In the evening I bathed after my father, standing in a wash basin full of soapy water as he scrubbed me with a rough washcloth and poured cold water over me to rinse me clean. Emo cooked a steak which Mahmi had gotten the day before and kept under a block of ice. My father was happy but uneasy. Even when he pierced the top of his Falstaff beer with the can opener, making that cold *crack-hissss* sound that used to make him smile, he seemed preoccupied by something.

I do not remember what he talked about that first night. I do not remember if the dinner was pleasant or if he had brought lavish gifts for everyone. I remember being shocked at the contrast between his burnt forearms and the paper-white flesh of his armpits. I remember thinking the damp curls of hair in his underarms were the color of the hairs around an ox's nostrils. I remember how his feet filled the entire wash basin and how the room became pungent with the familiar odor of his sweat. In his duffel bag he had brought back all the cigarettes he had not smoked or traded from his C-rations, the packets of acrid coffee, the packets full of toilet paper, salt, sugar, pepper, and cream, the metal can openers, the white plastic spoons—things that we would use every day in the house. He had brought my mother a red Vietnamese costume called an *ao dai*; he had brought fresh green wool socks for Hyongbu, grease pencils and yellow wooden pencils for Yongsu and Haesuni, and a leather wallet from my grandmother for me to hang around my neck. He asked me about school and I told him that I enjoyed it. I left out all the important things.

✧

"What you do in Vietnam, Daddy?"

We were at the edge of the parade field at Yong-san 8th Army Headquarters, just under the flagpole, and my father had put me astride the howitzer to take a quick picture. They fired deafening blanks out of the howitzer each day when the flag came down, and everything stopped to listen to the bugler play the sad taps music. The dark green barrel was hot under my thigh.

"You're sitting on top of Zam-Zammah!" said my father.

"Zam-Zammah!" I shouted.

"Thy father was a pastry cook!"

The shutter of my father's borrowed camera clicked and I quickly swung my leg over and leaped down. "What's a pastry cook?"

"Oh, that's someone who makes doughnuts and cakes. Like *ttok*."

"You not a *ttok* man, Daddy. What you do in Vietnam? You kill lotsa' number ten VC?"

"I was a red bull on a green field," he said quietly, still talking some sort of riddle I didn't understand.

"How come you not say?"

"I was on an Advisory Team near a place called Nha

Trang," he said. "I helped people called Montagnards fight the Vietcong. You'd like the Montagnards, Booby. They're like Indians."

"They got Indians in Vietnam? Make fire with sticks? Wow!" I took my father's sunburnt hand, and he led me across the street, past the Main Library, to the Snack Bar. I heard a raspy metallic sound and looked back over my shoulder at the parade field, suddenly expecting to see people ice skating the way they did when the field was flooded in winter. It was nothing, just a sound like the sound of a blade on ice, but it made me shiver.

My father was quiet. He had seemed happier since he returned from Vietnam, but he was also distant, as if a part of him had not made it back. I had seen my share of limp, black body bags and rigid aluminum coffins on AFKN television, and I imagined he had left something like that— some feeling that hurt like the sight of those containers— back in the highlands outside Nha Trang.

My father treated me to an early turkey dinner at the special buffet that afternoon. He wanted me to have the dark and white meat, but I found the sliced turkey loaf neater and less like a dead animal—more palatable under the lumpy gravy and the dark red cranberry sauce. I had never learned how to handle a full set of western silverware, and today was my lesson on how to eat European-style, keeping the fork in my left hand, the knife always in the right. My father corrected me and told me anecdotes while I sawed at the turkey with the dull knife and struggled to use the fork in its upside-down position without letting the food slip off.

"I used to go swimming out on Nha Trang beach," he said. "The water was so blue it was like looking up at the sky, and for lunch I used to eat a green dragon fruit."

"Green dragon? Like dinosaur?"

"Like a cactus—you know, like you see in the cowboy movies. Green dragon fruit tastes really good."

"Can I have one, Daddy?"

"You come to 'Nam with me sometime, Booby." He

tapped on his false front teeth. "One time I lost my partial plate when I went to the *benjo*. I dropped it in there and it was night, so I couldn't find it later even with a flashlight. In the morning I went out without my partial, and the Montagnards thought it was funny. I said, 'See, me Montagnard, too.' The chiefs got a real kick out of it. They file down their front teeth and they all smoke cigars, even the little kids your age."

I made a face to show him I didn't like cigars.

"Don't spill that. Pull your elbows in. That's right, and sit straight."

After I corrected my posture, my father took some change out of his pocket and put it on the table. "How about some chocolate cake?" he said. "Then we catch the bus home."

"Okay!"

The cake, I learned, was not to be eaten with a knife and fork, but simply cut apart with the fork itself. The crumbs could be compressed down and squeezed between the tines if you wanted to get them without touching them with your fingers. My father pronounced that I had made good progress, and we went down to the bus station where he bought his usual copy of *The Stars and Stripes*. On the bus we sat near the back, with the window open so he could smoke one of his pungent cigars even though the Korean women sitting around us grimaced and complained. He ignored them, but he knew what they were saying, and he actually enjoyed annoying them. He told me more about Vietnam as the bus droned on and I settled against his side, half drowsing.

"We used to go on patrol," he said. "We'd hump our gear up into the highlands and watch the big planes spraying the defoliants. Long clouds of it would come down. Agent Orange. It was beautiful. In a few days everything would be dead. Not a blade of grass for Charlie to hide under. And we used to take bangalore torpedoes—they're long tubes packed with plastic explosives—we used them to blow up bunkers and patches of barbed wire. We'd go out to the Montagnards and stick the bangalores down into the roots of their big trees and blow a few of them. When the trees fell over the Montagnard kids and women would run into the crater or to the roots that stuck out at the bottom of the trunk and catch all the stunned rats. That was a delicacy for them—a special food. They really liked us *taksan* for getting them those rats."

I fell asleep to the sound of my father's voice telling me something about a monkey and a shotgun. The pictures he took that day never came out.

My father stayed in Korea for eleven months after his return. Forty-eight weekends, and he came home on half of them. With the few three-day passes and holidays, he was home for less than fifty days before he left again. My mother and I visited him only once up in Camp Casey where he was stationed near Wijong-bu, and he wasn't at all happy to see us. He told my mother later that having his men see his Korean wife undermined his authority. We never visited again.

While my father was on leave for my birthday in January of 1968, the U.S.S. Pueblo, an electronic spy ship, was captured off the coast of North Korea, and all over the country, the military went on alert. My father went back up to his unit early after hearing the news on his transistor radio. Later that month, during the Vietnamese New Year's celebration of Têt, the NVA and the Vietcong simultaneously attacked over a hundred towns, cities, and military installations all over Vietnam. It was the bloodiest offensive of the war. The outpost where my father had served near Nha Trang was overrun, and many of his friends were among the Killed-in-Action. The mood among the GIs in Korea became thick and black, full of hate for Asian people and tense with the fear that the North Koreans might invade. The GIs were afraid to stay in Korea, but even more afraid that they might be shipped to Cam Ranh Bay to join some counteroffensive *against the North Vietnamese. Houseboys and prostitutes were beaten more frequently; there were more fights in the clubs. The Korean army stayed on alert and continued to mobilize more men to send to Vietnam. There was constant news about the White Horse Division, the Tiger Division, and the Blue Dragon Brigade.*

I don't think my father ever considered our house his home that year. We were just the family that kept him occupied when he wasn't working. Korea and Vietnam were both countries divided along their middle by a Demilitarized Zone, with Communists in the north and pro-American governments in the south. Both countries had Buddhists and Catholics and Animists, they farmed wet rice, they plowed fields with oxen, they were populated by people with yellow skin. When he took me to the Snack Bar that day to teach me how to use a knife and fork, he had said something about "The Great Game" when he sent me to buy my own slice of cake. "Heinz," he said to me, "what old man is going to teach you the important things while I'm off in The Great Game?" What was "The Great Game," I had thought back then. Was my father, like my mother, playing two slot machines, but one was Korea and the other Vietnam?

I think now that what he wanted was retribution. And that is why he volunteered for Vietnam again and left before the summer of 1968. And because I had not read the blue book he had given me, I wouldn't know what he meant by "The Great Game" or "Zam-Zammah" or bulls on green fields for another twenty years.

✧

Black hourglass against a field of red. Seventh Division—Bayonet. An Indian head in a feathered headdress superimposed on a white star. A field of black. Second Infantry Division. A black horsehead silhouette, like a chess knight, above a diagonal black slash across a shield of gold. The First Cavalry Division. In his German accent, he called it "The First Calf." These were the totemic symbols of my father, his military insignia. The four cardinal points in green, which the Germans in World War II had called "The Devil's Cross." Fourth Mechanized Infantry

Division. A white sword pointing upright between two yellow batwing doors against a field of blood. The Vietnam campaign. Golden chevrons, a white long rifle against a blue bar, oak-leaf clusters, a cross of iron for excellent marksmanship. Symbols of power. Totems of the clan that kills people whose skin is the color of mine. Indelible.

4

Metal

Image from a Stolen Camera

Some days the gang would gather at the mouth of the alley under the shade of the maple tree and we would watch Old Man Heaven and Old Man Earth play their long games of Korean chess; and when Yongshiggi's blind grandfather was there he would call us around him—he knew each of us, even how old we were, by our voices—and as we loitered around the maple tree he would teach us verses from the Thousand Word Classic until we could chant large portions of it, though we did not know the Chinese characters. The old men watched over us and kept us out of trouble when we stayed near Tatagumi, but on most days in summer when our parents were busy or away—which was nearly every day—we would leave the neighborhood for our adventures.

Since we had few toys, we made do with sticks and stones and scraps of wood and metal. We could spend entire days at a construction site, sculpting the piles of sand into elaborate mountainscapes with roads which we would traverse with our car-shaped stones. A few whittled tree branches or bamboo poles would be enough for us to transform into lances and swords, and so we would arm ourselves for week-long military campaigns. Unless we were an annoyance, no one seemed to mind us—though any adult would scold us to keep off the main street. In the alleys there were always adults about: Old Grandfather

Moneychanger whom we could spot in the distance as he wan-
dered the town in his white traditional clothes; Crazy ajuma,
who wore a tattered winter coat all year long; the traveling knife-
sharpeners and junk men with their bicycle-wheel wagons; the
seafood and nougat sellers with their odorous and fragrant carts.
They were there to break up fights and tell us to be quiet, to say
it was time to go home, to have a look at us if we happened to
get hurt—though there wasn't much they could do about it.
Occasionally, some boy would lose an eye in a rock fight or break
a leg leaping from an embankment or a scaffolding, and then we
wouldn't see him for a time until he reappeared, perhaps with
an eye patch or a limp. That was commonplace. Sometimes even
small accidents resulted in a death in our neighborhood, like the
time when Pyono's little brother sucked on a condom and choked
to death while his mother vainly pounded on his back.

I've often wondered what our parents would have done if they
had known the sorts of games we played—if they would have
been shocked or angered, or simply indifferent. Most of them,
like my mother, had grown up during the Korean War, when
the entire country was devastated, when ten million families
were separated forever as they fled from refuge to refuge on roads
lined with the dead. But my mother's memories of the war often
surprised me. "It's the most fun you can ever have in life," she
once said to me, "as long as you don't get killed."

The war was fifteen years past with Korea in an uneasy peace,
and yet Pupyong seemed to have some fatality nearly every day:
the shoeshine boy who was run over by a train as he tried to pull
scrap metal off the tracks; the delivery boy crushed between two
buses when he tried to take a shortcut through the terminal; the
bar girl killed by a truck as she tried to free her high heels from a
patch of fresh tar on the main road. At the site of each accident
there was inevitably a policeman waving the crowd away—and
always a straw mat, often with some appendage protruding from
underneath. These were mysterious and exciting things we all
went to investigate whenever we could, but on most days our
excitement was in creating our own potential tragedies.

✦

The light shone differently this morning, giving a fierce and almost painfully sharp brightness to everything, making the colors powerful enough to cut the backs of my eyes. Last night we had all breathed charcoal gas while we slept, but this time had not been bad. Mahmi said that Emo had once died and that my father had taken her out on the *maru* and breathed into her mouth until she lived again. This time we only had headaches. I had wakened in the late night, crawled to the outhouse to throw up, and gone back to sleep after all the windows were opened.

Early morning in Tatagumi, and like the old people and the birds, I was already up. I stood in the front courtyard, slightly dazed with sleep, trying to shake the dull ache from my head. Birds chirped from the tiled housetops, and outside in the quiet alleyway, the neighborhood dogs barked almost in rhythm with the pounding in my head.

I went to the red clay *chang* pots: one filled with water in case of a water shortage, one filled to the brim with black Japanese soy sauce, and one half full of bean paste. When I leaned over to wet my face in the pot of water, the ache in my head pushed down my spine into the small of my back, and I felt my bowels go weak. I clutched at the rim of the *chang* pot and moaned.

From outside the front gate came the sound of the dogs barking again. Someone was walking very slowly down the alleyway, breathing quietly, groaning an old groan after each few steps. When the dogs stopped barking, I heard a hum, and then some mumbled phrases of an old folk song. It was the Oilseller *ajuma*. I had not seen her in two months.

The Oilseller *ajuma* did not bring me things or even really speak to me, but her presence made all things tranquil. "Come in, please," I said, before she could knock at the gate. The small door panel opened and the Oilseller *ajuma* stooped in, ragged, gray-haired, and stained with the sesame-seed oil she sold. "Insu-*nuuun* . . . ," she said. "Insuuu-*nuuun* . . ." Her words were half question, half chant. Every time she came to our house, her greeting was the same.

"Hello, Oilseller *ajuma*."

She looked at me with her blue-tinged black eyes and nodded her head. "Insu-*nuuun* . . . ," she said again.

I ran into the house, trampling the floor of the *maru* without even taking my shoes off. "Emo," I called, "Oilseller *ajuma* is here!"

Emo came out of the kitchen, wiping her hands on her apron. She stepped up onto the *maru* after taking off her kitchen slippers. "Take your shoes off," she said to me. She greeted the Oilseller *ajuma* and helped her unsling the heavy oil canister she carried on her back. They sat on the *maru* and talked.

I jumped down into the kitchen and picked up our empty sesame-oil bottles, then crawled back onto the *maru* and walked across on my knees. My shoes did not once touch the floor, but Emo gave me an impatient look. "Bottles," I said.

The Oilseller *ajuma* had taken out our account book. She turned the pages which were transparent with oil, and finding the place, made another entry. Carefully and patiently, she filled our empty bottles and wiped their mouths and necks. She corked the bottles with dark corks and wiped her creased and callused hands on the oily green work apron she wore over her old-fashioned Japanese-style trousers.

Now the whole house smelled deliciously of sesame-seed oil. I took the slippery bottles back into the kitchen and licked off all the oil before putting them on the shelf. Then I went out by the back way and opened the gate to go out into the alley, but the straw-colored dog was standing in front of our house. I closed the gate door and sat down in front of the *chang* pots to let the sun warm me. I knew the day would be hot.

The Oilseller *ajuma* was resting on the *maru*. She drank a bowl of cold water and, as she shared an American cigarette with Emo, she told news from the city of Inchon. "This year the water is good," she said. "The fish sellers have a big profit."

"If only I were a fish seller, too," said Emo.

Breathing smoke from her half-parted lips, the Oilseller *ajuma* nodded and looked up, out through the open house doors, into the sky. "Today on the train I heard a curious story," she said.

I closed my eyes and breathed lightly so I would not miss the story.

Two lovers in Seoul had committed suicide. They could not continue living, each married to the wrong person. The woman loved her children but could not bear her husband's touch at night. The man could no longer look at his wife's gourdlike face, and he had taken to beating his unfilial sons. The lovers would meet in tea shops and often go to the private baths together, but they had been continuously unhappy. "How could they live so sadly," said the Oilseller *ajuma*. "They didn't know when they would be disgraced." They could not leave their families because of guilt, but one day, as they passed by the Seoul station, they decided to run away to another province. The man bought two tickets for Pusan. They cried as they waited for the train, and when it finally came, they knew they could neither leave nor live any longer in this world. The man composed a note, and clutching it in his hand, he walked with the woman, away from the waiting train. They lay down together on the tracks on the south side of the station, each holding one end of the note. When the Pusan train left the station, it ran over the lovers, taking their heads along with it all the way to the Yong Dong P'o station.

"Such sadness in the world," said the Oilseller *ajuma*.

I squinted as I opened my eyes to the bright light.

Emo was smoking a new cigarette. "Such a pity," she said.

From the alleyway there came a thud. The dog whimpered.

"Insu-ya, play!"

I opened the gate door and saw Piggy leaning on a long bamboo stick.

"Come out quick," he said.

I looked back at Emo and the Oilseller *ajuma* still talking on the *maru*. I didn't want to wait to explain where I would be playing that day, so I went outside and closed the small door of the gate quietly behind me. The dog was gone.

"Where's your stick?" Piggy said. He had gotten his hair cut again, and now it was so short it looked like flecks of pepper on his scalp.

"If I go inside, I'll have to do errands."

"Why didn't you come out a while ago?" He scraped his stick along the bottom of the wall as we walked out toward the main street of the neighborhood.

I remembered the straw-colored dog, but I didn't want to tell Piggy I was afraid of it. "I was listening to a story," I said. "Two people got their heads chopped off by a train! The heads rolled all the way to Yong Dong P'o and they were all bloody and mashed up!"

"I already heard that yesterday."

"Really?" Piggy always seemed to hear of things before I did.

"Let's buy some gum," said Piggy. "You have money?"

"*Ungh.*" I put my hand in my pocket and felt the coins

I had left from my spending money. When I pulled the coins out to count them, I saw that the straw-colored dog was just behind me, sniffing and coming closer. I stopped walking.

"A lot?" said Piggy.

I stood very still, holding the coins tightly in my fist. The dog sniffed at my hands, looking up at me and lolling its long, wet tongue. Its black lower lip was flecked with saliva. I could feel its breath all over my body, and my hand tingled in the spot where I was sure to be bitten.

"How much?" said Piggy.

I stopped breathing and looked down at the dog out of the corner of my eye. "Piggy-ya," I whispered, trying to look at him at the same time. He came back up the alleyway and hit his stick against a wall. The dog whimpered and ran out toward the street.

"You're afraid of a shit-dog?"

I swallowed hard and nodded.

"Stupid. That dog doesn't bite!"

"It was ready to bite," I said.

Piggy sniffed, then took my hand and sniffed again. "It wanted to lick the oil," he said. "Stupid! Rub your hands in the dirt. *Ya*, I'll hold the money."

I gave him the coins and rubbed my hands on the ground, making sure my palms became thoroughly dirty and they smelled like blood and metal. "Give me the money back," I said.

Piggy gave me the coins and made me put them away before I could count them. "I counted," he said. "There's enough to buy gum and pop-outs from the jam seller."

"Where are we going?"

"Going to get Dogshit," he said. Dogshit had an awful name because he had been very beautiful as a baby and his mother didn't want his good looks to bring misfortune from jealous spirits. "We'll play war," Piggy said when we reached the darker dirt of the street. "I found a really good place at the railroad bridge. Let's go and call Dogshit and

Kisu and Jani." He started to spin and make *ch'ok ch'ok* noises. "I'm a dragonfly airplane!" He ran erratically, but I still couldn't keep up with him.

We passed Chong's Wholesale Store, which had not yet opened. Mr. Chong had taken down the wooden night barriers and was splashing water on the ground to keep the dust down. He held the bucket between his legs and prompted the water out with little flicks of his fingers, pointing with his chin where he wanted to wet the ground. "*Ya*, little bastards, be careful!" he called after us.

When we reached Dogshit's house, we stood outside the gate under the old Chinese characters of the name plate and called, "Dogshit-ah! Play!" I called in a high voice, Piggy in a husky voice.

"Quiet!" said Dogshit's mother. "He's sleeping! Come later!"

"Dogshit-ah! Play!" Piggy yelled one more time.

"Go away!"

I could hear thumping on the *maru* inside, then a whine. Dogshit was awake. Piggy and I sat with our backs to the wall and waited. In a moment the gate opened and Dogshit emerged, rubbing his eyes and grimacing.

"Why did you sleep so late?" said Piggy.

"No."

"The whole day's gone by. Real soldiers get up while the sky is still dark!"

"What time is it?"

"Don't know. Go get your stick."

Dogshit yawned, scratched his head, and rubbed his face. "I was having good dreams," he said.

"What kind of dream?" I asked.

"I forgot."

"Two people got their heads chopped off by a train," I said.

Dogshit frowned.

"Their heads got all bloody and crushed and they rolled all the way from Taegu to Yong Dong P'o," said Piggy. I wanted to correct him, but I knew he would hit me with his stick if I did. "Their bodies got mangled and dogs ate them," he added thoughtfully.

"Oilseller *ajuma* came to our house," I said.

Dogshit went back inside and came out again with his rifle stick, looking more awake. His mother had combed his hair and tucked his white T-shirt into his blue nylon shorts. "My mother says to come back by lunchtime." He blew his nose on his fingers and threw the snot on the ground. The rest he rubbed onto his loose suspenders.

Piggy knuckled him on the head. "You dirty bastard! Doesn't your mother teach you good habits?"

"Ah! Son of a bitch," whined Dogshit. "I should tell."

"If you want to blow your nose, blow it right." Piggy pressed one side of his nose with an index finger and snorted his snot out against the wall. "Did you see?"

Dogshit and I were quiet. We had both practiced once until our noses bled, but we couldn't quite snort properly. We would usually get the snot on our upper lips or on our shirts.

"What are you waiting for, stupids! Let's get Kisu and Jani!"

At each of their houses we chanted their names. Kisu came out with rice cakes for us to eat, and Jani brought his extra rifle stick for me.

Jani had blond hair, blue eyes, and freckles, so even though he spoke no English, he always got to play the American general because he looked more American and was older than me.

"Now there's a Yankee leader and a Korean leader," said Piggy. "Insu, you be the Yankee private. Kisu, you're my captain, and Dogshit is the sergeant."

"I want to be a sergeant, too," I said. "My father's a sergeant."

"No."

"Why not? Why can't I be a sergeant? I'm bigger than Dogshit!"

"So what if you're big," said Dogshit. "You're too slow."

"Dog shit cow shit," I chanted.

Jani, Kisu, and Piggy joined me. We started the song and did a strutting dance.

> Dog shit cow shit!
> Rat shit horse shit!
> Pig shit chicken shit!
> Rabbit shit bird shit!
> YOUR SHIT MY SHIT!

On the last line, we all pointed at Dogshit, then at ourselves. "Dogshit is my shit," sang Jani, pointing at his ass. "I shat a big shit yesterday."

"Your mother's a fuck," said Dogshit, turning redfaced.

Jani slapped him on the head. Dogshit screamed and bit Jani on the shoulder. Kisu broke them apart while I watched Piggy scratch numbers onto the ground.

"*Ya*, you bastards, get quiet," said Piggy. "I'll teach you something." He pointed at the numbers one through ten and started to chant something he had memorized.

> One: A Japanese guy
> Two: Took a pretty maiden
> Three: And went across the 38th parallel.
> Four: Looking all around
> Five: He saw that it was deepest night.
> Six: That silly girl
> Seven: Took off her skirt.
> Eight: And on a prick as thick as an arm
> Nine: She put her hole
> Ten: And fucked.

We didn't say anything when he was done. I looked down at my sweaty feet and watched the ants crawl around my white rubber shoes. Jani tapped his stick against his knee.

"Kisu, you do it."

"One. A Japanese guy."

For the next fifteen minutes, Piggy made us take turns and recite the story. When we didn't remember a part, he slapped us on the insides of our wrists. Both of Dogshit's wrists were dark purple by the time he had memorized the story. It took me only two tries.

"Nine ten!" Piggy shouted. We were lined up in attention against the wall. "Dogshit!"

"She put her hole and fucked!"

Suddenly, an old woman came scurrying around the corner, waving a straw yard broom. "You damned little brats," she said when she neared us, "Let's see when I tell your mothers!" We scattered and ran circles around her like a pack of dogs until she screamed at us to go away.

"Eight nine ten!" said Piggy, and we all chanted the last three lines again before running down the street to the main road.

"That was Yongshiggi's grandmother," Kisu said as we all sat down on the curb. "She knows all our houses."

"Oh," whined Dogshit, looking frightened. "What are we going to do?"

"So what if she knows!" Piggy hit the ground with his stick, making a hollow buzzing noise. The bamboo had begun to splinter at one end.

"Think you'll get spanked?" asked Jani.

Dogshit sniffed. "Don't know. What to do?"

"I never get spanked," I said.

Dogshit frowned at me. A thin line of white snot peeked out of his right nostril. When he sniffed, it disappeared for a moment, then reemerged.

"We're going to play at the railroad bridge that goes into the American post," said Piggy. He told us how we could climb down between the ties and wait on the supports of the bridge while the train passed overhead. A week ago we had all swum in the sewer creek below the rail bridge and we had smoked our first cigarettes as we watched the train take supplies into ASCOM. Everyone had coughed except for Piggy. Piggy could blow smoke out of his nose, so we knew he had smoked before, but we pretended he hadn't. We had all been amazed when he chewed on a mouthful of smoke and then spat a large, egglike saliva bubble onto the plastic of the Pagoda pack. When the smoke-filled bubble finally burst, the cigarette mist danced for a moment and vanished like a ghost. No one else could make the bubble. We let Piggy smoke the rest of the pack by himself while we all chewed gum to hide the smell on our breaths.

"We have to be careful when we go across the bridge," said Piggy.

I looked across the road while Piggy talked. A Corona taxi and a *surikoda*, a three-wheeled pickup truck, passed by. To our right, I could see the neighborhood ice-cream seller wheeling his cart toward Sinchon. The straw-colored dog was on the other side of the road, sniffing and wandering in the opposite direction.

"*Ya*, the shit wagon's coming," said Jani. His soup-bowl haircut made him look like he was wearing a dirty blond helmet that was a little too large for his head. I wiped the sweat from my face and looked where he was pointing. From the direction of the train station came the ox-drawn shit wagon. Its owner walked to its right, matching his steps to the slow gait of the tan ox whose flank he tapped, from time to time, with a bamboo switch.

"Let's go see," said Jani. Three of us ran with him, leaving Piggy to sit alone on the curb.

"*Ya*," called Piggy, "where are you going?" Then he got up and trudged after us.

The sides and top of the wooden shit wagon were caked dark brown with the excrement that had spilled from it over the years. Black and gold flies swarmed sluggishly around the wagon and the ox, whose brushlike tail slapped at them rhythmically back and forth. Sometimes the ox's tail touched its owner, who would glance sideways and give a grunt.

The man ignored the flies though they landed on his wiry arms and even crawled under the dirty scarf he'd wrapped around his head. He wore a sleeveless shirt and baggy U.S. Army fatigue pants that were cut short and frayed around the ankles. His clothes were dusty and stained with dirt, but his slippered feet were caked with shit just like the ox's flanks. His thick toenails looked as tough as the ox's twisted horns.

The day's heat had not yet begun, and so we didn't smell the shit wagon until we were quite close. When the thick odor enfolded us, Piggy and Dogshit went, "Ayuuu! Ayuuu!" and held their noses. Jani went to the back to investigate the dripping shit-sluice.

"You kids are up so early," said the Shitwagon Man.

"*Ajoshi*, are you coming to our house today?" asked Kisu, flicking the flies away from his face.

"Whose house?"

"Behind the tailor shop with the rooster, sir."

"*Ya,* that vicious little rooster," said the Shitwagon Man. "Even if it pecks at me again . . . of course I'll come." He knew all the houses in Tatagumi because he emptied all the outhouses.

"Shit water's coming out the back," sang Jani.

"Piss water, shit water—it's all the same," said the Shitwagon Man. He tapped the ox again with his bamboo switch.

We all kept in step. Already, the odor of the shit had diminished, but its thickness was still in our noses like vapor. I walked to the front, and while the Shitwagon Man showed Jani and Kisu how to snatch flies out of the air, I studied the tired ox, whose thick nose ring dangled down to its upper lip and shook with each step. The corners of the ox's almost human eyes were gobbed thick with its dried tears. Flies settled there between blinks of its thick lids. I was surprised by its beautiful eyelashes.

"*Ayu!* Shit smell!" groaned Dogshit with his fingers still pinched over his nose.

Piggy tapped him with his bamboo stick.

I watched a fly on the ox's harness as it frantically rubbed its front legs together then leaned forward and rubbed its back legs just as quickly, its golden back gleaming in the sunlight. I waited to see if it could rub its two middle legs, too, but Jani came and captured it with a twist of his wrist.

"See," he said. "If you catch it from the back, it flies right into your hand." He let me listen to the furious buzzing in his hand, then he unclasped his fingers just enough to let the fly crawl out and fly into the swarm again.

"Let's go to the rail bridge," said Piggy.

"The Shitwagon *ajoshi*'s going to our house," said Kisu. "I'm going with him."

"Me, too," I said, pointing at myself with the borrowed rifle stick.

"I don't want to get pecked by the rooster," said Piggy. He and Jani and Dogshit decided to go to the rail bridge first. They marched down the street, leaving us to escort the shit wagon.

The tailor shop was still closed and the rooster, a retired fighting cock, was still inside. The shit wagon stopped on the street in front of Kisu's house. "Stay here," the man said. Kisu and I stood there until we realized that he had spoken to the ox, which was now thoughtfully going over its cud with side-to-side chomps of its wet jaw.

The man took the two wooden shit buckets down from the side of the wagon and hung them each, by their long rope handles, on opposite ends of a bowed pole which he then balanced over his shoulder. Carrying the shit ladle, which was made of a U.S. Army helmet liner attached to a long pole, he walked slowly to Kisu's house, his buckets swinging. Kisu opened the tiny outside trap at the back of the outhouse, and the Shitwagon Man put down his buckets. "Can you get me a bowl of cold water?" he said.

"Yes, sir." Kisu went in through the front gate.

Putting on a pair of worn hemp gloves, the Shitwagon Man smiled at me, then started ladling the shit carefully into his buckets. "Have to leave the hands clean," he said to me. The fresh shit poured like a watery soup and

smelled wet and powerful like the ocean. The Shitwagon
Man began to sing.

> That cold rain
> Endlessly
> Pouring through the night of Yong Dong P'o . . .
> *Jja-jja-jang ch'ang ch'ang.* . . .

He accompanied himself with instrumental noises and did
a little dance when he carried the full buckets back to the
shit wagon and emptied them in through the top.

> *Aaaah ah-ha ha ha* . . .
> Never could
> I forget that
> Rainy night of Yong Dong P'o. . . .

Kisu brought an aluminum bowl full of water. The Shitwagon Man put down his things and took off his gloves
before drinking. "Ah! Cold and refreshing," he said, emptying the bowl in a few gulps. "Is it well water?"

"Yes, sir," said Kisu, taking back the bowl.

"When I lived in the country there was a well that was
cold as ice in summer and warm as barley tea in winter.
Ah, the water was good. Can't compare the nasty spigot
water."

As the Shitwagon Man resumed his work, I recounted
to Kisu the story I had heard from the Oilseller *ajuma*. Kisu
only nodded when I finished; he wasn't impressed at all.
"It happens all the time," he said. "A lot of people die on
the railroad tracks. Usually, they're accidents." He told me
of the time a bus full of high school students was hit by a
train and the time a small boy was run over while listening
to the thunder in the rail.

"We should be careful today," I said.

"It's all right. The railroad bridge isn't dangerous unless
you're stupid."

When the Shitwagon Man was done, Kisu gave him the money he had brought from his mother. The Shitwagon Man thanked him and loaded his buckets and pole. "Good-bye," he called as he left. "Listen well to your mothers."

"Good-bye, *ajoshi*," we said.

The Shitwagon Man tapped the ox, and the wagon creaked and began to move again on its small wooden wheels. He would empty outhouses until his wagon was full, and then he would go to the outskirts of town and spread the shit onto the vegetable fields as fertilizer.

The air became lighter when he left, and the day seemed silent without the buzzing of the flies. Kisu took the bowl back into his house and came out with some dried burnt rice flakes which we ate noisily as we jogged toward AS-COM. We passed the first bridge that led into ASCOM and slowed down when we reached the patch of red peppers that grew on the side of the road opposite the Korean Sixth Brigade compound.

Kisu looked around for a moment before picking two tiny red peppers and putting them quickly into his mouth. "Did anyone see?" he asked before he bit them.

"No."

He chewed twice and hesitated.

"What is it?"

Kisu frowned, chewed a little more, and spat the peppers violently onto the roadside. "Ah!" he said, inhaling and exhaling large gulps of air. "Too hot!" He coughed and wiped his watering eyes.

"Drink some water," I said.

"Where?" His nose was already dripping, and he panted with his tongue protruding like a dog.

"There."

We climbed down the embankment and ran until I found the metal drainage pipe that led from the parade field of the Korean compound to the sewer creek. During the monsoon, the pipe gushed muddy water all day in a five-meter waterfall down into the creek, but now only a finger-width of clear water trickled out. Kisu cupped his hands at the lip of the pipe, waited, and rinsed his mouth several times. "*Ya*," he said. "Now I'll live." We each drank a bellyful of water so that we wouldn't get hungry later. We were sloshing inside when we reached the second ASCOM bridge and the railroad bridge, which were side by side.

"*Ppang!*" shouted Dogshit. "Die, you Yankee bastards!"

I looked, but couldn't see anyone.

"There," said Kisu.

Piggy and Dogshit crouched behind a concrete post on the bridge, aiming at us with their sticks.

"*Ya*, I'm your captain," said Kisu.

"The late ones are all Yankees," said Piggy, rolling a stone at us. He made an explosion noise when the stone reached my feet. "You're dead. Hand grenade! Our side has one point. Your side doesn't have anything."

"You can't do that," said Kisu. "We haven't started yet."

"Real soldiers are always ready. American soldiers are like bums."

"Where's Jani?" I asked.

Piggy stood up and motioned to the stone. Dogshit came over and picked it up, saying, "We won again." Piggy pointed over the rail bridge to where Jani was sitting on the far side, watching us. Jani waved when we all looked at him, then got up and ran nimbly to the middle of the rail bridge, sometimes skipping two railroad ties in a step.

"Look at that crazy guy," said Kisu. "If he keeps doing that he'll fall through."

"It's easy," said Piggy.

The other bridge was closed, so there were no guards to yell at us. We all went to where the railroad tracks turned into the rail bridge and stood there until Jani came all the way across.

"Show these guys," said Piggy.

Jani began to skip across the ties as if he were playing

hopscotch. Piggy followed him, stepping slowly but confidently on the middle of each oily railroad tie.

"How are we going to do it?" I asked Kisu, stepping over the rail. He waited for me, and when I stood beside him he said, "This way," and walked out onto the bridge.

I followed carefully. The first five steps were easy because I could still see the ground between the ties, but at the sixth step, when the embankment dropped off, there seemed to be a barrier made of air. I could see the shallow sewer creek far below, and I could hear the water gurgle over the stones and hiss over a small sluice. An invisible hand seemed to reach up from between the sixth and seventh ties, waiting to nudge me if I tried to pass.

"Come quickly!"

Kisu's footprint had left a light spot on the black oil of the seventh tie. Tiny strands of grass peeked like green hair from the dirt-filled cracks. I watched the grass quivering in a breeze too light to feel against my skin.

"*Ya*, what are you doing!" shouted Piggy. "Hurry! Stupid bastard!"

Jani came running back to get me. "Don't look at the bottom," he said. "Just look at the wood."

With his help, I managed to put my right foot on the seventh tie. When I lifted my left foot, it felt as if my entrails had suddenly fallen out. My rubber shoes squished when I finally stood firmly on the seventh tie. My feet were sweating badly.

"Again," said Jani, holding onto my elbow.

It was easier each time. I no longer felt as scared, and soon I was marching back and forth on the rail bridge. My shoes even stopped squishing after a while. I began to count a cadence so I could manage a slow and rhythmic jog.

Dogshit could barely walk on the bridge. Sometimes, when he got to the middle, he would have to put his stick down and crawl. I would shuffle by and scoff at him.

When the noon siren wailed, we all stood at the center

of the bridge, facing the other bridge, and pissed down into the sewer creek.

"The train comes in thirty minutes," said Piggy. "Let's practice getting down to the supports."

We left our sticks at the side of the bridge and practiced until all of us, except Dogshit, could easily drop between the railroad ties onto the top of one of the concrete supports. The wooden ties were slippery with oil in places, but none of us slipped. Jani could even dangle upside down by his legs from the ties at the middle of the bridge and then spit into the sewer creek.

Piggy led us all to the middle of the bridge when it was time for the train to come. "It comes slowly because it has to cross the street," he said. "When we see it get to the road, we go down and wait. It's fun when it goes over us. All the wheels and hoses are visible from down there."

"How long is it?" asked Kisu.

"Only has six cars. It looks like it's going slowly, but it's fast because it's so short."

Jani balanced himself on a rail and walked back and forth singing, "I'm a circus tightrope walker." Dogshit wiped his nose again and again with his oily hand until his whole face turned black.

"You look like a Black guy," I said.

"*Ya*, bastard. It's not so."

"You look like a charcoal seller!"

"Fuck! Shut up!" Dogshit raised his arm as if to hit me. "I'll push you!" He cautiously stepped one tie closer to me.

I opened my eyes wide and pointed at his feet. "*Ya*, the wood's breaking!" I shouted just as Jani sneaked up behind him and grabbed him.

Dogshit screamed, "Mother!" He was trembling uncontrollably even before Jani let go of him. He seemed to want to sit down like he usually did when he cried, but now he tried to stand still even while his knees kept buckling. We all laughed and started the Dogshit song while Dogshit squeezed his eyes shut and cried, but then each of us stopped in turn when we heard the scream of the steam whistle and the dull *puff puff* of the engine.

The red railroad crossing lights flashed on the street. The loud warning bells clanged. Traffic stopped and lined up as the black engine rounded the bend behind the Sixth Brigade compound and came into view, spewing smoke and steam.

"Let's go," said Kisu.

Piggy stopped him. "Wait until it gets to the road."

"If we don't wait it's no fun," said Jani.

My hands and feet began to sweat as the train came closer and the noise grew louder and louder. I felt another large fear inside my belly that grew with the size of the approaching train. I watched the black engine so closely that I almost forgot Piggy had already shouted, "Let's go!"

It took me a long time to shuffle over the oily ties and wait in front of the two that spanned the gap over the concrete support. I could barely hear anymore. Suddenly the headache I had forgotten pounded in my head with the rhythm of the train, and my vision became so sharp that even the dull color of the wood hurt my eyes. I trembled as I waited for Kisu, then squeezed between the ties and dropped down onto the concrete behind him. We squatted in a small knot and waited. Piggy left his spot on top of a large oil stain and made Kisu change places with him. My head hurt when they jostled me. I began to shake. The sound of the train covered us like a fog and I hid my face in my hands.

"Where's Dogshit?" said Kisu.

I looked up and counted everyone twice.

"Where's Dogshit?!" The train was almost above us now, and Kisu's voice sounded tiny and far away, but we could all see what he was saying. We began to yell, "Dogshit, hurry up!" I couldn't hear my own voice, but I thought I heard someone calling, "Mother!"

As the black engine passed overhead dripping water and oil, I suddenly imagined the severed heads of the lov-

ers rolling above us on the rail, dripping blood and grinning like goblins. Clouds of steam warmed and then
chilled me. The dull explosions of the engine, the roar of
steam, the groan of wood and the shrieking metal wheels
. . . the sounds receded and I could hear Kisu crying next
to me. He held his right foot, which was black with oil,
and rocked back and forth.

"What is it?" I said, reaching for his foot. He screamed
before I could touch him. "*Ungh,*" I said. I took off my
dirty T-shirt and gave it to him so he could wipe off the
burning oil. I looked up at Piggy, but he was staring off
into the sewer creek.

"Where's Dogshit?" said Jani. "Who's going to look
first?"

Kisu sobbed and Piggy didn't say anything. I could only
stare at the oil stains on the concrete. When I looked up
again, Jani had stuck his head up between the ties and was
looking across the bridge.

"What happened?" I asked.

"He's on the bridge."

"Alive?" Piggy said loudly.

"Don't know. He doesn't move."

I closed my eyes tightly, but then, fearing I would see
the severed heads in my mind, I quickly opened them
again. Kisu had stopped crying. Now he was grimacing
and breathing between clenched teeth, making a hissing
noise that reminded me of the train's steam engine. Kisu
had used the inside of my T-shirt to wipe his foot. When
he gave it back to me, the oil stains were still hot on the
fabric.

"Looks like he's dead," said Jani, crawling up onto the
bridge.

"Don't say that," said Kisu. "Say after we've gone and
seen him."

"I said it for no reason," said Jani, sniffing.

I crawled up from the support even though I didn't
want to be on the bridge again. Jani and I helped Kisu up
together. We stood quietly for a while, each not wanting

to move, and then, at some silent signal, we all walked carefully toward Dogshit.

"He looks all bloody," said Jani.

"*Ya!* You don't know if it's oil!" Kisu limped up to him and elbowed his side.

"I don't see any legs," I said.

We all stopped at once, and I knew that we were going to turn and run in a moment.

Just then, we heard a tiny noise come from Dogshit. Jani and Kisu went quickly, but I hesitated before I followed.

"Dogshit-ah," Kisu said when we stood over him, "are you all right?"

His legs were dangling between two ties—he had been hanging by his hands. Jani and I pulled him up until he was lying facedown across three ties. "Dogshit-ah," we said. He made the tiny little noise again, but that was all until we rolled him over and saw his wet pants and his contorted face. "Dogshit-ah."

"I'm dead!" he shouted when the sun touched his eyelids. "I'm dead! I'm dead!"

"Don't say that," said Jani. "You're alive."

"I'm dead, you sons of bitches!"

We laughed and picked him up. Jani and I helped him walk. Kisu followed slowly behind us. Dogshit didn't open his eyes until Jani pried at them, and when he saw us he began to cry loudly. "Mother," he said, "what am I to do?"

Piggy was waiting for us at the end of the bridge. "I knew he was all right," he said. "I've dangled from the bridge under the train just like that."

The four of us walked away without speaking.

"*Ya!* What's the matter?"

Dogshit crying and Kisu wincing with each step, we kept going.

"*Ya!* I have your rifles." Piggy got the sticks and followed us. "If you don't talk I'll break them!"

"Go ahead, break them," said Jani.

Piggy tried to snap Jani's stick across his knee, but the

wood was too strong. He threw it into the sewer creek. "Insu-ya, let's go to the jam seller. I have money."

We kept walking away. Piggy threw all the sticks except his own into the creek, then threatened to beat us up if he ever saw us alone. "You'd better not tell your mothers," he said. "If you do, you'll die." He threw rocks at us until he saw the shit wagon coming down the street. Then he stayed at a distance.

When the Shitwagon Man recognized us, he stopped his ox and called us over. "What's the matter with you kids?" he said. "You were all right just a little while ago."

Kisu calmly told him what had happened.

"It's all because of Piggy," said Jani.

"Yes, sir," I said. "Piggy took us there."

"What kind of talk is that?" said the Shitwagon Man. "You listened to a bad guy like that? Didn't you all play there? Stupid brats, you should know not to do dangerous things like that! I should stick you all in the shit wagon!"

We hung our heads. Dogshit kept crying.

"And you!" said the Shitwagon Man, pointing to Dogshit. "Why are you crying like that? Did your mother die, *ungh*?" The Shitwagon Man's voice was so loud it made us all cringe.

Dogshit stopped crying.

The Shitwagon Man led his ox to a sign at the roadside and tied it there. "Stay here," he said, patting its large head. Then, carrying Kisu on his back, he led us all back to Tatagumi.

✧

The picture is faded, overexposed, and poorly fixed, its blacks washed out around the edges, the bright summer light hanging in the air like a luminous white fog. It is a group shot, tightly arranged. Here is a blond GI who can't be more than eighteen; he still has a boy's smile, and the telling sword-emblem patch is absent from his left shoulder. He has not yet been to Vietnam, because if he had been, he would be wearing that campaign patch with a patriotic pride or a disillusioned resentment; he would have lost the quickness of his smile, and his eyes would have been empty with that prematurely ancient look they call "the thousand-yard stare." His name patch says, "McConnell" and he is crouching in front of a concrete bridge railing, holding a small, dark-skinned Korean boy in each arm as if they were bundles of wildflowers. Two other boys are standing behind him, only their dark, smiling faces and grimy necks visible, their shoulders bleached into the air because they are wearing white T-shirts. Standing in front of the GI are two boys who have their heads turned toward the camera, but their eyes are watching him. The boy on the left looks like he might be the GI's cousin—his hair is dirty blond and he grins with the same crooked teeth—but the subtle angles of his face mark him as an Amerasian. The other boy is also Amerasian, black-haired and darker skinned, but not as dark as the Koreans. He is a few years younger than *the blond boy, and his hesitant smile looks worried. I know why he is worried. He is thinking of the two other figures who are visible in the distant background in the shadow of a tin-roofed shack. The figures are only unfocused specks in the photograph, but I know that they are two teenagers waiting for the action to begin. I know, because the boy with the worried smile is me.*

For weeks, we had wondered how to get money to buy medicine for Kisu's foot. Kisu had grown pale since the accident at the bridge, his usual skinniness wasting away to leave him frail and almost birdlike. The whole top of his foot was covered with a clear, syrupy fluid that would dry into a transparent film, and his mother would skim it off each day with tweezers, leaving the raw and shiny skin underneath.

To get money for Kisu, Jani and I decided that we would have to do better at what we usually did for pocket change and candy. We would go begging from the GIs outside ASCOM. Since I spoke English and Jani had yellow hair, we usually got more than most of the other kids.

At the first ASCOM bridge, we were surprised to see two teenage boys smoking nearby. Usually the youngest boys came to beg and then hid what they made before the older boys found out and robbed them. The GIs never gave anything to the older boys.

"Let's go back," said Jani. "We won't get anything because of these guys." We stopped at the bridge railing and watched the two teenagers while they talked to each other. One of them pointed at a yellow-haired GI who was taking pictures of the naked boys swimming in the sewer creek below. "*Ya*, you *ainokos*!" the other teenager called to us, "Come here and earn some money."

Jani and I stayed where we were. They came to us. The one in the white baseball cap asked us how old we were.

"Eight," I said. "In American age."

"Eleven," said Jani.

"Good. Which one of you is the one who speaks English?"

"I do," I said.

"You?"

"Jani doesn't have an American father yet," I said.

"Well," said the boy in the baseball cap, "you stay with me then, while that older brother goes with your friend and brings more kids up here. You two will get a lot of money if you do as we say."

"How much?" said Jani.

"More than you can scrape by begging. Why don't you speak English, *ungh*? You're the one who looks like a Hello."

"So what?" said Jani.

The other boy, who wore the traditional black school uniform, but without a hat, grabbed Jani's shoulders and said, "Come with me, yellow hair." Jani went with him down to the sewer creek while the boy in the white cap explained the plan to me in a low voice. I wished I had been the one to go down to the sewer creek because it was hot on the bridge and I could hear the hiss of the water and feel the cool air coming up in little gusts.

"The Hellos like to take pictures of you little guys and send them to America," said the boy in the white cap. "So they have expensive cameras. Today we're going to swipe one of their cameras and get a lot of money for it." I sat up straight and listened carefully as he explained the plan. "Do you understand what you're supposed to do?" he asked when he was finished.

"*Ungh*, older brother. But who gets beat up? Do I have to?"

"No. You stay with the Hello."

"What if he beats us up?"

"He won't beat you up, stupid, because he'll think me and the other older brother are the bad guys. Now tell me what I told you."

I recited the plan. When the others arrived, the boy in the white cap asked if anyone knew how to use a Japanese camera. A small, frail boy volunteered, saying his father owned a camera shop in Sinchon. The boy in the white cap lectured us all, then had us get ready for a GI to come by. Jani and I waited near the middle of the bridge and the five others pretended to play rock-paper-scissors at the far end. The two older boys walked a little ways toward Tatagumi and waited there, sharing a cigarette.

Several GIs passed as we waited, sweating from the heat that rose from the tarmac, but none of them had a camera. Jani and I held out our hands and ran to them, saying, "Hello, you got gum? You got one cho-co-late? You got one MPC? Hello, you gimmee *taksan!*" Only one of the GIs stopped to give us some gum. The others simply pushed on the tops of our heads and shoved us out of the way so we wouldn't cling to them. It was a bad day.

We were about to leave when the yellow-haired GI we had seen earlier came back out of the gate and leaned down over the side of the bridge to snap more pictures. Jani gave the signal by wiping his forehead with the back of his hand. The other boys came running.

"Hey, Hello!" I called. "You want pitcher?"

Jani made faces and flipped his eyelids inside out to look scary. "Takee pitcher!" he called.

The GI pointed his camera at us, but we ran up to him before he could click it. "Hey, hold still," he said.

"No cho-co-late, no gum," I said. "We want pitcher!"

The other boys gathered around us chanting, "*Sajin, sajin,* Hello *sajin jjigo.*" I told them the American words, and they changed their chant. "Hello, pitcher takee!" they shouted.

"You kids want to be in a picture?" said the GI, grinning and looking down at us from his fantastic height.

"You all go line up over there and I'll take your picture. How about that?"

"We want Hello inside pitcher," I explained. "We like you *taksan*, Hello." We tugged at his sleeves and pants. One boy started climbing his back.

"Hey, you boys cool off a bit, okay? I likee boy-san *taksan*, too. Hang on and I'll call a buddy to take the picture." He looked toward the gate and waved at the American MP, but the boy on his back grabbed his arm and slid down.

"No," I said. "Hello, you stay." The camera shop boy stepped up. "He take pitcher," I said. "He be pitcher shop. He take pitcher number one."

"You're not shittin' me? This boy-san knows how to use a camera? He no breakee camera? This baby costs *taksan* dollars, you understand?" The GI knelt down, and while we all watched, the skinny camera shop boy showed in gestures that he knew how to use the camera. "All right," said the GI. "Let's take a couple pictures. Come on." He took us to the railing and lined us up in front of him, then selected the two smallest boys and held them, one in each arm. He bent down so the camera shop boy could take the camera from around his neck. "You takee a number one group shot," he said. "Get all of us." He motioned around. "Step back a bit. Over there." He pointed with his chin, and the boys in his arms giggled at the huge, dark stains of sweat at his armpits.

The camera shop boy looked nervously toward Tatagumi. The boy in the school uniform was standing near Long Legs's moneychanging store; the one in the white cap was running, already halfway to the bridge.

"There," said the GI. "Everybody say *kimchi*. Put on a smile, kids, this picture is going all the way back to The World."

Now the frail camera shop boy dangled the camera strap and glanced through the viewfinder, then up again. The GI put on a big smile that made him look no older than Jani.

"He's here," said Jani.

"Hey, you!" shouted the GI.

We all pressed against him to keep him from moving. The boy in the white cap grabbed the camera strap, shoved the camera shop boy roughly onto the pavement, and sprinted back toward Tatagumi without a backward glance. The GI dropped the two small boys, and pushing us out of the way, jumped awkwardly over the camera shop boy before he tripped and fell.

"Hey, you fucker! Come back here!" The GI got up and ran after him, but the boy in the white cap relayed the camera to the boy in the school uniform who sprinted into Tatagumi and disappeared down an alley. "You fuckin' Korean bastards! Come back here! Fuck you! Goddamn!" The GI caught the boy in the white cap and slammed him up against the wall of Long Legs's store, but before he had caught his breath or decided to beat him, an MP jeep came roaring past us out of ASCOM and pulled up behind him.

"They're taking him to prison," said Jani.

We walked slowly because we didn't want to look suspicious. The camera shop boy nursed a small scrape on his elbow, but smiled shyly with pride.

"The Hello wants to beat me up for no reason!" cried the boy in the white cap. "He's going to kill me!" He turned to the KATUSA MP, who was Korean, and started to cry.

By now, a small crowd had gathered to watch. The GI shouted at the KATUSA MP and the other Koreans while the boy in the white cap cowered against the wall. It looked like the GI and the KATUSA MP might start fighting each other, but then Long Legs came out of his store and said something that sounded authoritative both in Korean and in English—his English was better than most GIs'. The crowd moved back, and the giant yellow-haired MP, who had been sitting in the back of the jeep, came down and pushed the GI into the front seat. "Fuck you all!" shouted the GI. "Take your goddamn country and shove it up your ass!" As the KATUSA MP drove back into ASCOM, Long Legs slapped the boy in the white cap and shoved him violently into the street. The boy sat for a moment, nursing his bloody lip, but then he smiled, ran through the dispersing crowd, and was gone.

✧

The next day the boy in the white cap met us at the old village well and gave us our share of the camera money. The others each got a hundred *won*, but Jani, the camera shop boy, and I each got brand-new five-hundred-*won* bills. While the others ran to buy food and candy, Jani and I went to Long Legs's store to change one of our bills.

"Where did you get this money?" said Long Legs, puffing smoke and speaking through the side of his mouth. "Why are your mothers giving you this much when they owe me, *ungh*?"

"It's not from our mothers," I said. "We got it for the camera."

"What?"

"Nothing," said Jani, giving me a sideways look to be quiet.

"You two helped them steal the camera!" Long Legs pulled the cigarette out of his mouth and smashed it into the half-filled aluminum ashtray on the floor, scattering ashes everywhere. "You idiots! Is something wrong with your brains? Your mothers work so hard, and every day I see you on that bridge dangling from the Hellos and asking for money just like beggars! Isn't that enough? Now you have to steal? You should be studying to be great men to help your families, and you study to be thieves?"

"We got a lot of money," said Jani. Long Legs slapped him across the cheek with the tips of his fingers. I winced. Jani sniffed back his tears.

"A lot of money? A lot of money? Don't make me laugh, mister gang leader! Do you know how much a Pentax is? Over 500,000 *won*! That's over five hundred times what you made together. Five hundred times! Now get out! If I ever hear about something like this again, I'll tell your mothers! Get out!" He chased us to the door. I had forgotten about the money, but Jani asked for our five hundred *won*. "Here," said Long Legs, and he flung us a handful of coins as he slammed the door shut.

When we scraped the money—mostly fifty-*won* coins—up from the dirt, Jani counted seven hundred eighty *won*. He divided it for us, because I couldn't figure as quickly. "We got a profit," said Jani. "We each get three hundred ninety *won* now, and we can give five hundred to Kisu." We had planned to buy pop-outs, boiled squid with pepper sauce, and steamed beancakes, but Long Legs had ruined our mood and soured our stomachs. We ate a little *odaeng* soup before evening.

Later, Jani brought a flashlight from his house, and we decided to stay out till after dark to run the alleys and surprise the GIs with their *yang saekshi* girlfriends. They hated having lights shined on them because it scared them into thinking that we were MPs out looking for GIs in town without a pass.

At the Radio Shop, Jani and I paused to look through the taped window at the shiny vacuum tubes Mr. Paek had lined up like rockets along the sides of the dusty old radios.

"We have to buy new batteries," said Jani, holding up his black plastic flashlight. "We might need a light bulb, too. See, the one inside looks dark."

Before I could look, someone reached down and snatched the flashlight out of Jani's hand.

"*Ya!*"

"If you want to have it back, you two come out to the bridge tomorrow after the noon siren." It was the boy in the white cap. He didn't have his cap now, but I recognized him by his pockmarked forehead and the scab on his lip.

"*Ya*, give it back!" said Jani.

The boy slapped him. "You two come and we'll get another camera like last time."

"No, we don't want to," I said. "You didn't give us enough money. You got thousands and thousands, and gave us only five hundred."

"Who told you that? Shut your mouth and listen to me or your flashlight's mine."

"Give it back!" said Jani, grabbing for it.

The boy knocked Jani on the head and pushed him away. "Will you come tomorrow?"

Jani looked at his flashlight, then at me. "Give me my flashlight now, and I'll come."

"No."

"Then fuck your mother!" Jani kicked the boy in the shin. When he yelped and jumped back, I grabbed the flashlight and struggled to get it out of his hand. Jani darted away and threw a rock that hit the boy on the back of the head.

"I'll kill you!" The boy hurled the flashlight, but Jani easily dodged and picked it up. "Fuck your mother!" Jani said again. He was out of reach, so the boy turned to me and opened his mouth wide, showing his teeth as if to bite me.

"If you touch me, I'll tell Long Legs," I said.

Before I could say anything else, he grabbed me, turned me around, and shoved me, head first, into the Radio Shop window.

I heard a loud noise and felt a terrible heat wash over me. My body turned to water and splashed against the dirt. Then I heard something that sounded like a heavy rain going on and on in the darkness, roaring loudly, then quieting into a dull murmur. Through the one eye I could open, I saw a field of beautiful, sparkling glass that shimmered like snow crystals under shifting clouds. My mouth tasted salty and the terrible heat became a gentle and comfortable warmth that put me to sleep. I dreamt of my mother's worried face, a long taxi ride, and sudden bright lights.

I began to feel the heat again, in bursts, coming in turns from different parts of my body. Someone was moving me about and flashing something under the lights; and then a deep American voice said, "You're all patched up now, Tiger. Lucky you went all the way through, or you woulda' been sliced right in half." I opened both my eyes and saw the American doctor smiling down at me. He moved the bright light out of the way and offered me a cold can of Coca-Cola.

✧

Most of the scars from the window glass have disappeared; a few left faint marks that are obvious now only when my skin is cold—in winter, in a swimming pool, in a cold shower—but the large gashes on my hips that needed stitches stretched into long welts, and over the years, as I grew, they migrated upward and backward, obscured from both memory and vision.

I have mounted the picture back in its place, bracketed by its scalloped adhesive corners against the black paper page of my mother's old album; it faces a page on which an older Jani looks up from a later snapshot. For an instant, as I close the album, Jani's picture and I look together at the faded photograph of the camera thieves, and then he meets his own image, face to face, and is gone. I know that some restless night when my leg has grown numb from sleeping too long on the scars on my right side, I will awaken in the dark, expecting to see the sparkle of bright light on glass, the roar of distant and invisible water, the faces of dead friends.

My mother tells me the photograph was given to Jani's mother by Long Legs, who discovered it on a roll of film he developed for a GI friend. Jani's mother sent it to her with a glossy eight-by-ten of her son, twenty-one years old, his hair gone from blond to brown like that of so many of us. Jani's features hadn't changed much in all the years since I had seen him last. He still had the same crooked teeth, the same posture, the same glint in his blue eyes. He finally did get an American father—a sergeant named Peterson married his mother and took the two of them off to Minnesota in the summer of '70. For many years I wishfully imagined that Jani had escaped as I had, that he had survived into happiness, that he had avoided the misfortunes of other children like ourselves: Gannan's baby, who died still in the womb; Paulie, who apprenticed himself to a pimp and disappeared; Suzie, who ate rat poison after she was disfigured by a Japanese banker. All those years, not knowing where he was, I had imagined Jani somewhere in the vast and mythic America we had believed in as children—in the dream country that had vanished for me the day I set foot in the Westward Land—but then, along with the unexpected photos, came the report that Jani had died of leukemia just before his twenty-second birthday.

I remember now that when I heard the news from my mother, when she showed me the pictures, I felt no grief at all. Instead, I was suddenly preoccupied with the question of Jani's age. He had been three years older than me, but his mother had changed his age when she enrolled him in the American school at Yongsan. Because he spoke so little English, Jani had to enter a grade behind me; his mother had subtracted four years from his age so he would seem the right age for his grade. "When he died," I asked my mother, "was he twenty-one in his American age, or his real age?" "How would I know?" she said. "How can you ask that when I tell you your best friend died?"

I know that if I had truly wanted to, I could have calculated how old Jani really was when he died; but over the years I have let it remain a mystery—even the year his mother sent the photos to my mother has faded from my memory. I will not struggle to remember, and I do not want to be reminded. I would rather believe that Jani's mother slipped when she told his age, having believed her own lie for so long that she thought of him in his American years. I want to believe that Jani regained those four years she subtracted from his life—that he lived to the eve of his twenty-sixth birthday. I have missed him so much that if I knew,

I would grieve again for those four lost years. Even now I cannot bear to do the calculation. I would rather leave it to his ghost to count those years—the way he reckoned our profit from the handful of coins Long Legs flung at us in his guilty anger so long ago.

5

Wood

Dead in August

*This was the year they closed the Han River bridge. The dark,
muddy river crept up, meter by meter, darkening the concrete
supports to the color of fertile earth until it seemed to everyone
that the bridge would collapse or dissolve in the rising water.
Out in the country the rice paddies all vanished; parts of Seoul
and Wijong-bu lost whole neighborhoods, and though the American Combat Engineers worked day and night with their bull-
dozers and sandbags, the Han, the Imjin, and to the south the
Nakdong, which had flowed blood during the war, all swelled
with the heavy monsoon rain.*

*In Pupyong the sewer creek ran swift and high. We often saw
dead animals and strange pieces of things rush by in the current,
but other than the usual annoying flooding of kitchens, the mud-
clogging of the new sewage ditches, and pooled water in the
market streets, the town remained quiet. Everyone was glad that
the monsoon hadn't been so bad for Pupyong; the rice farmers
in the outskirts talked of how their paddies had flooded nicely,
how the crop would be good that year. But Yongshiggi's blind
grandfather, playing chess under the old maple tree, shook his
long pipe one day and said in his tired voice, "Even in good
years, a few bad things are bound to happen." And he was right
as he had always been right, ever since the Japanese had gouged
his eyes and left him to make a living as a fortune-teller.*

It began in August when a rich man from Seoul came down and built the Apollo Club at the site of the old neighborhood well across from Mr. Paek's Radio Shop. They said the Apollo Club would be a modern, shinshik *club with strip shows and all the latest drinks from America. The building itself was especially* shinshik, *with a wide concrete-paved yard in front of the entrance and what looked like large sewer pipes sticking out of the embossed concrete walls. The Apollo Club was supposed to look like an Apollo rocket, and if not that, at least a bunker. The club owner had paved the yard with concrete slabs that fitted neatly into one another, but for some reason he had paved around the well then put some boards over the rim and left it unfinished that way. The rumor was that in a few weeks they would stick a fake missile into the well and paint it like the Apollo rocket, but soon, despite their silence and their feigned lapses of memory, everyone—even the rich owner—knew that no rocket would ever fill the village well or erase the memory of what had happened there.*

✧

The fourth of August. The summer was about to end, and I would be starting the fourth grade. I was on my way home from ASCOM when I noticed the crowd near the first bridge; by the time I reached Long Legs's money-changing store I could see the fire truck, the police car, and then the hose—long and thick as a dragon—coiled out into the street twitching and gushing dark water. The dull sound of a pump beat like a drum over the excited chatter and screams coming from a crowd so thick it blocked traffic. Two policemen tried to clear the people so cars could pass, but more and more people came from Tatagumi and crossed the street to see what was happening.

Mr. Paek stood in front of his Radio Shop, flicking a paper fan at himself, trying to peer through the crowd. I asked what all the people were doing.

"Ku-ray-gee," he said in English. "They ku-ray-gee."

A policeman arrived with a megaphone. "Please clear the streets, ladies and gentlemen! We must get the traffic through!" Two police cars appeared from the direction of the north police station and tried to pass an Inchon-bound bus whose passengers had all run out into the crowd.

"It's a circus," said Mr. Paek. "Have you ever seen anything like this?"

"What happened, *ajoshi*?"

"Some maid dropped a baby into the well."

An ice-cream man and several ice-cake boys wandered through the crowd making sales. A man in a yellow shirt lifted his son into the air to let him watch as American MP jeeps and a truck full of soldiers from the Korean Sixth Brigade compound arrived and unloaded into the confusion.

"It's hot," said Mr. Paek, looking up the street. The owner of the tailor shop had brought a bench outside for her family to sit on. "Insu, go across the street and get some ice cakes, *ungh*?" He gave me some money. "I'll bring out some chairs and we can sit and watch."

I crossed the street and shouldered my way through to one of the ice-cake boys. "Sell some ice cakes!" I shouted.

"I don't have any!" said the ice-cake boy. "That way!" He pointed to his right.

I ducked under a policeman's arms and got out of the way as he shoved someone off the street. All the cars were honking now; a second megaphone roared instructions and the Korean Sixth Brigade soldiers pushed people away with their rifles. As I got closer to the Apollo Club I could hear women crying from the direction of the well, one loud voice wailing over and over, "Please forgive me, I didn't see, I didn't see." I paused to listen, but the megaphone came so close I had to cover my ears.

One side of the street had already flooded with water from the pump and another ice-cake boy had put his box just in front of the hose to keep it cool. He stood calf-deep in the rushing water and screamed, "Ice *kaekee*! Ice *kaekee*!" but I could barely hear him. I motioned to his open box and held up two fingers. He nodded, took out two cylindrical popsicles and gave them to me, but before I could give him the money someone yelled, "He's coming up!" and the ice-cake boy turned to look. I hesitated a second, then turned and ran into the crowd with the ice cakes.

I reached the other side of the street just as policemen

arrived with billy clubs. As the crowd scattered, the first of the honking Corona taxis sped forward, nearly running the stragglers down. Bus maids and passengers from the Inchon bus dodged policemen and soldiers to get back on board, and a police car, with its doors open, bumped a man who then leaped up onto the hood and shouted that they had tried to kill him.

Mr. Paek took one of the ice cakes and peeled the paper off. "*Ya*, what kind of a mess is this?" he said. "Things like this would never happen in another country."

I sat down by him and peeled my own ice cake. "Look there," said Mr. Paek. "They're pumping the water out and they've sent someone into the well again, but they'll never find the body today. That's the second-deepest well in Pupyong."

A policeman came across the street and stopped in front of us. I hid my face and leaned forward in my chair, getting ready to run. My knees trembled with tension.

"Have you seen a man in a yellow shirt?" the policeman asked Mr. Paek.

"People are swarming like ants," said Mr. Paek. "How is someone to notice one man in a yellow shirt? Why, what happened?"

"He's a pickpocket."

"No. I haven't seen him. Have you seen him?" He looked at me. I quickly shook my head. "What's happened at the well?" Mr. Paek asked the policeman.

The policeman took his hat off and wiped his forehead. "Three people went down, but they can't find a thing."

"Would you like an American cigarette?" Mr. Paek lit two Winstons and handed one to the policeman, who quickly glanced around before taking it. They spoke of various things until they noticed one of the police cars was gone. The policeman said good-bye and left in a hurry.

"He's from the Academy," said Mr. Paek. "A very young guy, *ungh*?"

I had been watching the thinning crowd. A group of

people who seemed to be the baby's family continued to wail, but most of the others had quieted down to listen. The pump still beat like an anxious heart.

"Go home," said Mr. Paek. "It's past dinnertime." He patted me on the shoulder. "Have to close the shop now." He got up with his hands on his protruding belly and went inside.

I said good-bye and went back across the street after making sure the ice-cake boy had gone.

The firemen had shut the pump off and pulled their truck out to make room for a three-wheeled pickup, which now made its way up the street with some wood from the nearby lumberyard. I walked past the pickup and got close enough to the well to see the men pulling someone out on nylon ropes. I winced, thinking they had found the baby, but it was a man in a diving mask who shook his head sadly when he noticed the eager expressions around him. The wailing grew louder; now that the pumping had stopped I could hear each separate voice.

Soon, the men with the wood had built a new top for the well. Most of the people had gone by now, and even the newcomers quickly lost interest and wandered away. "Before they even finished building," said one of the carpenters. "Very bad luck." He tossed away some fragments of the old, rotted well-top and climbed into the back of the pickup.

The sun touched the westward hills. In a moment the shadow of the building on the west side of the concrete yard reached the shadow of the well and merged with it. I realized, for the first time, that this was a grave event, that a baby had actually fallen into the well and drowned. I wondered how deep and dark it must be under the pale wood of the new cover. I remembered when I had dropped pebbles over the rim of the deep well in Samnung: the long pause and then the plunking noise—almost a swallowing noise, a wet, hollow sound—plunk . . . *plunk* . . . and then the ripples growing outward ring by ring. The well seemed to grow larger and larger as I looked. I thought I saw a corner of the lid move as if the drowned baby had crawled up and pushed but was too weak to lift it aside. I stared at the pale well cover, holding my breath, waiting; then someone grabbed me and I made a choking noise in my throat.

"Go away," said the policeman. "What are you looking at?"

"Nothing," I said.

"Go home. There's nothing to see here."

I crossed the street and watched for a little while longer before I left. The owner of the tailor shop told me that the maid had put the baby down for a moment to rest, and when she turned around to pick him up again, he was gone. "Not a sound, not a trace," she said. "Just a little hole in the wood."

✧

The next morning I met Jani and went into ASCOM, where we each bought eight one-pound bags of M&M's by stopping at all four of the PX stores. Before noon we biked down to Long Legs's store, sold him fourteen pounds of M&M's at twice their price, and took orders for things like Alka-Seltzer, Hershey bars, and Wrigley's chewing gum in ten-packs. Long Legs paid in crisp, new bills for the items he ordered. Despite his foul mood over our camera theft, he was nice to us once again.

We brought the last two bags of M&M's to Mr. Paek, who took them quickly and hid them, and then, out of nervousness, tried to sell us some new SONY transistor radios. "I'll give them to you at wholesale price," he said when we refused. "Jani, don't you want one before you go to America? Sony makes the best, and America is so far from Japan." He turned the volume up and dangled the small radio from the strap. We heard AFKN playing Don MacLean's American Pie song.

"No, sir," said Jani. "My father will get me one as a present."

"All right, then." Mr. Paek put the transistor away, paid

us for the M&M's, and scratched his belly. "Don't be around here at night," he said as we left. "The baby's ghost is calling people."

I stopped at the door. Through the glass I could see two women standing in front of the well. This was much more frightening than Mr. Paek's story.

"He's just trying to scare us," said Jani.

"It's no lie," said Mr. Paek. "Even Jani—even if you believe in Jesus—the ghost will call you, too. Korean ghosts don't care what you believe in."

"I still don't believe those things," said Jani, laughing.

Mr. Paek pointed across the street. "The baby's mother doesn't believe in ghosts. She believes in Jesus like you," he said quietly. "But she nearly jumped in last night."

Jani stopped smiling and looked out across the street with me. Though it was just past noon, the square around the well looked as if it were in an evening light.

"Have you heard it, Paek *ajoshi*?" asked Jani.

Mr. Paek shook his head solemnly. "They're bringing a bigger pump from Inchon to try again today. But it's no use. The body will wait and then it will float up in a few days."

We said good-bye and went out to unlock our bikes.

"I still don't believe any of it," said Jani.

"Me neither."

We biked back to ASCOM for lunch and spent the rest of the afternoon at the post gym practicing *tae kwon do* forms before lessons began at four. Then, under Mr. Kang's instruction, we went through our warm-ups, stretches, and three-step-defense forms with the GI class. He was pleased with us and told us we could begin sparring the following week.

In the shower after our lessons, Jani leaned his head against the wall and moaned with exhaustion under the cool spray. I lay flat on the floor, letting the heat ooze from my body into the cold concrete.

A GI walked in on us. I followed the curve of his calf with my eyes, up past his thighs, his wiry black pubic hair, to his foreshortened face. It was our friend, Williams, with his afro pick still protruding from his hair. "Hey, you cats looked pretty fuckin' good out there tonight," he said. "You take your belt test soon, huh?" He was so tall the shower nozzle only reached his chin.

"Right on," said Jani, pushing himself away from the wall. "We get the test next week and then we get to kick your ass, man."

Williams laughed and lathered himself with his bar of yellow Dial soap.

"You want to practice with us?" I asked.

"Yo," said Williams.

I got up and scrubbed his back for him. "We're just Fuckin' New Guys in the class, you know. You could show us some of the hard shit."

"Sure, no sweat," he said. "You all just come by when I get off duty and we'll come here on the double. Cool?"

"Yeah."

"You cats wanna' catch a movie with me tonight?"

"What's on?" asked Jani.

"Some zombie shit," said Williams, turning to us. "You know, dead folks coming alive and eating people's guts. This one's supposed to be big-time scary."

"We'll go if you buy us Chinese food," I said.

"You got it."

We put on our clothes and walked with our bikes out to Sinchon. After dinner, Williams took a post cab from the restaurant and met us at the theater.

There was something peculiarly frightening about the movie, even before the gruesome parts began. I wanted to leave shortly after the beginning, but I didn't want to seem afraid in front of Jani and Williams, so I huddled in my seat and watched with one eye closed because I felt safer that way: A crowd of walking corpses grabbed through boarded-up windows at the people inside a house; a truck exploded at a gas pump and the dead people picked the burnt bodies apart like pieces of chicken; a small girl in the basement stabbed her mother again and again with a trowel and then ate her before the mother came back to life herself.

At the end of the movie Williams yelled out "Fuck you!" because the Black hero, who had survived all of the zombies, was shot down at the very last minute by the white men who were supposed to rescue him. As the credits rolled, the screen flashed a series of still pictures of the Black man's body being dragged away with a meat hook to be burned in a pile with the zombie corpses. Williams was in a foul mood, and he left us to go down to the Lower Four Club and get drunk with some brothers. Jani usually played and joked after watching American vampire movies or Korean ghost movies with me, but tonight he just walked out, not waiting for the theater to clear so we could look for lost money in the aisles.

Night had begun to creep down from the westward hills. Some of the GIs looked sullen or numb, as if they hadn't quite woken from sleep. "Come on," said Jani. "Let's go before it gets dark. I won't be able to go to the outhouse for a month now." He didn't say anything more as we unlocked our bikes at the bottom of the theater stairs and rode down the hill.

Despite the colors, the day was fading into the overcast twilight gray of the black-and-white film. I imagined the drowned child again, blue and bloated, crawling up the well with its water-swollen fingertips. I pedaled faster to catch up to Jani's three-speed. "Slow down!" Jani just glanced at me over his shoulder.

By the time we reached the gate, the colors had gone. To the left, the bleak Quonset hut–lined street that led to the post morgue seemed much too quiet to be deserted. We looked that way and shuddered. As soon as the guard waved us through, we sped out into the street and raced toward Tatagumi.

I lived farther away since we had moved from our old neighborhood in Tatagumi to a house near the north district office. I knew already that the last street to my house would be dark when I reached it. The streetlamps went only as far as the police station. As I pedaled faster and faster to keep up with Jani, I wondered for a moment if I should leave my bike at his house near the market and take a taxi home. No, he would laugh at me.

We passed the Korean Sixth Brigade gate, rattled over the railroad tracks, and then, just in front of us to the right, we saw the dark street up to Samnung, the two houses, the warehouse, and the black yard of the Apollo Club with the pale wooden well cover glowing faintly against the shadows. Jani pedaled even faster; I followed him, splashing through the gutter which was still wet from the day's pumping.

As I stood up off my seat to pedal as fast as I could, a shadow stepped out from the darkness, directly into my path. Fear leapt up in my throat and I wrenched my handlebars to the left. I was too close to the curb; the front tire skidded against the edge, the bicycle lurched under me, and I crashed into the ground. I got up instantly, but I had scraped my knee and elbow against the curb and I limped for a second as I shook the numbness out of my right palm.

"Are you all right?" said a voice. I looked up quickly, ready to run. It wasn't a walking corpse at all. A young woman in a red scarf had picked up my bike, and she was holding it for me, tentatively, by the twisted handlebars. "I'm sorry," she said.

"It was my fault," I said. "I should have been looking more carefully." I took my bicycle, and holding the front wheel between my knees, turned the handlebars back into place while she stood close by and watched.

"Are you really not hurt? I'm very sorry." She looked familiar and sounded very concerned.

"I'm fine. Nothing's wrong," I said. "I'm sorry." I got on my bicycle, nodded to her, and pedaled slowly up the street. My knees, my elbow, and my palm all hurt now. I looked back and saw that I had fallen just beyond the Apollo Club yard. The woman was already gone, but a peculiar odor lingered after her.

Jani was waiting at the end of the next block. "What happened?" he said. I explained about the accident and he laughed. "There's a funny smell coming from you," he said.

"What is it? I've smelled it before, but I don't remember."

"*Hyang.*"

We rode quickly again. It wasn't until Jani said good-bye and vanished down the dark market street that I remembered where I had smelled it before. *Hyang* was funeral incense.

When I reached the police station, I rode a little farther to the edge of the last streetlamp and waited there for a car, another bicycle, or just another person walking down into the dark street toward my house. I saw no one for the longest time and I began to feel as if I might be the only living person out that night. The sparse traffic passing in the street a block away made hardly any noise at all, and though the lights were on in the police station, there didn't seem to be anyone inside.

I heard a noise and turned to see moths tapping against the streetlamp, and beyond that a man walking slowly toward me. I hoped he would cross over and go down the street where I lived, but he came closer, not slowing or quickening his step, until I knew he would walk right into me if I didn't move. I stepped up onto the pedal, getting ready to escape. When the man walked into the light I stared into his blank face and yet he didn't seem to notice me at all.

The wind changed. I smelled the *hyang* again and I wondered if the woman had heard the drowned baby's ghost calling to her. Why had she smelled so strongly of *hyang*? I looked down for a second and sniffed. The smell came from my clothes and maybe even from the handlebars of my bike. I leaned forward to sniff again, but my glance turned and I saw the blank-faced man standing right behind me now, looking at me, not moving, not blinking. I smashed my foot down on the pedal, but I was leaning so far forward I slipped and stomped on the ground. And just as I tried to get my balance back, the man bent forward, opening his mouth full of crooked teeth, and reached out a pale hand. The dirt under his fingernails looked horribly black.

"What time has it gotten to be?" he said.

The night felt suddenly clear and cool. I coughed and looked at my watch. "It's nine-thirty, sir."

He lowered his hand and slowly walked on toward the police station. My sides and stomach shivered violently. A little huff of breath came from my throat. "Goddamn," I said to myself. The words in English had an odd power in the night.

In a moment, a bicycle with a headlight went past me down the street to my house and I followed close behind, avoiding the potholes and rocks. When I reached my house I jumped off and pounded loudly on the gate, again and again, until Emo asked who it was.

"Me!" I shouted. "Emo, open the door!" I looked behind me at the darkness, my legs trembling as I heard Emo's footsteps. I burst through the gate before she had even opened it all the way.

"What's the hurry?" she said. All the fear disappeared when I saw her. The darkness was simply night once again. "It's nothing," I said.

I woke up very early, and I went out to the kitchen and poured some water in the basin to wash and brush my teeth. The water was too hot; I used the bathroom first and came back.

The morning air smelled cool and clean after I blew the thickness out of my nose, and I enjoyed just squatting over the basin like this, listening to the morning, feeling my sleepiness slowly float away like the steam from the water as I washed. After a while I got stiffly to my feet, dumped the water, and walked quietly through the house out to the front.

Emo had already watered the garden patch along the wall. I helped her spread the red peppers, which would dry later when the sun was high.

"Why are you up so early?" she said. "Aren't you cold in just your underclothes."

I shook my head. "I'm going to Yongsan on the first bus to buy things."

My clothes still smelled of *hyang*, so I wore cleaner, less comfortable clothes. The memories of last night seemed quite far away now; the *hyang* still disturbed me, but I could choose not to think about it. I could even imagine scenes from the horrible movie and not be afraid.

Emo told me to be home before dark.

"I'm coming back on the six o'clock bus," I said.

"Be careful. Don't get into trouble." She went into the house to make breakfast.

Two women from the poor neighborhood passed by me as I walked to the bus stop. They were on their way to fill their water cans at the nearby well, but they didn't remind me, even for a moment, of the drowned baby.

I slept on the bus and spent the day in Yongsan buying tool boxes for Mr. Fatso and Mr. Chong, a pair of blue jeans for Mr. Panji Lee, and Phillips Milk of Magnesia for Mr. Paek.

When I returned at seven, I got off at the first ASCOM gate. I took the jeans and tool box to Mr. Panji Lee at the Crafts Shop. Mr. Chong was gone for the day and Mr. Fatso was in the bathroom showering. I could hear the spraying water and see the steam creeping out from under the door.

Mr. Panji Lee paid me in brand-new bills. "What's in the bag?" he said.

"Stomach medicine for Mr. Paek at the Radio Shop."

Mr. Panji Lee nodded. "Bad digestion from all that trouble across the street, isn't it? First the baby, then the maid."

"The maid?" I said. I folded the money into two wads, putting one in my front pocket and the other in my back pocket.

"You haven't heard?"

"I was in Yongsan all day."

Mr. Panji Lee tapped a ring mold against the counter and blew off the dust before he told me how they had found the note late last night, in the maid's handwriting, saying that she was going out to look for the baby. "She said he must be hiding from all those divers because he was afraid of them. She was going to go down and get him herself. When they went down this afternoon, they found her scarf."

"Scarf," I said. "What color?" A pulse of heat seemed to hit me suddenly as I realized what I was asking. I could smell the *hyang* again.

"How would I know?" said Mr. Panji Lee.

But I was already looking down at the brick-red countertop and feeling sick and distant. I tried very hard to give a natural shrug. It seemed that everyone in the shop, even the GIs, suspected I was hiding something. I tried to smile.

A GI suddenly stood up in the lapidary section and looked at me; he put down his work and came toward the counter. Mr. Panji Lee followed my eyes to the GI. "You want silver now?" he asked. I took my things and left while they calculated how much silver it would take to make a punching ring.

Outside, the wind was blowing and darker clouds had gathered in the direction of Sinchon. I stopped running and sat down on the grass to think about the red scarf, the *hyang*, the pale new cover of the well, and in a moment the images grew into something quiet and terrible. They must be so lonely down there in the cold, dark water. I breathed rapidly and opened my eyes wider. Almost desperately, I took out my wallet and folded out the pictures until I found my favorite—the one of Abebe Bikila running the marathon. I pulled it out of the plastic sheath and stared at it, trying to push everything else out of my thoughts until the black-and-white turned into vague color, the stillness to motion, and I saw him again, as I had

seen him years ago through the crowd in Samnung, glid-
ing like a spirit over the narrow road to Seoul.

Swallows swooped low over the grass. It would rain
soon.

I got up slowly, put the picture away, and carrying the
paper bag like a football, I jogged to the gate. Outside, I
paused a moment, deciding whether to take a cab and
have it wait while I delivered the medicine to Mr. Paek.
But the cab would drive on the right side of the street—
too close to the Apollo Club. I could walk instead and stay
on the left side.

I jogged along the sewer creek until I was sweating and
breathing hard in the humid air. When I reached Tatagumi, I slowed to a fast walk, keeping my eyes on the
storefronts, trying hard not to glance across the street toward the Apollo Club. The comic book store; the drug
store; the butcher shop with its red, hanging meat; the
Korea House, where they translated letters for Korean
women writing to their GI husbands in Vietnam. The Korea House was closed, the interior dark. On the window,
under the white letters of KOREA, I saw the reflection of
the Apollo Club yard closed off by white cloth tape
stretched between wooden poles. I stopped. If I squinted I
could see the spot where I had fallen from my bike, the
place where the woman had disappeared. The pale
wooden well cover still glowed, and the white cloth tape
moved gently up and down like waves in the wind. I
turned away.

Three junior high school boys stood just in front of the
Radio Shop, looking at me. I stopped. "It's him," said one
of the boys. He pointed at me. "You!" he said. "You thief!"

"What's the matter?" I asked. But I already recognized
him as the boy I had stolen the ice cakes from. One of the
others, I knew, had a green belt in *tae kwon do*—I had seen
him running with one of the classes that met near the coal
store. I would never make it past them into the Radio
Shop.

"Give me my money, you son of a bitch," said the ice-cake boy. He held out his hand as the other two stepped forward. I knew they would beat me up anyway, but I reached into my pocket and pulled out half the money Mr. Panji Lee had fronted me.

"I'll pay," I said.

The green belt stepped closer. Even if I shouted for Mr. Paek now, they would hurt me before he came out. I recognized the third boy from the scar on his neck; he had once tried to stab Jani with a pocketknife. The new bills crackled in my trembling hand as I took a step backward.

"Give me the money!"

I looked at the ice-cake boy, then at the green belt. The third boy had his hand in his pocket. "Here," I said. I threw the bills into the air, and before they could grab for them, I smashed the Milk of Magnesia into the green belt's knee and ran back down the street.

The green belt cried out, but in a moment he was scuffling and arguing about who had the money first. I turned before I reached the butcher shop and ran up the street until I reached the first alley. There, I paused to pick up two stones and looked behind me before I ran again, turning up toward the street of the prostitutes.

No one was out; the alley was quiet. In a minute, I heard the footsteps behind me. "This way!" shouted the ice-cake boy. "You go around and catch him when he comes out."

I paused. If I turned left I would circle back into the prostitutes' alley; if I turned right I would pass the alley of the biting dog. I ran to the right, clutching each stone more tightly, my breath wheezing. I couldn't run much faster. Luckily, the dog didn't notice me until I had passed the mouth of the alley. When it finally leaped out and snapped after me I turned and hit it with one of the stones.

They heard the yelping dog. "Here!" shouted the ice-cake boy.

I had reached the main street again. I ran across hoping to hide somewhere before they saw me, but two of them ran together out of the alleyway and the green belt followed, half limping. It was too late. I would have to run into an unfamiliar neighborhood. While they waited for a bus to pass, I cut into the alley beside the Chinese restaurant, and ran as quickly as I could down the strange alleyways until I lost track of the turns and found myself at a dead end. I stopped in front of the last house gate, counting my quick breaths to relax the wild tension in my belly as I looked for a wall to climb over. But each house had carefully arranged their shattered glass shards, leaving no place even for a handhold.

"Fuck," I said in Korean. I turned around and walked slowly to the last branching of the alleys, listening carefully for the sound of footsteps. With my mouth open all the way to breathe more quietly, I crouched to peek around the corner.

The ice-cake boy and the green belt were creeping around the far corner; the other boy stood a few meters in front of me, covering the mouth of the alley. Now he was looking in the wrong direction. I waited until the two were gone, and then, clutching my stone more tightly, I stepped out. The boy turned around and smiled.

"Don't shout," I said. "I'll throw this." I lifted the stone higher.

"Let's see," said the boy. He pulled his hand out of his pocket and clicked open a thin switchblade. "Here!" he called to the others.

My stomach twisted when I saw the knife. I threw the stone as hard as I could, aiming for his face, but he must have ducked sideways or I must have missed, because he took the impact on his shoulder, letting out a grunt of surprise and pain. As the boy faltered, I ran at him, grabbed his knife arm and shoved him against the wall. He tried to smash my face against the bricks as we struggled, but I turned so that I only scraped the side of my head. I felt a burning sensation flare downward across my cheek and hesitated, distracted just long enough for him to pull his arm free and slash me somewhere with the knife. I staggered away, but then I threw a sidekick into his belly, knocking him away from me as I stumbled down the alley.

One entire side of my head felt numb and my hip burned, and yet I felt as if I were only skimming the earth with the barest touches of my feet; I ran down the long, narrow alleyway toward a brightness at the end, and now the brightness stretched and thinned into a tape at the finish line. Abebe Bikila arriving in Seoul, head pounding, vision dimmed, breath too quick for the lungs. The footsteps behind me grew fainter and fainter as I bounded over pieces of rubble, passed a long concrete wall, and burst through the opening at the end, breaking the white tape across my thighs. But as I took the last exhausted steps, I realized what I had broken—what I saw in front of me through my blurred vision was no finish line, it was the pale wooden top of the well in the middle of the dark Apollo Club yard.

I couldn't run any farther; my heart pounded so fiercely I had no more capacity for fear. I looked behind me, and before the footsteps reached the entrance to the yard, I staggered hopelessly behind the well, collapsing with my eyes closed.

In a moment I heard their voices.

"Fuck, he got away!" Something thumped against the well cover and spattered like sand onto the concrete yard. "Ya! Stop that. There's still corpses in there." Silence. Sand trickled into the well. The boy with the knife complained of pain in his ribs. "Shut up," said the ice-cake boy. He decided that they would go around again and catch me in the street. "It's quicker if we just go over the yard," said the green belt. "The police put that tape up. And the dead bodies. . . ."

I curled myself into a ball, squeezed my eyes tighter, and gasped with my mouth between my knees. I was sure they had heard me and were talking just to torture me before they caught me. I waited.

But there was no kick in the kidney or the cold pain of a knife in my back. Instead, only the sounds grew louder moment by moment—my breath, my pulse, and the strange wet noises that followed the echoes in the well. The bodies were still inside, under the cold, black water—the maid with her red scarf and the horribly bloated child. But they had taken the scarf, and now, with the wet dripping sounds, the maid would be climbing out to find it. "Where's my scarf? Who took my scarf?" Her cold, water-soaked fingers clawed in the cracks of the well stones. She crawled up, bit by bit, dripping water from her soaked dress. She reached the top and pushed up at the pale wooden lid. "Did you take the scarf? It's you. You've come to stay with us. It's so lonely down there." The lid thumped as she reached out to grab me with her icy hand, and I felt the water drip against my neck. I screamed and looked up, but the cold water fell into my eyes and I couldn't see until I twisted to my side, crashed against the well, and heard a sound like the crackling of crisp paper.

I blinked the water out of my eyes. Rain spattered in the concrete yard, thumping against the top of the well. I started to laugh and cough all at once until soon the pain in my side was too much and I threw up with my chin scraping against the cement. I was shivering inside. The right side of my jeans was slashed open at the hip, but only a little blood had oozed out of the rash-like welt on my skin. Both sides of my head pounded now as I ran my fingers across the numb side and pulled out a tuft of hair. I wasn't hurt very badly.

For a long time I lay there, feeling the cool rain against my face, getting slowly warmer and sleepier until I knew that I would have to get up or lie there until someone found me cold and pale in the morning. Could death be so bad, I thought, even the coldest water grew warm after a while—and suddenly the shock put me on my feet and I was walking stiffly out to the road.

I took a cab home, sneaked in through the back gate, and washed in the kitchen before I went inside. Emo, Hyongbu, and my cousins had just started dinner. Mahmi was probably still out in ASCOM or up in Yongsan.

"Here's your rice," said Hyongbu. "Got wet in the rain, *ungh*?"

I nodded. Before I sat down I smoothed some hair over the scrape in my head, then I ate quietly until Emo told me my nose was bleeding. She gave me a napkin, which I ripped and used to plug my nostrils.

"Got in a fight," said Hyongbu, without looking up from his food. "Good thing your mother's not back yet."

"No."

"Then you must have been in such a hurry to get home you bumped your nose against the gate." He laughed and waved a chopstick at me. "Tell me about it later."

"Yes, sir," I said. And I tried to eat dinner as if nothing had happened.

✧

Later in the evening when we had had our tea of burnt rice, Hyongbu sat with his back against the couch, and smoking a Pall Mall—which was his favorite brand this week—he told me a story.

"In the old days, out in the country where we lived, there was a strange incident," he said. "It was before the war when tigers still wandered in the forest and the buses had just come to Korea. Terrible buses. And the roads were even worse." He mashed out the stub of his cigarette. "Are you wondering what this has got to do with your fight?"

"I didn't fight," I said.

"All right, then." Hyongbu tapped another cigarette out of the pack and lit it. "One day a brim-full bus was going up the road near our fields. It was making a terrible racket and throwing dust in a thousand directions. The people inside were all worrying about getting to where they were going so they could see to their business—selling eggs at the market or visiting relatives in Seoul, or just going out to the city to make a living.

"So as this bus passed by, making all that racket and rumbling, a huge tiger jumped down from a hillside and followed it, leaping first this way, then that way in front of the driver's window. The driver and the people inside were so scared they stopped the bus. But when the bus stopped, the tiger stood in front of it and grumbled.

"Everyone thought they would be eaten. They shouted and cried and chattered until someone came up with an idea: 'Instead of all shaking in here, let's go outside!' Everyone knew the tiger would eat only one person anyway."

I scratched my head, accidentally touching the painful part. "Why did they go out if they were afraid of being eaten? Wouldn't the tiger just eat the first one out?"

Hyongbu smiled. "With a big selection like that?" he said. "A whole bus full of fat people and skinny people and plump babies and lunch-size children? They figured the tiger would take a pick. The fat ones were scared and so were the mothers of children, but eventually they all went off the bus.

"And the tiger just stood there until this one man came out, and then it took him over that way. The poor man cried and begged for help, but the others got back on the bus and left. They didn't even take a message to his family."

"It just ate him? What had he done wrong?"

"Ah, that's exactly what all those people said. 'What had he done wrong to deserve such a terrible fate? He must have been a truly horrible man.'" Hyongbu blew a long plume of smoke out of his nose. "But a strange thing happened. The tiger just sat with the man for a while, then slowly went back up into the hills, leaving the man behind. And the bus full of happy people fell off a cliff that same day. Everyone in it died."

I waited for Hyongbu to go on, but he just sat and quietly puffed his cigarette. "So what happened?" I said loudly.

"That's all." He smiled and showed his gold-banded teeth.

"The man the tiger took—what happened to him?"

"That man lived a long and peaceful life."

I frowned. "And so what's the meaning of this story?"

"It was just a true story you needed to hear." Hyongbu picked up the old yellow aluminum ashtray, got stiffly to his feet, and went to his room.

For the rest of the evening I was angry as I tried to figure out the meaning of the story and why Hyongbu had told it to me. Yongsu said it meant that even what looked like a great tragedy could be good luck, but that seemed much too simple.

I woke instantly the next morning and turned the pillow over to hide the bloodstain from the scrape in my head. When I went outside and squatted over the basin to wash, I realized my dreams had been quiet. I had fallen asleep thinking about the story, and now yesterday seemed distant like the half-memories I had of my infancy.

The Milk of Magnesia—had it broken, or had someone found it? Had Mr. Paek stumbled on it as he walked home after closing the store? And what of the money—had they fought over it, or had they divided it evenly among themselves? It was far, far more than the price of two ice cakes, probably more than the ice-cake boy could earn in a month. I felt myself going tense, so I sat on the steps with my back against the cold wall, breathing carefully, counting, and letting the horrible pictures fly through my thoughts. I imagined everything again and again—until the pictures made me uneasy but no longer fearful. I memorized the faces of the three boys: the fat bottom lip and the pockmarks on the ice-cake boy, the slight downward slant of the green belt's eyes, the scar and the pointed chin of the other. I would make sure they never again saw me alone.

Now the pale wooden top of the well, the drowned bodies, the wet echoing sound of dripping water, the crackle of rain—I went back into my memory and made myself open my eyes while I crouched behind the well. I saw the rock hit the well's top, I saw the rain touch my neck and then my eyes. The slither of dirt falling between the boards into the well, the echo, the cold first drops of rain, the fresh smell of wet dust—that was all. I opened my eyes slowly and watched the last wisps of steam rise from the dirty water in the basin.

The clouds had begun to clear. To the east, the sun reached down through the blue gaps of sky, touching the distant fields.

✧

They came up with the bodies two days later. The divers didn't say anything, but a rumor spread that the baby had been in the maid's arms when they dragged her up by her long, tangled hair.

In the next week, the cholera deaths began. From the neighborhood behind the Apollo Club the disease spread each day into the other neighborhoods—into Tatagumi, Samnung, the market, and soon toward the police station near our house. The drowned baby's uncle died of cholera. A *mudang* at a nearby exorcism rite said in her trance that the cholera had come because the Apollo Club had polluted the water and offended the guardian spirits of the well.

But the club had opened by then. They had paved over the well, forgetting about the Apollo rocket, and they had already had their grand ceremony with the important people from City Hall all hesitantly entering the yard to cut the yellow ribbons with their oversized scissors. They had already served the American drinks, showed the strip shows, and hauled away the first victim of a knife fight.

The Apollo Club made lots of money. From early evening to early morning, Arirang taxis from the American Army post and Korean Corona cabs parked in front of the yard, bringing customers, taking drunks home, haggling over fares to Paekmajang and Inchon.

Everyone tried to forget. When I finally took the Milk of Magnesia to Mr. Paek, business had picked up; he didn't even mention the drowning. "Look at that," he said. "That yard gets full of people in the evening. I stay open longer and they come over to buy transistor radios and batteries." He never spoke of the baby's ghost again, even after the second knifing and the man who was strangled one night with his own necktie and left dead on the spot over the well. Even Jani seemed to avoid what had happened. On our way back from ASCOM in the evenings, he would stop at the club and run errands or sell things to the cab drivers and the waiting customers. Though I made less money, I would leave him there and go home, remembering the drowned baby and the maid with the red scarf.

Each time I passed the Apollo Club I became very uneasy. I thought, at first, that it was fear and sadness, that I was afraid of my memories and the ghosts that might dwell there now, that my sadness was for the Apollo Club; but then I realized that my fear was of the Apollo Club and my sadness was for the ghosts of the dead. "It's so lonely down here. Have you come to be with us?" Everyone so quickly tried to forget. The ghosts of the drowned maid and the drowned baby, the ghosts of all my friends who had gone away forever—I often saw them in my dreams and they were always so lonely.

✧

The dreams came night after night as August drew on and it came near time for school to begin again. Sometimes the dreams were simple, like the vision of the moon-faced leper man or the image of my face receding deeper and deeper under a rippling current of clear water, but there was one I recalled from earlier —from when we had lived in the house of the Japanese Colonel —and this one repeated itself in many convolutions, although it was always essentially the same:

There is a shadow in front of the curtainless window. I look, moving only my eyes, and I see an old woman standing there, hunched almost double. She is wearing white, a bright white blouse and a yellowed white skirt, her white poson socks, gray with dirt at the bottom, hesitating in midstep as if she is suspicious or undecided about something. She turns, and in her hand I see a gleaming kitchen knife just sharpened on a spinning stone. I know with dream certainty that she has come to kill someone. If I cry out to warn the others, she will surely plunge the knife into my heart, but if I remain still, if I close my eyes into slits and remain silent, she will kill someone else. I do not know what to do. I cannot make a sound, I dare not think a thought. My body has become rigid and the slow stiffness creeps up my throat. Perhaps if I make no sound she will kill someone else and let me live. Or will she kill everyone? What if she knows

I am awake, that I am too frightened and too cowardly to warn the others, and she kills us all, one by one, saving me for last to plunge the already bloody knife into my eye? I am sweating. The stiffness has become wood, and the wood is beginning to creak like a branch blown by the wind. Slowly and suspiciously, the crone turns toward me, raising the knife. I must decide. Now. Now. And her eyes turn toward the sliding door, open just a crack. Her eyes widen. She sees someone standing in the opening. She smiles, and without a sound, she steps between our bodies to follow the figure in the doorway.

I would always wake from the dream wondering who that figure was in the doorway. He looked so familiar—so much like myself—that I tried to imagine he was me. But he was not me. He was too old in that place to be me, and he was too thin, his ears a bit too wide, his face too narrow. He was a stranger in my skin, and each time I saw him I was terrified and unspeakably sad.

Once I dreamt that I had died with my eyes open. I could see the whole room—the silk blankets, the papered walls, the sliding doors, the quiet face of my mother as she looked down at me. I wanted to tell her that I had died in my sleep, but nothing, no sound, would come from my closed throat. The sadness welled up inside me until it overflowed through my eyes and the world turned into blurred colors, shimmered, and cleared again into a brighter, cooler world. My mother was gone. I saw a flickering shadow on the far wall; and only then, in my death, did I hear the quiet flutter of swallows' wings and the distant sounds of morning. It was morning and I was awake.

✧

6

Earth

The Ginseng Hunters

Eight-thirty in the morning, and my mother already had visitors. I could hear them coming in through the gate, Emo greeting them. "Insu's mother!" they called. "Are you up?" Mahmi sat on a cushion at her vanity applying makeup and Emo was across the *maru*. I turned over in bed and hid my face under a pillow.

Shoes scraping outside. Footfalls on the wooden floor. The sound of water and the clatter of cups and spoons in the kitchen. I recognized one of the voices as Changmi's mother; the other was new to me, and she didn't speak much, but I could tell she was younger—maybe a new apprentice to Changmi's mother.

The distinctive wood-on-wood rumble of the sliding door opening and closing. "Have you had breakfast?" Mahmi asked.

"Breakfast?" said Changmi's mother. "Whatever for? Today's the pancake special at the NCO Club. Why don't we just have some coffee and get going?"

"I need my morning cigarette," said Mahmi.

"Here." There was a pause, the metallic flick of a Zippo lighter lid and the dull scrape of the wheel on flint. "This is Mijong's sister from Paekmajang," said Changmi's mother. "You know, the friend of Motorpool Sister."

They said hello and had their coffee and cigarettes once Mahmi finished with her makeup. The rising and falling tones of their chitchat put me back into a state between sleep and waking, and I lost track of time and place, rising back into consciousness only when I heard the tinkle of a cup or some especially loud laugh.

I was thinking of cable cars. Out of boredom, I had finished my sixth-grade English workbook half a year early, and my teacher was concerned about what to have me do. She had taken me and another boy, the son of a diplomat, and arranged for us to go on field trips with other classes or work in the library. Last week I had found a picture of a cable car in a book in the high school library, and it had recalled something in me so profoundly that I had stared into it long enough to make the image move. It was an alpine cable car strung from some mountain in Europe, but the cable car I remembered was hanging over a pond. It had been so vivid I could see it even now—the sun glinting off the glass of its windows as it glided slowly along its drooping steel cable. Suddenly I felt a pain in my right palm. I was hurt. I had slipped on the slate paving stones only inches from the border of the pond, and I was lying on my belly, stretched out, reaching for someone I thought was my mother; but when I turned my watery eyes upward and reached up with my skinned hand, I saw a young boy in white standing there, tentatively shifting from foot to foot, looking down at me as if he knew me. I knew I had seen him before in a family photo album. He was wearing that same white outfit and holding a pillow in his hands, looking up at the camera, and the light glinted in his dark eyes. He looked like me, but he was not me. His was the face I often saw in my dreams, the face that always frightened me with its mysterious familiarity.

I did not want to think of the boy in white, so I shook off the images and tried to follow the conversation though I was still only half awake. I found that when I heard some distinct word, I would see an image, and when I heard a

name I would see a face. If I caught a piece of some an-
ecdote I remembered, I could suddenly see its entirety—
the story of each detail, the secret meanings.

Changmi's mother had come to ask Mahmi a favor. She
wanted Mahmi to take Mijong's sister to Yongsan with her
because she was too busy that day. She had a meeting with
a sergeant. "You know, *that* sergeant," she said. She had
managed to marry a Black sergeant who loved her very
much and even liked Changmi, whose father was Korean.
But the husband wanted desperately to have children, and
after failing for over a year, Changmi's mother had secretly
gone for tests at the 121st Army Hospital. There was nothing wrong with her, and the medic—an old customer doing her a favor—told her that it was her husband who had
the problem. She feared now that he might be infertile, and
she was terribly afraid he would divorce her if she didn't
produce a child, so she had scouted the Army clubs until
she found a man who looked just like him. "Close enough
to be his brother," she said. She was meeting the man today, and she still hadn't decided whether she should simply seduce him or tell him the whole story about why she
needed him to make her pregnant. "It seems somehow dis-
honest just to sleep with him without telling," she said.

Mahmi pointed out that if she told him, there was a
chance that he might know her husband, and that word
would somehow get back to him. "What if you have an
argument? Or what if he wants you for himself?" she said.
"Telling your husband would be a good way to make him
divorce you. Do you want this man to have that kind of
power?"

Changmi's mother made up her mind simply to seduce
the GI. "Even if my husband finds out, then it would only
be a butterfly issue," she said. By "butterfly," she meant
fooling around. "He's a kind man. I can't imagine I would
find anyone better than him."

"But why does it have to be a Black GI?" said the young
voice. "There are plenty of handsome white men you
could catch."

"Oh, you don't know anything," said Changmi's mother, rather impatiently. "Black men are much nicer to women. And you have to decide, before you start, whether you're going to date the Black or white GIs. They won't let you date both."

"Who won't?"

"The GIs, the women—what does it matter? The white bastards won't touch you once they see you with a Black man. They think the color comes off on you or something. And the women who go with Black men won't associate with you if you go with a white man."

"Oh, you're being too hard about it," said Mahmi. "It's your business who you go with. Just stay with the right group of friends."

"But Insu's mother, you're married to a white man and you're friends with Changmi's mother."

Changmi's mother *tsk-tsked*. "We've known each other a long time. Insu's mother used to help collect the money for Numbo and Kaksaka before they knew what was what."

"What odd names. 'Kaksaka'—is that Japanese?"

"Japanese?" Changmi's mother laughed loudly. " 'Kaksaka' is what we used to call her because the GIs said she was such a good *cock sucker*. And Numbo, well, how was it she got that name?"

"I don't remember," said Mahmi. "That's something James's mother would know. Say, have you seen her lately?"

"James's mother?"

"The mother of the Black boy?" said the young voice. "Motorpool Sister mentioned her."

"Did she find another husband?" said Mahmi. "I haven't seen her in years. Her son and Insu used to be good friends in the first grade."

There was a moment of silence, the slurping of coffee, a cough. From under the pillow, I could suddenly see James—his legs sticking straight out on the seat of the bus, his reddish kinks of hair, his wide nose and bright teeth.

I saw the girls' stockings he used to wear in winter, and I could feel their texture, smell their cottony smell. I remembered losing bites of our Eskimo Pies to the gate guard, the teachers' notes we threw away, our mutilated lunch tickets. I wondered if James had gone to Oklahoma or if he had moved somewhere in Korea after finding a new father.

"You mean you didn't know?" said the young voice.

"Know what?" said Mahmi.

"James's mother found someone and went to America until her husband got stationed here again at Taegu. But her son—he died years ago."

"What? How tragic."

"He drowned in that sewer creek behind their house. She said he went out one day to play and fell in."

"How awful."

"But fate is fate, don't they say?" Changmi's mother sighed. "That man never would have married her if she had such a troublesome Black son, now would he? Isn't the husband white?"

"Oh, he's very tall, with yellow hair. 'Those skinny ones like their women with some meat' is what she said. Their new daughter's an angel. Her name is Suzie, so now we also call her Suzie's mother. She doesn't like it when we call her James's mother, but everyone still calls her that who knew her from the old days."

I was awake now, but I lay there with my eyes tightly closed, as if I could deny what I had heard by forcing it into the world of dreams.

✧

If it had been possible, I would have remembered James back to life. Things I had forgotten rushed back to me, as if I were flying through scenes in a movie in which he and I were the heroes. I thought I'd recall the images through my eyes, but in each fragmentary scene I was looking obliquely down from somewhere just above us, just beyond the periphery of our vision, as if I were someone older and taller. As I lay there in bed, listening to the murmur of conversation, drifting toward that twilight area at the border of sleep, I was in some timeless state, in the past or caught there, seeing beyond memory. I see James sharpening a dry popsicle stick on the sidewalk in front of the bus stop, his hair full of dust. I see his lips smeared with chocolate and cream. I see him wiping his eyes on the back of his right arm, grinning proudly as he comes out of the principal's office after his first paddling. He tells me the giant spoon the principal uses for a paddle has an African carving on it, that the principal called him a little monkey, and he wants to go play on the monkey bars after I return from my paddling. I see James weeping, looking down at the tiny puncture on the upper part of his left arm as he pulls his sleeve up after his cholera shot—we had gone into the gymnasium in a long procession, seen the Army medics in their white uniforms standing in front of boxes full of what we thought were ball-point pens with red caps. I see myself stumble and grab onto James's waistband, pulling at his pants to stop myself from slipping as we make our way through the sewer pipe, avoiding the trickle of water that drains from the officers' swimming pool. I see us dangling from the bottom of the highest row of seats in the bleachers of the football field where the Army bus makes its last stop before the elementary school. We play there for an entire morning, sneak into the lunch line, then disappear from the playground once again before the teachers know we are there or missing. I see James snatching up green tree frogs with one flick of his hand and then worrying about warts because his mother had told him a frightening story about a green frog and his dead mother. I see him unable to sound out the words to *Green Eggs and Ham*, although he memorizes it with me the first time around when I read it out loud. I see his white teeth, the pale pink of his tongue, the white scrapes on his dark skin, the scars where his mother hit him with the metal comb. I see him balancing on a soccer ball or flying through the air as he leaps from a swing. I see him slapped in the head by the playground teacher for doing a dangerous trick, the way he turned his head away from it, smiling so she couldn't see, and then turning back and pretending to cry. I see the purple Seoul American Elementary School lunch ticket pinned to the front of his striped shirt, the handful of change he stole from his mother's purse while she was sleeping on the bus, the pack of cigarettes we smoked over the course of a week, the gum we chewed to take the foul taste out of our mouths. I see James climbing the maple tree across from the Commissary, dangling upside-down by his legs, trying to drink a Pepsi from that position and finding, much to his surprise, that it doesn't just gush out of his nose. I see him looking back at me as his mother takes him home to Paekmajang, where he has no friends and the Korean children throw stones at him because he is part Black. I see him wincing as his mother wipes the trickle of snot from his upper lip, coughing into his snow-covered wool mittens on the coldest day of winter, blasted by the icy Siberian wind. But the wind against my own flesh is warm—it is late spring—almost summer—and James is dead.

Before going out for the day, my mother reminded me that it would soon be my father's birthday. I sat up in bed, rubbing my eyes, and watched her leave with Changmi's mother and her young apprentice. I hated them at that moment. I wished that James had escaped to Oklahoma with Jongsu, that he was there, waiting for me and we would meet again, without our mothers, when I finally flew to America.

I got up and made myself a coffee with the hot water left over in the kettle. When Emo came in to take the tray away, she rinsed off the sugary spoon by stirring it in my coffee, and as she left the room I thought I could still hear the sound of the tinkling in my cup.

✧

My father always carried two wallets. One of them was full of pictures and identification cards, so thick I wondered how he could sit with the lump in his back pocket. His other wallet, which he carried in his right back pocket, was always much thinner. That was the one in which he carried his money—Korean bills, American bills, and change, all in their separate compartments. He used the money wallet much more than the other and the leather, where it folded, had begun to crack.

I had learned how to work with leather at the ASCOM Crafts Shop, so for his birthday, I made my father a new billfold. On one face of the billfold I stamped in his name in the kind of lettering you see on WANTED posters in Westerns. I did not know what design to put on the other face. My father liked to wear a cowboy hat and hand-made suede cowboy boots when the weather was good, and he would often come home in his civvies—a Wranglers jean jacket and Levi's with the legs folded up—chomping a dead cigar in the corner of his mouth. I had already made him a belt with his initials stamped into it, with elaborate tooling and a two-tone dye job in monochromatic brown. He showed it off to everyone, and I needed a design he would like as much, something more interesting and respectful than a horse's head, a horseshoe, or a cluster of oak leaves and acorns.

Sitting hunched over on a stool in the leatherworking corner of the Crafts Shop, I flipped through the stencil book again and again, but found nothing that seemed exactly right.

All the Korean employees were busy, and I didn't want to bother them, but suddenly the far door opened and Mr. Chong entered with the Cokes he had bought at the bowling alley. "*Ya*, Insu," he said, "you want one of these? Tomorrow is your turn so you'd better have one."

"Sure," I said. I took the ice-cold can halfheartedly as Mr. Chong sat on the stool at my side to peruse the stencils. He knew how to do everything—from photography to woodwork to jewelry casting—and he often raced model airplanes with me when Mr. Panji Lee, my regular dogfight partner, was busy. "If none of these looks right to you, I have an old book of designs in the back," he said. "Go take a look, *ungh?*"

Mr. Chong took me behind the counter and opened a cabinet stacked with old catalogues and manuals all yellowed and stained black to purple by various leather dyes. He pulled down a slim volume without a cover and handed it to me.

Corners of the pages flecked off in my hands as I flattened the catalogue on the counter and opened it to some random point in the middle. It was a North American buffalo like the one on the back of an Indian head nickel. It was the old, stately buffalo patriarch like the one I had read about two years ago in my fourth-grade advanced-reading book.

"You're smiling," said Mr. Chong. "It's the one you want?"

"Yes, sir." I paused. There was no plastic stencil in the catalogue and I knew I couldn't draw the buffalo on the leather.

Mr. Chong understood my hesitation. "They didn't make stencils back then," he said. "Come on, I'll show you how it used to be done."

At the leatherworking station Mr. Chong laid out the leather for the billfold and inspected the letters I had already stamped into one side. "Good," he said. "Next time don't wet the leather quite so much. See how you get the edge of the letter block here?" He expertly tore the page out of the catalogue and placed it over the leather, glancing up sideways at me with a gold-banded grin. "It's a virgin design," he said. "No one's used it yet." He rapidly traced over the black lines with a hard pencil, then removed the page and checked to see if the faint impressions were visible on the surface of the leather. "You could do this easier if you used a sheet of carbon paper like the stupid white boys, but then it would stain the leather when you tool it. Here." He showed me how to look from an angle and follow the outlines with the swivel knife. After I was done with the cutting, I was to tool the entire design before coming back for help with the shaggy fur on the buffalo's hump, which seemed to be the hardest part. "And be sure to give it the right size *chaji*," he said. "You wouldn't want to insult your father's manhood, *ungh*?"

I spent the next hours so engrossed that I didn't realize I had skipped lunch. It was five o'clock when I cut the last line of the buffalo's penis, tooled in the outline of the last hoof and called on Mr. Chong.

"Good work," he said around the cigarette in his mouth. "Now this part all has to be done with the knife, and you have to wedge the cuts so it looks like fur, see? Not too regular." He made rapid cuts with the very tip of the swivel knife, moving from the top of the hump to the bottom so that the cuts would not overlap. There was no pattern. Mr. Chong simply cut at random until the chaos of slits had turned the buffalo's hump into a patch of fur. "You tool this very lightly," he said when he was done. "Then you're ready for the lacing. You'll be done before we close."

By the time I had tooled the fur, hammered in the slits, and laced the billfold together with yards and yards of leather, woven and interwoven in a pattern like my father's blue infantry braid, it was eight o'clock. Mr. Chong taught me the final splice, and then it was done, so new it creaked when I folded it.

"You want to roll it a few times with the lawn roller?" joked Mr. Chong.

"How about if I tie it together under two blocks of wood?"

"That wouldn't be smart, Insu. Remember, it's a wallet. Your father will put it in his back pocket where it will take on the shape of his ass. Tailor-made, this one!" He opened and closed the billfold a few times, adjusting the lacing so that it folded properly. "It's getting late. Why don't you go eat dinner with Panji Lee before you go home? We owe you for getting those cans of film out last week."

"Okay," I said. "Thanks for the help, Chong *ajoshi*. I think my father will like this a lot." I hesitated.

"Forget something?"

"Ah, could you lend me a pack of cigarettes for my uncle?"

"You brat," said Mr. Chong, mussing my hair. "Panji! Fatso!" he called. "Got any unopened cigarettes?"

"Buy your own damned cigarettes!" called Mr. Fatso.

A pack of Kents came flying from across the room. "That's all I have!" called Panji Lee.

"You had Marlboros today! Where did they go?"

"Smoked them all!"

"Well, sorry," said Mr. Chong. "Will your uncle smoke these?"

"I think so."

While Mr. Chong closed up the Crafts Shop, I wrapped up the billfold and went out to unlock my bike. Mr. Panji Lee came out, and we walked together off post. I carried a bag out for him as usual—a few ring molds and dental tools this time. When the gate guard asked me what they were, I told him I was making something for a school project.

Mr. Lee treated me to dinner at a Chinese restaurant not too far into Sinchon, and afterward, we walked back to Tatagumi together, into the narrow street that went through to the main bus stops.

✧

They were lined up on either side of the street, some of them standing at the entrances to their borrowed rooms, all wearing hot pants or miniskirts in garish colors. Because the light was dim and irregular in the street they had made their faces up to look whiter, like the full moon, and their eyes and eyelashes were exaggerated in black the way their lips were highlighted in red or hot pink. "Hey, *ajoshi*," they called to Mr. Panji Lee, "let's go together." They reached for his arm and he swatted them away with a gruff word or a "Let go!"

It was dark and some of them were drunk. I was almost as tall as Mr. Panji Lee, tall enough to be a Korean man, and some of the prostitutes grabbed the handlebars of my bicycle or pulled at the hem of my jacket. "*Ajoshi*, come with me. *Ajoshi*, don't you like me? *Ajoshi*, just listen to me." I looked from their pale faces to their bare midriffs and thighs. It was unusually cool that night and they must have been cold in their thin clothes. I didn't recognize any of their faces. These were women whose customers were Korean men from the Sixth Brigade compound down the road. They looked down on the GI prostitutes although they made less money from Koreans, and sometimes if a *yang kalbo* wandered into their neighborhood they would beat her up as a message to the others.

One of the women stepped out in front of me and straddled the front wheel of my bicycle, placing her hands over mine on the handlebars. "*Ajoshi*, your skin is so soft. Where are you leading your shiny bull?" she said to me, her words slightly slurred. Her pink angora sweater was too small for her, and its buttons were undone to show off her black lace brassière. Her face was squarish and her white teeth flashed as bright as the chrome of my handlebars as she squeezed her thighs together and trapped the bicycle. She giggled.

I suddenly found myself alone. Mr. Panji Lee had walked ahead and didn't see me caught there behind him, surrounded by drunken women who didn't know I was just a boy. There was something hungry about them, and as they converged on me I had the sudden feeling that they would pick at me like a flock of crows on a dead animal, tearing me into shreds of meat. I looked from one face to another, more frightened than I had been when the boys with their knives had chased me down this very street. My heart pounded and my hands trembled, drowning on the handlebars under the hands of the woman in front of me. She was leaning forward now, thrusting her breasts at me, and I nearly choked when I smelled the sharp fumes of *soju* on her breath. "*Ajoshi*," she said again, pouting her lips and drawing out the last syllable into a long, husky sigh, "my room is hot and cozy." I let go of the handlebars and let my hands drop to my sides, throbbing from her feverish touch. "I . . . ," I began to say. "I'm . . ."

Suddenly the woman's head snapped back and I was looking into the night as if the pockmarked face of the moon had disappeared. Mr. Panji Lee was there. He had yanked the woman by the hair, and when she was standing upright again, grimacing and whining shrilly from the pain, he dropped her hair and shoved her out of the way, back into the dark doorway from which she had emerged. "Listen, you fucking bitches!" he shouted. "He's only a boy, understand! He's only a boy! He's got no money! Now let us through!" I heard laughter and some grumbling, but the women scattered and let us by. I picked my bicycle up from where it had fallen and followed Mr. Panji Lee out to the main street. "Are you all right?" he asked.

"Yes, sir."

"Don't concern yourself about it," he said. "They're just stupid, drunken whores. Only in sixth grade, but I guess you look like a man to them, *ungh*?" He patted my hair. "You'd better get home." He gave me a little push when I got on my bike and waved good-bye.

I didn't look behind me when I reached the street, but I had the sudden intuition that Mr. Panji Lee would go back down into the prostitutes' alley.

✧

"Why did you run away?" said Hyongbu. "I would have had fun if I were you. Afraid of a hot little hole around your pillar?" He laughed and slapped the floor by the ashtray, meaning I should produce his cigarettes. "What makes you afraid of them, *ungh*? You see those Yankee whores all the time with your mother, and they don't scare you, do they?"

"They don't," I said. "But they're nicer."

"They just know to keep their hands off you"—he took the pack of Kents without even complaining that they weren't the Marlboros he had wanted—"at least till you're old enough."

"They kept grabbing me."

"Korean soldiers don't have money to throw away like the Yankee bastards. The whores have to fight over customers." Hyongbu smiled. "Want to know a secret?"

"A secret?"

"It means they're a lot cheaper."

"I don't spend money on that sort of thing. I don't need to know," I said, leaning away from him to put my back against the wall. I could feel the trembling from the refrigerator.

"Their pussies are tighter."

"You're lying, Hyongbu!"

"Korean men have smaller pricks, you know. Why do you think they don't go to the Yankee whores, *ungh*? It's because their cunts are stretched by those Yankee phone poles and it doesn't feel very nice." He squeezed his eyes shut and lit his cigarette, savoring the first draw. "Ah, I would have stayed if I were you."

"I made Daeri a wallet," I said. I took it out of my pocket and spread it flat in front of him on the floor. Under the dim light of the bulb the leather finish glistened, as if it were still wet.

Hyongbu picked the billfold up, admiring it as if it were a present for himself. "You've got clever hands," he said, running his fingers slowly over the lacing. "Ah, and I see there's no mistake it's a male, *ungh*?"

"Well, it's for my father."

"He'll like it. From you he could get a sack of shit, and he'd brag about it to everyone because you're his son—but this is a fine present." Leaning back against the arm of the couch, Hyongbu lifted himself slightly up and repositioned one of his shriveled legs to keep the circulation going. He had suffered a stroke a few months ago after having acupuncture treatments during a drunken binge; his speech had returned after a round of Chinese medicine, but his legs were still useless. Sometimes he joked that he should become a Buddhist since he had to sit around in the lotus position all day, but his humor could never mask his rage at being crippled.

"Don't consort with those black marketeers or whores, Insu-ya," Hyongbu said, suddenly changing his tone. "None of them. They're just criminals and women selling their cunts to earn a living. Yongsu's gotten a whiff, and he's already ruined. Suni's clever, but she's learned all the wrong things." He reached down and lifted one of his knees, then let it drop like a dead weight. "You don't want to end up like me."

"It wasn't your fault, Hyongbu."

"My fault, my fate. It doesn't make any difference. You stop wasting your time with that small-time peddling and study hard. You could be a doctor or a scholar."

"I'm going into the Army like Daeri. He said I could go to the U.S. Military Academy."

"You have to study hard for that. Otherwise, you'll be a grunt just like him. You'll wind up in some no-name country with some war going on and you'll knock up some dark-skinned whore and end up marrying her. You're too sensitive."

"I wouldn't do that."

"In your dreams, Insu. You're kinder than a black *kkomdungi*."

"I gave you a pack of cigarettes, Hyongbu. Tell me a story."

"I ever tell you about my great uncle, the ginseng hunter?"

"No."

"The best ginseng looks just like a little man, down to the tiny prick."

"I already know," I said.

Hyongbu tapped a couple more cigarettes out of the pack and set them up on the floor. This would be a long story.

I smiled and slumped back, watching the smoke unravel as it reached the ceiling. I listened to Hyongbu's voice without looking at him.

✧

"A great uncle of mine was a *shimmani*—a ginseng hunter. He was a man with a pure heart, because only the pure-hearted can truly see the ginseng flower. Before he went searching he didn't drink and he didn't touch his wife. He kept his spirit and his body clean and he prayed to the old man of the mountain. He was the most successful ginseng hunter in the province. He was a great man.

"But one day something happened in the mountains, something strange, and he became very sick. For months he had a fever and he would wake in the darkest time of night in a delirium. Each morning it seemed he would get better that day, but then when evening came the fever would return and he would sweat a cold sweat and stare with round eyes into the back of the room as if he could see through the wall. Sometimes he would shout out, 'No! No! Don't take it! Don't pluck it!' and then he would fall back against his pillow, nearly lifeless.

"His wife and everyone else were sure he would die. He withered and began to look like an old root. His fingers grew twisted like brush twigs. The villagers stopped helping and began to say that he had committed an evil sin against the mountain spirit. They stopped lending money. And his wife sold everything, borrowed money from over the hills, cut her hair for the wig makers. She spent everything on the best medicines, but nothing worked, not even the most expensive things from China. Soon there was no money, no place to borrow from. Nothing.

"Now they were starving. Their house was no longer theirs. My great uncle was sicker than ever, and even his wife was going to be sick from hunger. There was nothing left to do but die.

"But my great uncle's wife did not want to die. She had heard of a magical stone Buddha in the mountains that would grant one wish to the devoted, and so she decided to go there and pray to it. She could only take a few grains of rice and a piece of her fine dowry cloth as an offering. It was almost nothing, hardly an insult of an offering, but those things were more to her then than ten thousand *yang* to a rich man. She walked into the mountains following the moon until she could hear the water, and then she followed the sound of the waterfall until she could feel the cold, and then she followed the cold until she saw the big stone belly of the Buddha that had grown from the cliff-side. In the shadow of the belly, she opened her *pojaegi* sack and lit an incense stick and made the offering of the uncooked rice grains she had brought. Then she began to pray, and she rubbed the stone belly where thousands of hands had rubbed it before. She rubbed at that smooth and shiny spot that unhappy women had rubbed for hundreds of years. She rubbed and prayed and cried. And that night the Buddha did not come to her.

"At dawn she returned to my great uncle to see if he had improved, but he was the same. Still delirious and feverish. No worse—the same. All day she took care of him, begging for the food to feed him his daily bowl of gruel, and when night fell she went to the mountains again with the few grains of rice she had left as an offering and prayed to the stone Buddha. And that night the Buddha did not come.

"The next day and the day after that, and the day after that—all the same. My uncle ranted each day and his wife prayed each night, and it went on and on until it seemed forever. On the ninety-ninth day a whole season had passed, and still the Buddha did not come. But then, on the one hundredth day, something happened. It wasn't the Buddha who appeared to her—it was the *sanshin*, the old man of the mountain himself. Under the moonlight his white robes glowed and his white hair and beard were like tufts of cloud around his wise old face.

" 'Listen,' he said. 'I have heard your prayer because you are a sincere and devoted woman. Listen carefully. There is only one thing that will cure your husband of his sick spirit. You must go away this very night into the mountains to such-and-such a peak. There you will find an abandoned grave mound that has grown wild. You must search carefully to see it. Dig there. Dig until you have unearthed the coffin, and when you see the body inside, you must take its right leg. Remember—the right leg. Cut it off and bring it back with you. You must cook it and feed it to your husband, and he will be cured.

" 'But once you have cut off the leg, you must never let it out of your grasp until you are home. Never—not if lightning strikes you, not if a tiger attacks you—or it will be all in vain and it will simply crumble to dust.

" 'Now go, before the night is any older, for you must return before dawn. Go in peace.'

"And the *sanshin* was gone. Where he had stood was a shiny reflection, like water in the moonlight. My great uncle's wife reached out to touch in wonder and found that it was a knife with a silver handle. She took it and offered her eyes up in gratitude one last time before she got up and ran into the charcoal-black mountains.

"It was terrible. She could hardly see where she was going on the trail, but then the moon was covered by storm clouds and it began to pour like the monsoon. She found her way by the flashes of lightning, and sometimes the lightning struck so close it burned, and she thought the spirits must be testing her. She went on and on into the mountains with branches tearing at her clothes and poking at her face. Her hands and her forearms were bloody from covering her face. She went on and on until suddenly she saw two bright lights like the headlights of a jeep in front of her and she stopped.

"It was a goblin. He was hideous, and he held a club

as thick and long as a horse's leg, with a shiny steel spike in it. My great uncle's wife tried to run back the way she had come, but the goblin grabbed her and held her so tight she felt her bones begin to give. 'I know where you're going,' he said to her. 'I could kill you and eat your scrawny body, woman, but I will let you pass if you let me and my brothers have our way with you.' She struggled and even thought of using the silver knife, but she knew the goblin would just kill her. The knife was no match for the spiked club, and the *sanshin* had given it to her for a special purpose. 'Then have your way!' she said to the goblin. 'Just be quick because I have to be back before dawn!' In tears, she lay back and spread her legs for the goblin and his brothers.

"She had expected a few of them, but there must have been a hundred, and their giant penises tore at her like swords and burned like hot *yontan* tongs. She would have died, but she kept her sick husband's face in her mind and she lived, though she was bleeding and could hardly walk when they were done with her. 'Here!' the goblin leader said when they had finished. He tossed her a sack of money. When she bent over to lift it, she collapsed from weakness. She tried to gather the strength to get up again, but then, suddenly, she felt a painful tug on her hair and she was lifted high into the black night. Then suddenly she tumbled back down and collapsed again, and when she came to her senses the night was clear. The moon was out again, lower in the sky. It was calm, and she was sitting in front of a flat circle of grass which she knew was the grave the *sanshin* had spoken of. She would never have been able to find it by herself.

"She started digging. She had no shovel, so she dug with branches and with her bare hands until her fingers were cut to the bone. The grave was not very deep, and soon she had uncovered the lid of the coffin. The wood was rotten, and she easily tore through it and found the body.

"She was shocked. The body was fresh, as if it had only been buried that morning. She thought for a moment that the goblin might have tricked her, but this was clearly where the *sanshin* had told her to look. Now she drew the silver-handled knife and got ready to cut off the leg. She hesitated. The *right* leg. That was the leg on her *left* side. She gathered all her courage and stabbed the knife into the corpse's right thigh, and it went in all the way to the hilt.

"Suddenly the dead body opened its eyes wide in surprise and lurched up in the coffin, screaming, 'My leg! My leg!' My great uncle's wife drew back in terror. She nearly let go of the knife, but then she remembered what the *sanshin* had said. She gripped the handle in both hands and started to saw away at the leg as gout after gout of hot blood covered her face and the corpse continued to scream in pain. 'My leg! My leg!'

"She tore the leg from the corpse and climbed out of the grave, slipping on the blood that had turned the dirt all muddy. The dead man grabbed at the hem of her skirt and tried to pull her back, but she slashed at him with the knife and ran, clutching the leg to her breast as if it were a baby. She ran into the woods just as the starry sky clouded again and the rain began to pour. She hunched over, not even bothering to cover her face against the branches, and she ran back toward her village.

"Then she heard a thumping sound behind her. Lightning crashed all around, and it left her nearly deaf, but she could hear that persistent thumping sound coming closer and closer. Once, she turned to look back, and she saw what it was. It was the dead man! He was hopping after her on his one leg, reaching out his arms and shouting, 'Give back my leg! Give back my leg!'

"My great uncle's wife ran and ran. Her breath was hoarse, her heart pounded like it would burst her throat, her legs gave out, she coughed blood. But she ran on somehow, drawing strength from her spirit that her body did not have, and finally she reached her house. No one was

awake in the village. No dog barked. It was as if everything had died in the night.

"Before the dead man could catch her, she ran into her
kitchen, and still clutching the leg, she put on a pot of
water and stoked the fire until it roared. There was no
sound outside. She relaxed. As she moved to put down the
leg so she could cut it to fit the pot, suddenly it was gone.
She drew back in alarm, but then she saw that it was still
there. It was a ginseng root. The largest ginseng root she
had ever seen in her life. Larger than any she had heard
of, even in legends.

"It was a ginseng root that looked just like a little man,
perfectly formed. And she could have taken that root to
Seoul and sold it to the King, and she could have lived the
rest of her days in a palace with servants to wait on her.
She could have worn the finest silks and eaten the finest
foods with that ginseng root. But she prepared it for her
husband, and he was cured.

"From that day on my great uncle could see ginseng
flowers where others saw nothing. He could smell the fragrance of ginseng from ten *li* away. He became the most
famous ginseng hunter, and his family prospered from his
ginseng and the sack of money the goblin had thrown to
his wife. But from that day on, he knew that all his success
came from the devotion of his wife. She had undone the
offense he had committed against the ginseng spirits, and
it was she who was responsible—even for his life.

"And that is the story of my great uncle, the ginseng
hunter."

✧

Hyongbu's cigarettes were stumps in the ashtray. He
tapped another one out of the pack of Kents.

"The story was more about the wife than your great
uncle," I said. "What does it mean?"

"You always ask me what it means," said Hyongbu.
"And I always try to explain to you that the meaning of

the story is in the story. If I could tell you what it meant, I'd just tell you the meaning and throw the story away, wouldn't I?''

"But with Aesop's Fables, there's a message at the end."

"Aesop? What kind of name is that?"

"Greek, I think. I read some of his stories in a book."

"Well, professor Aesop can eat my shit. And you can wipe my ass with the pages of your book. We tell stories because they're meant to be told. Just remember the story, and you can worry about the meaning later, understand?"

"All right, Hyongbu. It was a very good story. I liked it."

"Whether you liked it or not doesn't matter to me. Fuck it. Bring me a drink of cold water."

I went out to the kitchen and scooped a metal bowl full of water from the storage pot. The kettle on the stove was still hot, so I made myself a cup of Lipton tea and an instant coffee for Hyongbu. I put everything on a tray and went back to the room.

"Be careful," said Hyongbu. "You keep fixing refreshments and carrying trays, and your balls will fall off." He downed the water in a few quick gulps and immediately took a sip of coffee from the plastic U.S. Army mug. "Good," he said.

"Hyongbu, do you remember James?"

"*Jae-im-su*," he said. "Another odd name."

"It's an American name."

"I know, I know. That's that mixed-blood kid you used to play with a few years ago. His father was a *kkomdungi*."

"Do you think he could have drowned in the sewer creek out by Paekmajang?"

"During the monsoon?"

"No. I don't think so." I pulled the tea bag out of my cup and squeezed it with my fingers, wincing from the heat before I put it down on the tray.

"Ah, that's a nasty habit you have there. Why would you want to burn yourself like that?"

"It doesn't hurt."

"I can see it hurts. Use a spoon next time." Hyongbu slurped at his coffee. "So the Black boy drowned in the sewer creek?"

"Do you think he could have?"

"The water's pretty shallow out by Paekmajang. Not much higher than your ankles most of the time."

"That's what I thought, too," I said.

"So how did he drown then?"

I told Hyongbu the story I had overheard from the young woman who had come with Changmi's mother that morning. I told him how James and I used to play in the sewer creek under the first ASCOM bridge, where the water was deepest, how we used to sneak into the Officers' pool in Yongsan together until they fixed the fence.

"It's terrible that he died so young," Hyongbu said, "but why are you telling me all this, *ungh*? Is there some mystery here?"

We looked at each other for a while without speaking. Hyongbu found a cigarette butt in the ashtray and lit it. "Don't look at me like that," he said, waving the match at me until it burned out in his fingers.

I sipped my tea and watched Hyongbu smoke the bitter Korean cigarette.

"Think about it," he said. "You're a dungwhore and you catch yourself a GI by getting pregnant with his brat, but then he goes off to Vietnam and gets himself killed. That leaves you with benefits from the great Emperor of America, but now you have a Black brat to feed, and it's not enough money. So now you want another GI husband to start things over—maybe a white guy with a higher rank, *ungh*?—but who would marry a whore with a Black kid?"

My head hung lower and lower until I was staring glumly at the undissolved sugar at the bottom of my mug.

Finally, Hyongbu said, "Maybe she was trying to scrub the color off and she held his face down in the washbasin too long."

I wanted to lift my head and say something back to

Hyongbu, but I was tired and full of shame, and I sat there rather helplessly, listening to him go on about dungwhores and Black GIs, children of mixed blood, the devious conniving of Korean women. When I had the strength finally to look up again, Hyongbu was quiet, absently twirling his finger around a red cord. He told me to get to bed.

I remember a tragic and ironic story of wartime. There are many versions, set in many places and many eras—Christians fleeing Romans, Jews fleeing Nazis, Koreans fleeing the North—but they are all basically the same: It is the dead of night, and a rowboat full of refugees makes its way, unseen, past a hostile sentry. The occupants of the boat anxiously eye a mother and her baby, and for fear of being discovered, the mother places her hand over the mouth of her child, smothering a cry of hunger. She clasps her hand tightly, more tightly, because she knows that the slightest sound from her baby will alert the sentry and that would be the death of them all. But when they are safely past the guard post and she can remove her hand, when everyone on the small boat draws a relieved breath of air, she looks down and sees that her child is deathly still. She has suffocated her baby. And yet she cannot cry, because even then the danger is not fully enough past to allow her that anguished cry in the dark. We all forgive this mother her unwitting sacrifice because it is for the good of the many, but what if she were alone in that boat, if she covered the baby's mouth not at someone else's behest, but merely out of her own shrewdness? What if she had done the pragmatic thing, anticipating the danger, and drowned the child before entering that critical stretch of black water? Could we ever forgive her then? Or would we forever condemn and hate her?

To say I hated James's mother would be inadequate. Somewhere, running through my tangled emotions there might have been a single thread of hate, but my feelings were too incoherent and too frayed for me to examine so concisely. Looking back— or even now—it would be easier for me to feel vengeful, to wish her ill, and be done with it; but what I felt in my heart then, and what I feel now, is a great blank emptiness. It is a profound sadness, a fatalism, a knowledge that the world is the way it is, and that the path of blame is not an arrow's flight, but the mad scatter of raindrops in a storm. I could have blamed James's mother, but that would have been too simple to do her justice. In the end there is no blame, only endurance.

For the longest time, I had not realized what it meant that James was Black. I had seen it, of course. I had chanted the chocolate rhyme at him, compared the tones of our flesh, called him a kkomdungi. And he had chanted the chocolate rhyme himself, singing about the Negro men from Africa and their kindness. He did not seem to notice, any more than I, that his difference went further than simply being of mixed blood. To both of us, I think his Blackness was lost under the labels we heard —ainoko, chapjong, t'wigi—and that commonness obscured the fact that when people looked at us oddly, they looked at him more oddly than at me. Even a decade later, I could not look back and see that James's tragedy was in the fact that his father was Black. The irony and the symmetry of what his mother and Changmi's mother had done never struck me until twenty years later. How pragmatic was that balancing act: James's mother destroying her half-Black son to find a white husband, Changmi's mother plotting to bear a half-Black son to keep her new Black husband. Bartering sons for their own welfare. It was unfortunate that the rules of blood would not permit one mother simply to hand her son to the other, to keep the balance sheet in the world of the living and not in the sad realms of ghosts and memory. I would learn that women—even seemingly devoted mothers—will traffic in children for the mythic promise of America. And they would all look back in regret from the shores of the Westward Land.

And despite all the things I knew and would learn, I would never truly believe Hyongbu's vicious descriptions of black marketeers, bar girls and prostitutes—even after his death, which is when I finally understood his stories. Hyongbu died the year after we left Korea of a stroke like the one he had suffered after his bad acupuncture treatment. Already paralyzed and lame, he had left this world with a gesture as noble as it was pathetic. Haesuni had found him slumped against a cabinet with a red cord looped around his neck, the other end secured to the brass handles. It wasn't possible for him to hang himself in that sitting position and it was another stroke, and not the hanging, that killed him. But perhaps he had suffered the stroke and, in his last moments, decided that he would rather die than burden his family the rest of his days as an even feebler invalid. After his philandering, his drunkenness, and his violence, they did him the honor of putting his memory to rest, believing that his heart had finally failed from the effort of putting his head through his improvised noose.

My father carried his buffalo wallet for over ten years, until the leather turned a shiny black and began to break apart. And because the profits were better once the U.S. Army introduced real greenback dollars to Korea, my mother continued her black marketing.

The year I turned twenty, I saw a girl at a family wedding; her face was criss-crossed with pale lines her makeup couldn't hide, and though I had never seen her before, she looked familiar to me—more familiar than a distant relative with some slight family resemblance. I learned later that she had been a teenage prostitute until a Japanese banker had disfigured her with a straight razor. It was Suzie—the half-sister James could never know.

❖

7

Sun

Memories of My Ghost Brother

When my mother turned 39 by the lunar calendar, a numerologist told her that she was at a critical juncture in her incarnation because her age could be written out as a string of four threes: 30 + 3 + 3 + 3. In Korean the number three sounds similar to the word for life, but the number four is the same as the word for death. My mother consulted a fortune-teller after a long bout of worrying, and she was told that she would be devoured by a flying serpent with a scorpion's tail. She couldn't be certain, the fortune-teller said, but if the serpent flew, it might be a dragon—a dragon with scales of silver and the nose of a dog would eat the family and fly into heaven. And it was strange, she said. The dragon flew east—she knew that because there was a morning sun over that horizon—but she sensed somehow that it was flying west. In the end she could not say whether these complicated and contradictory signs were good or bad; she advised my mother to hire a mudang *to perform a* kut *for good fortune. My mother was frightened, and she stopped gambling for a while to save money for a* kut, *but then she started again with a passion brought on by an unexpected winning streak at flower cards. And then it all seemed to make sense when she learned that she was pregnant and a friend told her that the child would be born a Scorpio under the solar zodiac. That November she delivered a daughter.*

My father's mother had already named my future sister Anna. But because she had clung so long to my mother's womb, not wanting to leave that world for this one, everyone spoke the two syllables of her name in Korean, imbuing them with accidental meaning: An-na—"not to birth." An-na: it sounds like an-nwa—"not to let go." In the ninth month of her pregnancy and approaching the tenth, as my mother's large belly stretched tight and shiny as a plastic ball, I had tried to imagine my sibling inside that dark, watery world, suspended in fluid and sound, curled like a giant prawn in a self-contained ocean. Sometimes I would lie at my mother's side, tucked into a fetus shape, and ask her if she thought I would fit inside.

I know that my father had wished for another son; I remember, because the name he had picked was "Helmut"—helmet— a name that would have been even more terrible than mine in a schoolyard full of English-speaking military brats. I had secretly wished for a boy as well, but when An-na fell into this world I knew that she had willed herself into being, that nothing could have changed her from being anything but herself.

Because she had lingered so long in my mother's womb, An-na was heavier and larger than I had been at birth. But she was also denser, as if she existed fiercely, as if she were so much realer than other things that her flesh had assumed the substance of stone.

They say the oldest child is jealous of younger siblings, that the relationship is a mixture of love and hate. I did not hate my younger sister, and I was not jealous of her. I think I loved her at first the way a child will innocently love an infant—it is the most natural thing to do. But if I had to describe, in a word, how I felt toward her afterward I would say that I respected her. She learned to speak much later than I had, so late that we might have believed her mute if not for the frightening knowledge in her eyes. Until she spoke, her eyes were an unearthly bottle green, and I knew with the certainty that only children possess that she could see into the other world. Like those fated to be great Buddhist masters, she had been born with memories of her previous lives and a vision that cut both forward and backward through time. When she looked at me as she sucked on her bottle of Similac, one hand worrying her hair, she saw me as an infant, an old man, a brother, a stranger. She smiled at things the rest of us could not see or turned her head attentively toward things we could not hear. When she finally spoke, she would always call me her "little" older brother no matter how many times we all corrected her.

When An-na's eyes were still strange, Hyongbu said that she must be haunted by some malignant spirit. But that was not true. She could see spirits, but I knew they did not inhabit her because, until she spoke her first words and her world became mundane, I could see those spirits reflected in the wet algae color of her eyes.

✧

After my father's second tour of duty in Vietnam the Army had sent him up to the Joint Security Area in the DMZ to be the sergeant of the Honor Guard at Panmunjom. On his visits home he talked about applying for Fort Ord, California, or Fort Lewis, Washington, when his time in Korea was up because he wanted me and An-na to be raised properly, away from what he called the barbarism and the pagan ceremonies he saw in our house. He wanted us to be going to church, saying confession, being confirmed as good Catholics, though he himself certainly was not one. He had seen the Virgin Mary during a malaria fever in Vietnam, and since then he was concerned about our spiritual welfare. It wasn't enough that we had all been baptized—since the Virgin Mary had come to him, he felt that he owed it to her to take us all to church and worship her son.

I had read the Bible by then, but in the church I had no sense of how each bit of the Jesus story was supposed to teach a lesson. What I remembered was that Christ had knocked over the table of the moneychangers, he had let a prostitute annoint his feet, he had saved the life of an adultress by pointing out the hypocrisy of her accusers, he had healed the sick and exorcised the possessed, and then his people had let the Romans hammer him to a cross. I imagined Christ in dusty robes and dirty sandals walking through the desert, but in church there was the priest in a gold-trimmed, pure white cassock telling men—whose job it was to kill other men—that they should be Good Samaritans and build their houses on stone. The priest made the Jesus stories into riddles, but he was not as clever as Hyongbu, and his ploys did not fool me. I thought perhaps he could not say what he really meant because he was an Army priest saying mass in a chapel used by the Protestants, who were an enemy of his religion; the Protestants would call him an idol worshipper even when they shared the same God and prayed to the same murdered son. I understood the way each Buddhist temple up in the Korean hills had a separate shrine dedicated to the old man of the mountain, how Buddhists prayed to nature spirits and honored their ancestors, how Korean Christians often lapsed and called upon a mudang to perform healings, how everyone would give alms to the mendicants tapping their hollow nokttak—but the American religion I could not understand.

I went to a Korean Catholic church once to see if their priest was more logical or if he told better stories about Jesus, whose stories were, after all, very beautiful. But there I saw Christ's dead body on the cross, blood dripping from his crown of thorns and the nails through his palms and feet, a red gash under his ribs and tears of pain and abandonment dripping from his eyes. And the sarcastic banner above him—INRI: Jesus of Nazareth, King of Jews—the gross insult of the Romans. How could these Catholics worship under this thing? Their savior abandoned by his father and left to die alone between two thieves? How could they line up under his body and eat the white disks that were supposed to be his flesh, sip the red wine that was supposed to be his blood, and go away healed? How could I worship this man with the unbearable agony in his eyes or the father who sent him to earth to be tortured to death? I could make myself pray to the Madonna, the mother of Christ who was also his father's mother, whose name as the great Virgin was the same as the name of the prostitute. I could understand that if the Father and the Son and the Holy Ghost were separate and yet one, then the mother of God could also be both the mother and lover of his son. But I also understood that my father's religion was one whose miracles were old; they were in the stories of the healing, the walking on water, the multiplying fishes and loaves; there were no miracles now. My father's priest could not lead the souls of the restless dead into the other world or heal the man whose arm was paralyzed by his ancestors because he had beaten his wife once too often. He could not bring luck to a family whose house was full of tragedy or bring sons to a woman who could only bear daughters. My father's religion wallowed in stories and pictures of tragedy and suffering, but it could not heal what happened every day outside the gates of the U.S. Army post. And so I could not worship his God or the murdered son—I believed in ghosts and ancestors and portentous dreams of serpents and dragons because those were the things I could touch in my world.

Soon after he began taking us to his church, Mahmi started to lose money again and my father grew sick with what the Army doctors thought was a relapse of malaria but which they eventually diagnosed as cancer. I stayed away from home as much as possible, returning only in the evenings to sleep, and sometimes I was away for days at a time under the pretense of staying with a friend. But I had no real friends by then—they had all gone to America or moved to Seoul. I would sleep in the crawl space under the roof of the GIs' shower house in ASCOM, sometimes in the company of a classmate who visited from Yongsan. It was the year before we left Korea, and the imminence of our departure hung over us like a cloud of danger.

❖

My mother was sick; she lay on the bed mat in the center of the room with an IV dangling from an improvised wooden rack, its needle tip puncturing a vein in her wrist. The clear solution that dripped from the glass bottle, trickling down the tube into her arm, reminded me of sand in an hourglass, and I was afraid of what it might be measuring. A piece of white gauze wrapped around my mother's wrist kept the plastic tube in place; she had another strip of gauze wound around her head, the way she did for her headaches. It was quiet in the room and a faintly bitter hospital scent lingered from when the nurse had been there.

Mahmi's eyes were closed, the expression on her face calm but also pained, as if she were thinking something regretful. Her flesh looked pale against the dark blue silk of the blanket, and with her head angled like that on the pillow and her hair a mess, she looked uncomfortable. I did not know what to do or what to say—whether I should weep in the corner or be in the other room playing with An-na to keep her happy. I felt a desperation I had never understood before, like someone hurtling toward a steep ledge, knowing that the fall was inevitable and yet unable to do anything to stop it—that fall in the future, unavoidable as mortality. I remembered a movie—no, two movies—I had seen years and years ago; though only a couple of scenes remained in my mind, they were fixed there as if the black silver specks on the celluloid were indelibly etched onto a metal plate. In the first scene a squad of North Korean soldiers—Communists, lean and harsh in that North Korean way—marches a young woman toward a post standing in a barren courtyard. The woman is wearing only her slip, and she is disheveled, as if she has just awakened from sleep or was interrupted in the middle of some intimacy. She is weeping, and her mascara runs as the soldiers handcuff her to the post, march back with their rifles and take aim. The title of the movie is *The Dead and the Living*. The soldiers take aim at their officer's sharp command. But do they shoot? Is the woman the "dead" of the movie's title? Or does the hero suddenly appear with his Thompson submachine gun and blast all the Communists into sprawling oblivion, spewing their black blood onto the white dirt of the courtyard? I could not remember. In the other scene a poor father, obviously a common laborer—since he is in a white sleeveless T-shirt and wrinkled, baggy pants—is with his little boy at a crematorium. They are weeping, the man with the corners of his mouth grimly downturned, his eyes nearly squeezed shut; and the little boy is sniffling, wiping his eyes with the length of his forearm as the crematorium attendant pulls a drawer from the oven to show the glowing white bones of his dead mother. Gray and white ash, glowing white bones, overexposed and washed out to look ethereal against the uneven black shadows inside the crematorium. The little boy and his father break into awful sobs, their chests heaving simultaneously, and the man must restrain his boy from embracing the hot ashes and burning himself. The crematorium attendant closes the drawer and the remains of the boy's mother return into that brilliant white part of the screen and shuts into black, leaving my eyes with afterimages, blurred by tears.

I was sobbing, my head nodding up and down like a

pigeon. Mahmi didn't even open her eyes. She looked grim lying there, as if she were finally tired of everything—the black-marketing, the gambling, the debts, the friendships and antipathies, the matches she made, the ungrateful friends and business partners. The gauze around her forehead was the same off-white color as the fabric of funeral clothes. I was afraid and all I could do was leave the room and sit by myself on the *maru*, hoping that she would want to live again.

✥

"Look," said Hyongbu, "you're almost in high school. You're old enough now to know what's going on. Did Emo tell you what the problem is?"

"No."

"All those clots of blood that came out of your mother —they were babies. Twins. A boy and a girl."

"What happened?"

"They died inside her belly. They came out early."

"Will Mahmi be all right?"

"That all depends on how she feels. She needs a reason to live now."

"I didn't know she was pregnant," I said.

"Only Emo knew," Hyongbu said, scooting himself closer to me. "Even your father didn't know—that bastard. He's the one she got pregnant for in the first place, as if it's not enough to have two of you in this awful world. She wanted another son for your Yankee father so he could call him 'war helmet' or some nonsense. You have to go up to Panmunjom and tell him why your mother isn't meeting him this week."

"What am I going to tell him? I don't want to go."

"You know where your mother always meets him, right?"

"Yes."

"You go up there on the bus tomorrow and you play the good son for him. You tell him it's that time of month and your mother is sick. Can you do that?"

"I don't know."

"What? This is serious business! You go up and tell him she's sick but don't mention a word of anything else, understand? He would be terribly upset if he knew he'd lost a son."

"Why did the babies die, Hyongbu?"

"Sometimes they just die. Your mother wasn't ready to have twins, especially so soon after An-na. There's barely enough money to feed you and your nasty little sister. Here. Take this pocket money and get yourself something good to eat while you're up there. One of those *hama*burgers or those *chaji*dogs, *ungh*?"

I took the money and folded it to put into my pocket. "Is Mahmi so sick because she's afraid Daeri will find out?"

"*Ya*, you just go up tomorrow and do what needs to be done. Let your Mahmi worry about the rest. And have that father of yours buy you some cigarettes before you come down."

"All right."

I lay out on the *maru* that night, rehearsing in my head what I would need to say to my father, but what kept coming into my mind was a scene from a news report I had seen years ago at some war movie with Kisu. A woman on a hospital gurney, covered in a sheet except for her disheveled black hair, and a fragment of voice-over saying, "This frightening patient." I had been afraid of wigs ever since I had seen that report. "This frightening patient." Each time I tried to come up with something to say to my father, that piece of voice-over intruded in my ear—"This frightening patient"—and eventually I drifted into a disembodied sleep.

There are times when the soul is filled with a desolation that stretches out like a surface of stone going on and on forever, farther than the eye can see, farther even than the reach of imagination. It is a barrenness borne of speechless tragedy, a river of silence having worn everything into a smoothness like the polished face of a marble slab.

Early in the morning, I awoke from a vision I had had years ago in the house of the Japanese Colonel, and as before, I found myself conscious and yet unable to move, paralyzed by the vividness of a dream I believed was not yet over. I opened my ears wide, trying to gulp in the crisp sounds of daybreak, but I heard nothing, no telltale of the thick-socked feet I had seen pass my face only moments before. In my dream I had been awake: The sparrows made me open my eyes, and I was lying on my side, looking toward the center of the room where the others are still asleep. Mahmi looks toward me, her face large and pale, sagging slightly, beautiful and unconscious. There is Emo, Haesuni, and Yongsu; and Hyongbu is drunk in the other room and my little sister, An-na, is not there. She is yet to be born. All the same images are there: the shadow in front of the curtainless window, the hunched old woman in white, the *poson* socks gray with dirt at the bottom, the suspicious look, the gleaming kitchen knife just sharpened on a spinning stone. I know with dream certainty that she has come to kill someone; I am too terrified to make a sound; I close my eyes into slits; my body is rigid and the stiffness creeps up my throat. The crone turns toward me, raising the knife, but just then she sees someone else in the doorway; she smiles, and without a sound, she steps between our bodies and is gone.

As before, I could not move my head, but this time I forced my eyes up, so far back the muscles ached, about to snap my vision into the back of my skull, and I saw him there, looking calmly at the old woman. He was the stranger whose face I had seen many times before under the surface of rippling, clear water. His was the face I so often took for my own, and this time I knew his name— Kuristo, my ghost brother—and just then the crone's foot stepped in front of my face, and when it came up again, Kuristo was gone. The old woman was gone.

And now I lay there with my soul full of silence, having

passed from dream to waking without a pause. I turned my head, and through the open door of our room, I thought I saw a smile on my mother's sleeping face, a smile just formed in her dream; and at that instant I hated her, and I hated Kuristo for having saved us from the crone's gleaming knife. The hate was so strong that all the wooden stiffness in my body burst at once, with an audible *crack!* in my throat, and the hate splinters flashed like cold needles into every part of my body, back into my memories, and as the cold tears streamed from my eyes, one eye emptying into the other, then down to soak the sleeping mat, I knew that I would hate myself most of all.

In the morning I took the first bus to Yongsan, sleeping all the way to fragmentary and unpleasant dreams. I woke with a headache because the bumpy ride had pounded my temple against the window. RC-4 was a Recreation Center, an R & R camp I could get to without special clearance needed in the DMZ area. While I waited for the transfer I drank coffee at the Service Club and looked through the latest Johnson Smith catalogue for Vietnam grunts. Around 10:30, after I had had my fill of coveting .22-caliber pellet rifles and BB pistols, I went out to the bus, jittery from too much coffee and walking awkwardly because I had rolled up a few Sad Sack comic books and put them in my back pocket to read on the bus.

My night rehearsals had failed, and now I wondered how my father would react when he saw me instead of Mahmi. Would he have some present or money for her that he would ask me to take back home with me? Would he be angry?

Once the bus left the brief outskirts of Seoul I found myself staring out the window at the paddy fields; the passing bicycles so overladen with merchandise it didn't seem possible that the skinny men could pedal them; the women late on their way to market with heavy metal basins on their heads, balanced as steady as rock though they carried parcels in their hands; dirty children squinting in the dust kicked up by the bus, all of them with trails of watery snot leaking from their noses; storefronts of sandy gray brick, roofs of corrugated tin, thatched barns and dun-colored oxen in fields fertilized with human feces. I belonged out there. I should have been watching this bus go by, running alongside in my white rubber shoes, my feet squelching inside from their own sweat. I should have been carrying a gray bookbag with the characters of some middle school painted on it in white, worried about my school uniform and whether my hair was short enough to pass muster under the stern eyes of my schoolmaster. But I was on this bus, sitting behind freckled GIs who spoke with accents from places I had only imagined, whose sweat smelled thick and nauseating, whose eyes were the color of the sea and sky, whose boots and tanks trod the earth of this country to bitter dust. I wondered if Chongsu and Jani were happy in America with its dustless streets and sparkling nights. I could taste the bitter dust on my tongue, and today the Sad Sack stories, which usually amused me, seemed repulsive and simple-minded. A pot-bellied sergeant, a skinny buck-toothed private. Women with circles for breasts and eyelashes as thick and black as bootlaces. Names like Slob Slobinski and Killer. And always explosion after explosion that seemed to resolve even the most complicated dilemma. I remembered hunting for artillery brass one afternoon near a place the GIs called Mickey Mouse Village, finding wads of C4 plastic explosive, manual fuses, unexploded shells. Earlier that week some boy had dug out a shell and dropped it on a stone, and he had blown himself to pieces, scattering fragments of himself so far they could not gather him together again to hide under a straw mat. He had died so suddenly they said he didn't have time to realize it and his ghost was still drifting back and forth across the range wondering why no one could see him or speak to him. But sometimes someone would hear his voice whispering in their ear or feel his breath on their neck, and they would have to say,

"Tong-su, go away, go away," and listen to his weeping. That afternoon I had found scraps of cheap clothes black and stiff with dried blood and I had walked gingerly back to the road, carrying my armful of brass all slippery with my sweat as I followed my own footprints back and counted my breaths to keep calm. Later that afternoon I had taken a post bus and gotten off in Itaewon, where I sold my brass to a dealer who would turn it into ashtrays, bedposts, deep-sea diving helmets, and gaudy decorations for spendthrift GIs to take back to "The World." I had walked down alleys where girls not much older than me would suck a GI's penis for a few dollars, where boys my age would let a man fuck them and then pretend to be their family friend. I had seen a man stabbed in the gut with a sharpened afro pick, had my shoulder slashed by a fast straight razor, smashed a thief's head with a brick. And we were all doing our best to get money from the yellow hairs, the long noses, the Yankees. The *yang saekshis*, the slicky boys, the hustlers, the pimps—all after the same things—skulking through narrow alleys running with sewage and piss and wafting with a stench so awful that it gagged you.

I met my father at the Snack Bar in RC-4. It could have been any Snack Bar on any small U.S. Army post—the same pastel-colored, vinyl-padded metal furniture, the same plastic trays, the same china, the same food. He was drinking coffee in the far corner, reading a paperback book he had folded backward, breaking its spine. He was in his ODs, his flight jacket draped over the back of his chair, his cap on the table next to the ashtray in which a cigar butt still smoldered. I could smell it from the doorway—a Dutch Masters.

"Daddy," I said.

He looked up at the sound of my voice, scanning instantly from my face to the empty air behind me. "Heinz," he said, in his German-accented voice. "Where's Lee?"

"Mahmi's sick," I said. "She said I should come to tell you." I sat down at the table, draping my own flight jacket over the back of my chair.

"Get yourself something to drink. I'll finish this chapter." It was a Louis L'Amour Western, something like *Hondo*, a thin paperback he could read in a couple of hours. He was half done with it, which meant he had probably bought it in the Stars & Stripes Bookstore next door. He had been waiting an hour. I got myself a cup of Lipton tea and sat back down.

"What's the matter?" he said.

"Mahmi said it's that time of month when she gets the headache. It's bad this time, and so she couldn't come." I felt an odd thickness in my voice, a constriction in my chest. I wanted to tell him what was really wrong.

"How's Anna?"

"She's okay. She said, 'I wan come Daddy.' "

My father grinned with pleasure. "She reminds me of my mother. I ever tell you that?"

I shook my head. "Daddy, you want to go bowling? I broke 150 last week."

"No kidding." He was looking down at his book. He turned the page, folded the book back over on itself, and put it in the inside pocket of his jacket. "Hey, I have a better idea," he said. "I brought a jeep down from JSA. How would you like to have a look at Panmunjom, where I work, huh?"

We put our matching jackets on and walked out to the EM club where we found Private Jones, the driver my father had brought down with him.

"I have to take a leak," my father said as he went toward the back. "Jonesy, you can show him the jeep."

Jonesy was taller than my father, almost two meters tall, I thought, and he looked like one of the football players I had seen playing for the Kansas City Chiefs on *Pro Football Highlights*. "Howdy," he said. "Come check out our noble steed, man."

The open-topped jeep, parked behind the Quonset hut,

had a small flag mounted on either side of the front bumper: a white surrender flag on one side and a black flag decorated with a skull-and-crossbones on the other. The Jolly Roger was emblazoned in red with "Alpha Company" and "Angry Alpha" in quotation marks.

"What do you think?" Jones said. "The pirate flag is to annoy the North Koreans. They call us 'Hooligan Fenkl and his Gang.'"

"Why do you have a white flag?"

"That's so they don't shoot at us in the DMZ area. Usually the other flag is the UN flag, but the old man didn't want us to seem like pussies. It's against regulations to fly this thing. The gooks fuckin' hate his guts."

When my father came back, he adjusted his cap and stepped up into the passenger seat. "It's gonna get windy back there," he said. "There's a poncho liner on the floor if you need it."

Jonesy got in on his side and started the engine. "Panmunjom, home away from home," he said.

What I wanted more than anything when I climbed onto the jeep was to go home, but that was not something I could say. "Ready to go, Sarge?" Jonesy said, popping the clutch.

"Proceed," said my father, and Jonesy shifted gears and lurched us forward.

When I looked curiously down at the sandbags that lined the bottom of the back where I sat, my father laughed and explained that it was to keep the jeep steady, to avoid rolling because jeeps were notoriously top-heavy.

"Had a greenhorn lieutenant in 'Nam who rolled one at twenty fucking miles an hour," he said. "Twenty fucking miles an hour! Can you believe that?" He looked over at Jonesy, and the private replied with a sheepish smile. They shared a laugh.

"It's in case we run over a mine, too," Jonesy said. "The sand keeps the shrapnel from coming through and ripping your balls off."

"Not that we're gonna hit a mine," said my father. He

pulled out a cigar and Jonesy lit it for him one-handed, flipping his Zippo open and shut with a casual precision; I could smell the momentary bite of lighter fluid even in the wind.

In the back, crouching between the two front seats, I felt oddly light and heavy at the same time. It was cold, and as the wind whipped through my hair I was glad I had worn my flight jacket that morning.

We exited the gate past the saluting guards, and then we were outside, down a road that was oddly well paved for its distance from Seoul. As we drove I had the sense that we were somehow winding backward through time, along the band of black tarmac, to some earlier, less inhabited Korea.

Shortly past RC-4 there were no more houses. We followed a streambed for a while, passing a few outposts and bunkers, but there were no signs of people, only the landscape and this odd stretch of good road. I was frightened. And then we approached an eerie concrete monument that felt like it existed in the middle of nowhere although I could see paddy fields off in the distance. The two gray embankments had huge stone slabs balanced over them, forming a precarious-looking square gateway. It reminded me of pictures of the ancient dolmens I had seen on Kanghwado Island, the place where they said Tan'gun, the mythic father of Korea, had descended from heaven. "Daddy," I said over the wind. "Is someone important buried here?" Jonesy laughed.

"Negative," said my father, leaning backward and squinting toward me. "That thing is wired so they can blow it up in case there's an invasion from the North. The top parts fall on the road and keep tanks from getting through." We passed several more structures like it, and each time, even after I knew what they were, I thought of mythic places I had read about—Stonehenge, the Pyramids, the ruins of Machú Picchú. I could not imagine Russian tanks crushed under those slabs of concrete any more than I could quite imagine being on a jeep with my father, speeding northward to the three-mile-wide line that sliced this country in half.

By the time we crossed the Imjin River, over the bridge wired for instant demolition, I had pulled the camouflage poncho liner around me, leaving only my head exposed to the wind. My cheeks felt fresh, but slightly numb where my hair beat at my skin, and my nose was beginning to water. Down below, along either bank of the Imjin, stood concrete obstacles to prevent amphibious crossing during an invasion. Everything, it seemed, was awaiting that imminent invasion from the North. Even the landscape felt wired for destruction—trees, branches, leaves, flowers all set to explode in the faces of North Korean invaders.

"Jonesy, what do you say we sing my boy the old Angry Alpha song?" my father said through the thick air.

They sang together, and even through the wind and the sound of the jeep's engine, my father's deep bass voice harmonized with Jonesy's tenor with an unexpected beauty.

> Every place we go-*oh*
> People want to know-*oh*
> So we tell them
> We are the Alpha
> Angry, angry Alpha
> Mad, mad Alpha . . .

They must have sung this together a thousand times, I thought. They must work together, eat together, sleep in the same barracks, worry the same worries and fight the same fights to have their voices merge like this. I could not imagine my voice joining with my father's the way Jonesy's did. I could not imagine how I would ever understand their secret language of knowing glances and inside jokes. That was something that only yellow-haired soldiers could do. I would forever be tainted by a Koreanness that would make the words "gook" or "dink" sound strange coming from my lips, like the word "nigger" spoken by a Black GI to anyone but his brothers.

When we reached Panmunjom in the Joint Security Area, my father showed me the famous conference room with the microphone cable running down its center, the final divider between North and South. In the safety of the room, with Jonesy watching the far door, I stepped across the line and looked out through the north-facing window at the brown-uniformed North Korean soldiers on guard. Later, I was taken down an interception shaft into the infamous infiltration tunnel, hundreds of feet below the earth, and I stood in the icy cold, dripping stone corridor through which they said an entire division could sneak undetected to invade the South. I saw The Bridge of No Return through periscope binoculars, the fire pole in the American soldiers' barracks set up so they could respond instantly to emergencies, the pick handles they kept by the door to fight axe-wielding North Koreans without firing their weapons and inadvertently reigniting the never-finished War. I heard about a dim-witted lieutenant who set a booby trap while on patrol one day and then fragged himself when he forgot about it and tripped the grenade while he was taking a piss in the bushes the following week. But what I remembered most vividly was what my father showed me after we ate at the NCO Club—his BEQ—the Bachelor Enlisted Men's Quarters he lived in though he was married. My father's room.

The Quonset hut was like a giant tin can laid on its side and half-buried in the ground and the walls inside were arched. My father had built long rows of low bookshelves to go up and down the length of his half of the hut, and he had put up plywood partition walls, dividing the space into a sitting area, a working area, and a sleeping area. In the sitting area he had set up a Panasonic console with a built-in turntable, an AM/FM tuner, and a reel-to-reel tape deck; a collection of a hundred jazz records of Louis Armstrong, Count Basie, Lionel Hampton, Charles Mingus; one entire wall of paperback books—murder mysteries and private dick novels with scantily clad women on their covers, but also books whose titles and authors I would never have thought to name in the same breath with my father: *The Rise and Fall of the Third Reich, The Decline and Fall of the Roman Empire, The Conquest of Mexico, The Inferno, The Iliad, The Odyssey, Plato's Republic, Kim, The Seven Pillars of Wisdom, The Naked and the Dead, Death in the Afternoon;* Friedrich Nietzsche, Karl Marx, Heinrich Heine, Thomas Mann, Hermann Hesse. In the working area were commemorative plaques and awards presented to him by the various units he had served in, including one made out erroneously to "Eldridge L. Fenkl." He had a collection of stamps both stark and beautifully elaborate, from countries with names like Qatar, Norge, and Maygar; and coins— pfennigs, lire, francs, and dong. Had I walked into this room, and had I not seen the small pictures of my mother, me, and An-na in frames on his desk, I would never have believed this could be his life away from us.

On the partition wall that blocked the sleeping area from view, my father had strung an assortment of small silk flags of the UN countries, and under the bright and colorful banners hung two black X-shapes formed by a set of crossed Montagnard swords and their metal-banded scabbards—his mementos from Vietnam. On his desk, on top of a stack of cream-colored Army field manuals all labeled with the letters "FM" followed by some hyphenated number, sat rings of brass and aluminum. They looked like piston rings I had once seen at the ASCOM Motor Pool.

"Those are bracelets the chiefs gave me," said my father. He was sipping his second can of Falstaff beer while he waited for the hotplate to warm up water for my C-ration cocoa. "Made by Montagnards."

"You told me they were like Indians," I said.

"You remember?"

"Yes. You told me the day you put me on the howitzer at 8th Army HQ."

"What else did I say?"

"You said I would like them," I said.

"Yeah, I guess you would, though they're unhappy and they don't quite live in this world. They're superstitious people and they don't trust nobody. But if you got fucked over by everyone who said he was your friend, you wouldn't trust anybody, either."

"Who fucked 'em over?" I said.

"The French, the South Vietnamese, the VC, us. That's about everyone. Watch your language." He motioned to a beret on his bookshelf. "I was on an Advisory Team, a special A-Team. We worked with the Montagnard Strikers. Those guys aren't much bigger than you, but they're tough as hell. I trusted them a hell of a lot more than any Vietnamese. You could never trust a Vietnamese, especially the interpreters."

"Why not?" I asked. The aluminum pot on the hotplate made a sort of whining sound and steam had just begun to curl from the top. I ripped open a pack of hot chocolate with my teeth and made myself a cup.

"Let me tell you something important," said my father. "If you ever count on someone to do the talking for you and you don't know what they're really saying, you gotta assume he's covering his own ass. Interpreters always tell each side what they want to hear or they tell each side what's good for themselves. Sometimes they lie to both sides and benefit from it. I always kept two interpreters who hated each other's guts, and that kept them honest. The ones who fucked up and got caught—we gave them to the Montagnards out in the slopes and looked the other way."

I knew the Montagnards had tortured them and then killed them, but I wanted to know how. I wanted to know if they had used their swords or sharpened bamboo stakes, whether they had cut out the men's tongues as I might have done because they had used them to tell lies. "What did they do?" I said. "They must have been really pissed off."

"Never mind," said my father. "Hey, I know Emo's old

man tells you stories all the time. Let me tell you a story I heard from a Montagnard chief in An Lac. Well, it was across the Krong Kno river from An Lac, a village called Buon Romen.

"It's a story about the men and the monkeys," he said. "In the old days the monkeys and men lived together. They were friends. But the men were jealous of the monkeys because the monkeys had number one fields with lots of rice and the men's fields were number ten. The men knew that if you looked at their fields from the ground they looked very good, and if you looked at the monkeys' fields from high up from a hill, they looked small and shitty.

"So the men showed the monkeys the fields from these different heights and tricked them into switching. And when harvest time came, the crops were bad for the monkeys and they had nothing to eat. So they went to their friends, the men, for advice, and the men told them, 'You have to kill your children for food.'

"Now the monkeys still trusted the men for their wisdom, so they went home, and crying all the while because they were so sad, they butchered all their children. That night the men sneaked into the monkeys' village and stole all the meat. The next morning, when the monkeys came to the men's village, they saw them eating some meat. The men said it was just bird meat.

"But the monkeys recognized the flesh of their own children—how could you not?—and now they were afraid of the men. They ran from the men's village into the deep forest and from then on, they lived wild. Now the monkeys steal corn and rice from people and they're always screaming in anger because a long, long time ago the men lied to them and stole the spirits of their children."

◈

Why had my father told me this? I stared silently down into the chocolate dust that had congealed on the sides of my plastic U.S. Army mug. What did he expect me to say, caught here in the boundary between the two Koreas, caught between North and South and East and West with my own blood mixed from the blood of enemies? I could tell he wanted me to say how much I liked the story. He had liked my questions in the past—he had enjoyed explaining the difference between Zeus and Jupiter, Odysseus and Ulysses, Argus and the Argo—but what could he expect me to say to this?

"Daddy," I said after a moment, "I had a dream I had a brother. His name was Kuristo and he was a ghost. Why do you think I had that dream?"

When I looked up, my father's face was red—I couldn't tell if it was from the beer or because he was angry at me. He sat there, swishing the beer around in his nearly empty can, glancing from the crossed swords on his partition wall to the pictures on his desk. "What did Lee say?" he said finally.

"I didn't ask Mahmi."

"Well, don't ask her. You don't ask nobody. That's just a bullshit dream, you understand? Sometimes we just have bullshit dreams where we appear and we think it's our own brother."

"But he saved us. And his name was Kuristo."

"Kuristo—what does that sound like to you?"

"Christopher."

"It's Christ. Jesus Christ. He saved us all, and you just saw him like he was your brother, *nicht wahr*? Remember the time I was sick with fever and I saw Maria when my mother had her church pray for me?"

"Yes."

"It's like that, but it's just a bullshit dream, too, and you don't need to tell anyone else about it." He was leaning forward in his chair, his elbows on his knees, holding the red beer can in both hands, staring at a point just beneath my feet. I gulped down the rest of my lukewarm hot chocolate and wiped my lips with the back of my hand. "We gotta' get you out to the bus," said my father. "You want to get back in time to catch the last one back to ASCOM."

We walked to the bus stop without speaking. I had said the wrong thing to him, something as bad as telling him why Mahmi was really sick, something as bad as asking Mahmi whether she had lost the twin babies or had aborted them.

At the bus stop my father reminded me to take Mahmi to the hospital if she got any worse, to give An-na a kiss for him. "Hey, Booby," he said as I stepped onto the nearly empty bus, "I'm glad you got to see all this. We're gonna ship stateside next year." He watched at the door until I sat down and then walked away without looking back. He didn't know the schedules as well as I did—I hadn't told him I would reach Yongsan too late to catch the last bus home.

I fell asleep as soon as the bus left Panmunjom, but I was jostled awake at the next U.S. Army post for my ID. I left my wallet open with my military dependent's ID card visible on the green vinyl seat at my side so that I wouldn't have to wake up for every MP gate guard on the way to Yongsan. I drowsed, and after a while I realized I was awake, but I stayed in the same position, my head angled into the space between the seatback and the cold window, my eyes closed, my breath the breath of sleep. I watched the darkness turn to flashes of light with each post we approached, I listened to the dull hum and rattle of the bus, the hiss of air brakes, the opening and closing of the pneumatic doors, the sound of footsteps and murmuring voices. Through my eyelids—though they were closed—I could see the MPs checking name tags and IDs with their flashlights, their khaki uniforms, their boots laced horizontally with white parachute cord, spitshined to a black gloss that reflected their flashlight beams. I could smell the gritty odor of cigarettes, the sour yeasty smell of beer, the thick yellow smell of American bodies.

When the bus finally killed its engine, when the motion

ceased and the vibration died to stillness I opened my eyes to see the bus driver looking down at me in the empty bus.

"Last stop," he said to me in English. "You wakee up now. Yongsan."

"Thank you, *ajoshi*," I said to him in Korean.

"What were you doing coming back from Panmunjom so late?" he said without surprise. "You're not old enough to be a GI yet."

"That was my father who brought me to the bus," I said. "He's the sergeant of the Honor Guard."

"You must be proud then."

"Proud?"

"He's in a dangerous place doing a good thing for our country."

"He hardly ever comes home since he's been stationed up there," I said.

"Where do you live?"

"ASCOM."

"You missed the last bus. Do you know how to get back?"

"I was going to take a share taxi from Seoul Station."

"Save your money for something to eat and take the last train from Yongsan Station. You still have over an hour to make it."

I thanked him and said good-bye. I knew they would be worrying about me at home, but since I had spent so many nights away, I hoped they would simply think I was at a friend's house. The bus driver's advice reminded me that I had forgotten to ask my father for cigarettes, so I walked up to Itaewon and bought a carton of black market Marlboros for Hyongbu before taking a taxi down past the Samgakji Rotary to the Yongsan train station. I ate some fishcake soup at a covered wagon, watching the flickering light of a carbide lamp while I waited for the last train to Inchon.

Every passenger on the train seemed exhausted by life. Here was a young man with four tall stacks of books bound with straw rope, a woman in a market apron and head scarf with a huge metal basin still half full of rice cakes, an old man in round glasses with nothing but a small bundle centered like a child on his lap. The compartment was full of people like them, all faces creased with wrinkles of worry, suffering, and permanent exhaustion. People usually talked to me on trains, but tonight everyone was grimly silent, everyone nodding off or sitting with eyes closed, thinking. I tried to sleep again, but what I noticed was the smell of squid, the texture of the frayed fabric of my seat, the rhythm of the rail and the sound of the wind gently mothering me as we departed Yongsan, the mountain of the dragon.

When I got home, wide awake, just before the midnight curfew, everyone was asleep except Haesuni, who had stayed up to wait for me; she answered the gate even before I knocked and followed me back up to the *maru*, dragging the mashed-heeled sneakers she wore like slippers. She had set up a sewing table on one side of the couch; An-na was asleep on the other side holding a still-warm bottle of Similac as if it were a stuffed animal. She was too old for a bottle, but she refused to give it up.

"I missed the last bus," I said.

"That's what we figured. An-na said you'd be home tonight before the siren." The curfew siren blew just then, and An-na's eyes flickered momentarily in the dim light. Haesuni laughed at my expression. "Are you hungry?"

"No. I had some *odaeng* at Yongsan. Here." I produced the carton of Marlboros for Hyongbu. Haesuni took the cigarettes and sat down on the floor at the table, using the couch for a backrest the way everyone else did.

"Why were you so late? Were you hanging around Itaewon again?"

"Daeri took me to Panmunjom and showed me around. He doesn't know the bus schedule and I forgot to remind him."

Haesuni lifted a black wad from the table and let it fall open into a pair of fishnet stockings. I didn't see how she could mend them with black cotton thread. "Here, take this," I said, giving her the two thousand *won* I had left. "It's a contribution for a new pair. You can't fix those."

"I got them caught on a nail sticking out of a chair," she said, nodding as she took the money. "Thanks."

"Why don't you ask Mahmi to buy you new ones?"

"She doesn't want me going to the clubs, so I don't tell her. Last month I had to hide when she showed up to find one of her friends at the Star Club."

"You go all the way up to Itaewon?" I was surprised. Haesuni was seventeen now, old enough to be in the clubs, but I couldn't quite imagine her in Itaewon. She had quit school years ago to help Emo, and now she had to earn money for Hyongbu's medical expenses. "How do you afford the fare?" I said.

"I take the post bus like you."

"But you don't have an ID card. They wouldn't let you on."

"I know a bus driver—Widow *ajoshi*. I always take his bus up in the morning and take it back down. The GIs just think I'm going to school or something."

I laughed. "Suni," I said, "do you remember the time Hyongbu took you and me and Yongsu out in the boat? That time we went down to the country to move Gannan's grave?"

"I remember the water was so clear," she said.

"Do you think he would have let you drown if you had really fallen in?"

"He was splashing us, wasn't he? I wanted to get out because he was drunk, and the water was so clear. I thought I could just step down, but the bottom was so far away. That's all I remember. And I was cold. The water was so clear and cold."

"But what if you had lost hold of the boat? Do you think Hyongbu would have saved you?"

"He was too drunk. He would have drowned, too."

"So you think he would have jumped in to save you?"

She looked down at her unmendable stockings and she picked up something else, something silky and red, like a scarf or a sheer blouse—I couldn't tell which. "No," she said finally. "What I should say is 'Of course!' but I know the true answer is no. He probably wouldn't have done a thing."

"But you're his daughter," I said, and then I remembered what he had told me about women.

"That's right. His daughter." She scanned the room quickly, as if to see if anyone were around, then reached under the couch and produced a pack of Lucky Strikes. "You want one?" she said as she lit one for herself.

"No. Why are you smoking the bad luck cigarettes?"

"Someone got them as a present and didn't want them. Like she was afraid she'd be shot by a Viet Cong sniper if she smoked them in Korea," she mumbled with the cigarette burning between her lips.

"I had a dream about Kuristo," I said.

"What?"

"I dreamed I had a brother named Kuristo, and he saved us all from an old crone who was going to kill us. I asked Daeri about him and he got mad. There are things he doesn't want me to know, but I think I remember things. Pictures in our album. The Ring Boy picture."

"Mahmi never told you?"

"The Ring Boy is him, isn't it? And those other pictures I thought were me—they're him, too. I don't remember having them taken."

"How could you? You were little."

"I would remember." I reached out, and Haesuni gave me her Lucky Strike. I took a drag, inhaling deep into my lungs, almost coughing because I hadn't smoked since I was nine. "Tell me something," I said with a cloud of smoke rising in front of me. "Did he die? Is that why no one wants to talk about him?"

Haesuni lit herself another cigarette, and as we both smoked, I felt suddenly older, as if I were some middle-aged black marketeer talking about our next deal. In the dim light I could see how the GIs in the Itaewon clubs would have no idea of Haesuni's age when she wore her makeup—they couldn't read a Korean's age anyway and often went with women old enough to be their mothers. I wondered if Haesuni remembered Gannan, or Gannan's room, or the way she used to dream out loud.

"He wasn't your father's son," said Haesuni, not looking at me. "Daeri wouldn't marry Mahmi until she gave him up for adoption. Kuristo was sick with something in the chest, and no one wanted him. Eventually he got adopted by some American doctors, but after he got to America, they only sent two pictures."

I was clenching my teeth on the filter tip of my cigarette. "Why wasn't I supposed to know any of this?" I said.

"What would it have helped?" said Haesuni. "They wanted you to be the oldest son. And Mahmi was upset enough. She cried and cried. She gave him up and took him to the orphanage in Sosa, but then she went back for him. She did it twice, and then the orphanage threatened not to take him again and the whole family had to keep her from going back. They put him in a different place that she didn't know about, where she couldn't go get him. It's all because of your father. He didn't want some other man's son in his family. Why do you think he treated you so oddly when you were little? He almost dropped you when my mother gave you to him that first time. Maybe he was afraid it was that other man's son."

"So he's my older brother with a different father? What's his father's name?"

"We don't know. Nobody knows. Even Mahmi doesn't remember his name." She got up and opened the window to let out the smoke. "I shouldn't have told you any of this," she said. But then we ended up talking through the night, not only about Kuristo, but about other things— Gannan's suicide, Hyongbu's failing health, Yongsu's problems with the police, Mahmi's debts. We smoked the entire pack of Lucky Strikes. When we were exhausted and our eyes were red and dry, I helped Haesuni clear the smoke out and dump the ashtray into a paper bag. Haesuni put the sewing things away and lifted An-na up. "Sleep well," she said. "There's gum over there to get the smell off your breath."

"Sleep well."

As Haesuni took An-na to sleep in the other room, I sat on the *maru* watching the sun rise outside beyond the gate, beams of light sparkling against the slivers of colored glass that protectively spiked the wall, and I was as empty as when the Japanese Colonel's ghost had split my head and opened me up to the sky. I was more empty than clear water is empty of shadow, as empty as the sky after it has unleashed the monsoon and stretches pure blue as far as the eye can see. That was my emptiness, and I knew that nothing would ever fill it.

✧

By early spring my father had been diagnosed with cancer, and the Army doctors told him to wait until he was back in the States to have his surgery. They shipped him out early, leaving me and Mahmi and An-na to wait until summer to join him. The day after we watched him leave from Kimpo, Mahmi started packing our mementos.

I was flipping through one of our photo albums, and I paused on a page that included a faded black-and-white Polaroid of the two of us: She is twenty-eight, but she looks no older than eighteen, and she is holding me in front of her, leaning so that her cheek touches mine. I am four years old. We are partially obscured by a bush that grew in one corner of our courtyard, which was a garden of sorts, in the house we had lived in before we moved to the house of the Japanese Colonel.

"I never took pictures like that with him," Mahmi said over my shoulder.

At first I thought it was just a slip of the tongue, but then I wondered who she was referring to. There was only one other him in our family, and it was my father as far as I was supposed to know. As I stared at that page in the album, I remembered the other pictures I had always assumed were of me, ones that made me pause at the absence of recall. There were times when that absence was so palpable I had sat and stared into the distance of memory and time, and I had tried to look down upon my past like some predatory bird circling its prey. But now I felt like a carrion bird waiting to pick at something whose stillness marked its end. I looked at my mother's face and back down at her younger face in the photograph.

Then I had a flash of memory—something I knew was not quite real because it simply could not have been. My father had brought a slide projector home one day to show us his slides from Vietnam, and I had met him in ASCOM, on the way up to the Service Club. The pebbles on the path had a gloss on them that morning, as if the dew had never quite evaporated, but dried into a glaze of melted sugar.

Everything shimmered as it did in my dreams, everything too bright, and I remembered watching slides projected against a silvered canvas screen, and I remembered looking into the projector to examine the magic that made those pictures leap across the span of darkness and appear on the flat canvas like a luminous, square world. I had seen the bright light, the vague blobs of color, and against the lens, when my eye could focus there, the disenchanting strands of glowing dust; it was the same dust I had seen in the lenses of cameras, the same dust that gathered in the corners of the Army bus windows. I had turned away with watery eyes, blinking away the afterimages as the projector clicked briefly into darkness and I had recalled my first memory—not of myself, but of Kuristo as he stood there, shifting from foot to foot in a white ruffle shirt and white trousers. He had just put on his shoes, though we did not wear shoes in the house, and their glossy blackness shone nearly as bright as his clothes. He carried a pillow, upon which something golden caught the morning light. And then, suddenly, Kuristo is gone, and there is me, stretched out on a paving stone, reaching out with my skinned hands, crying for my mother as the sun glints against the glass of a cable car hanging over a pond. He was there. If I had only turned my head, I could have seen him again, spoken to him, but then the voice of my father had cut my name through the air, and I could hear only the scraping of table legs on the floor, a cough, the soft hum of the projector fan.

"What's the matter?" said Mahmi.

"Nothing," I said automatically, but it took me a moment to realize where I was. My father was in America. I was sitting on the *maru* with my mother. I realized Hae-suni had told my mother about our talk that night, and now Mahmi was telling me about Kuristo. "I was just wondering," I said. "Mahmi, do you really want to go to America?"

"I've dreamed of it since I was a little girl during the War," my mother said without hesitating. "That's where all the wonderful things come from, and that's where he is." She turned in the photo album to where Kuristo's pictures had been, but now the page was empty and black, only the scalloped corner mounts indicating what had been there. "Someday I will find him," said Mahmi. "That's why I'll go to America. I know that someday your father will be gone and I can look for him. And then I can finally tell this secret to your sister, too."

"Why did you marry Daeri?" I said. "How could you marry someone who made you send your son away?"

"When I first met your father I thought he was the most beautiful man I had ever seen. His skin was white like milk and his hair was like gold—real gold. I had never seen anyone so beautiful. It was like the way the Catholic fathers said angels of the Lord were up in heaven. I didn't know about his temper then. But he's a kind man despite his temper. And really, I did think the streets in America are gold or something. I used to think every American was a millionaire and everyone owned his own house and had a car and drank Coca-Cola instead of water and had meat for every meal. I don't know where I got those ideas, but

I had them. My friends who came back tell me that everything will be a disappointment, but I don't care. I have to go there and see for myself."

"But you don't know anyone where we're going, Mahmi."

"I can visit them by bus."

"It would take days. It must be a hundred times bigger than Korea. People have to take airplanes to go from one state to the next, and there are two hundred million people there."

"I don't care," she said. "It can't be that big. Korea is three thousand *li* from end to end. How much bigger can America be? But I have to go for him. Even if we never find him, that is where I belong—in the place where I might find him. Even if he's dead, in the ground, it's that ground I'll walk on. It's the ground that has half of my blood in it, and even if I don't know his last name or the name of his father, I know that he's there somewhere. He's there."

But she had only three photographs. She had removed them from the family album and hidden them somewhere.

✧

As long as I could remember, I had wondered about America—that clean and oddly bright world of the Dick and Jane *books I had read in elementary school. But I had also seen the grim America of urban ghettos in movies and the oddly flat America of TV shows, and in the end, as the secret day of our departure approached, I knew that I did not want to leave. I knew, even without seeing that the streets were not gold, without turning a faucet and feeling water—and not milk—on my hand, that I would long to return to the place of my birth and the language of my mother.*

When the time came I went not with a struggle but like a dutiful son. I went the way I had seen Korean prisoners march to their execution in movies about the Japanese Annexation, with determination and grief and a sense of hopeless purpose. I went trying to name the dead to give them peace: Gannan, Cholsu, James; and if I could not name them with a word, I could name them with their stories: the young girl who came from the country and sacrificed herself for her family, the boy who was run over by a careless taxi driver, the boy who might have been drowned by his mother; and there were others, and there would be others: the baby who fell in the well, the maid who leaped into the well, the boy who died of leukemia, the uncle who died of a stroke as he tried to hang himself, the father who died of cancer from the beautiful powder that fell from the sky.

I did not need to go to America. I needed a place to go where I could be with these thoughts, where I could look up, through the clear glass of a window, up through space into the black, star-filled night and follow the arch of the bridge of stars. I felt helpless, like the abyss beneath those stars, with my cry of sorrow echoing up at the moon. But there was no other way. Sitting there one day, flooded in sound and tears, with the scent of tragedy and nostalgia mixed together in my memory, with the bitter taste of metal and blood in my mouth, the texture of sorrow at my fingertips, shadows falling over the darkness of my heart, I was helpless and prepared to leave.

I remember we went to Kimpo suddenly—Mahmi hadn't even told me until the day before—and when we got there and had our bags loaded and documents stamped, I held An-na up to the rail so she could look out of the second-floor window at the jets taking off and landing with their unbelievable languor. She watched quietly for a while, and then, as our plane approached the terminal building, she waved her bottle and said, "Dragon! Dragon!" I looked out onto the runway and saw a Northwest Orient 707 with its red, spiked tail and its scales of silver—the giant serpent, the scorpion-tailed dragon.

And in the end, just before our departure, when I stood beneath the belly of that giant serpent, I would look back to see Kuristo waving a sad-eyed good-bye. He is turning away from me when I see him, and he is always in white, a pure white that seems to throw off more light than the sun, and the air around him is bluish and darker than the rest of the world, like the air in a tunnel, like the air at night between the treetops and the moon, like the air between our two worlds. He is walking away from me into that next world, and I cannot see him emerging. He recedes into that fixed direction, and always, no matter how brave I have made myself by that time, I am too terrified to run forward and look at his face because I know it will look too much like my own. Kuristo, my ghost brother, gone already into the Westward Land. Kuristo, a family dream from a time before my golden-haired GI father. This was the dream that had affixed *itself in my mind, and I would wonder—could my mother have known that she would be standing with me and my sister looking up at the belly of a giant white serpent with scaly wings of silver? The heat and the dampness of summer would be rippling behind its wings; its scarlet tail, with its scorpion spike pointing westward, its blind eyes, its black dog nose, its shrill whining —is that what would become of her portentous dream? As I stand there, looking up at the jagged stairs that will lead us up into the dragon's belly, I remember—yes, I remembered, I will remember—I was born from a dream, and now I will fly into the heavens, to the West, into another dream; and if I am awake now, perhaps I shall sleep and wake again to dream this new dream with my mother and my sister.*

ACKNOWLEDGMENTS

I would like to thank the following people for their inspiration and assistance in the long and difficult process of writing this book: my professors, Ann Imbrie, Bill Gifford, Diane Johnson, Marian Ury, and Daniel Rancour-Laferriere; my agent, Regula Noetzli; my editor, Julia Moskin; my friends and colleagues, Indira Ganesan, Shan Wu, and Walter K. Lew; the many members of my extended family in the Lee, Fenkl, and Chong clans; and my tranquil, bright moon, Anne B. Dalton, without whom there would not have been reason enough to write this.

· A NOTE ON THE TYPE ·

The typeface used in this book is a version of Palatino, orig-
inally designed in 1950 by Hermann Zapf (b. 1918), one of
the most prolific contemporary type designers, who has also
created Melior and Optima. Palatino was first used to set the
introduction of a book of Zapf's hand lettering, in an edition
of eighty copies on Japan paper handbound by his wife,
Gudrun von Hesse; the book sold out quickly and Zapf's
name was made. (Remarkably, the lettering had actually
been done when the self-taught calligrapher was only
twenty-one.) Intended mainly for "display" (title pages,
headings), Palatino owes its appearence both to calligraphy
and the requirements of the cheap German paper at the
time—perhaps why it is also one of the best-looking fonts
on low-end computer printers. It was soon used to set text,
however, causing Zapf to redraw its more elaborate letters.